PRAISE F

The Widow

A deliciously diabolical take on marriage, politics, and the lies that bind."
—*Library Journal*

"[A] wild mix of intrigue, secrets, and corruption."
—*Publishers Weekly*

"What happens when 'the woman behind the man' has a dark secret of her own? Slick and rocket paced, *The Widow* by Kaira Rouda is a top-notch political thriller. With hairpin twists and turns, insider knowledge, glamorous settings, and a whole cast of untrustworthy characters, Rouda expertly ratchets up the tension, keeping her readers breathlessly turning the pages. And the deliciously devious Jody Asher is as cold and calculating as she is riveting. A captivating read!"
—Lisa Unger, *New York Times* bestselling author of
Secluded Cabin Sleeps Six

"*The Widow* pulls back the curtain to reveal an insider's look at the fascinating and duplicitous world of DC politics. This stunning page-turner has a cast of characters with dangerous secrets and hidden motives. Rouda's best so far!"
—Liv Constantine, internationally bestselling author of
The Last Mrs. Parrish

"Known for her fiendishly cagey characters, Kaira Rouda introduces readers to her most diabolical cast to date in the cleverly crafted *The Widow*. Tense, sharply written, and ticking with suspense, *The Widow* is a killer edge-of-your-seat thriller with an eye-popping glimpse into DC politics and simmering grudges. Rouda is at her best with this devilishly smart novel that kept me guessing to the very end. Clear your calendar; you don't want to miss one scintillating minute with *The Widow*."

—Heather Gudenkauf, *New York Times* bestselling author of *The Overnight Guest*

"Kaira Rouda is back with another delicious and darkly comedic tale, this time pulling back the curtain on the glamorous and backstabbing world of Washington politics. Rouda takes her readers into the heart of a messed-up marriage, where scandal threatens to sap a congressman's reelection campaign. Packed with juicy secrets and intrigue, *The Widow* is a propulsive, unputdownable tale of a couple's battle for power, and an incredibly fun ride."

—Kimberly Belle, internationally bestselling author of *My Darling Husband*

"With her signature dark wit and clever insights, Kaira Rouda takes us deep into the fascinating world of power and politics, where ambition and manipulation reign and shameful secrets become weapons. *The Widow* is a breathless page-turner with a ruthless and conniving protagonist that you can't help rooting for. This might be Rouda's best book yet!"

—Robyn Harding, bestselling author of *The Perfect Family*

"Kaira Rouda is on top of her game with her latest thriller, *The Widow*, a suspenseful tale filled with backstabbing, page-turning goodies: Capitol Hill shenanigans, manipulative lobbyists, adulterous politicians, opportunistic interns, and dirty backroom deals. In other words, welcome to Washington, DC—a place where the secrets have secrets. Rouda's 'I'm not a bitch, you're a bitch' protagonist is an overly seasoned, 'supportive' spouse living her best life in the hallowed halls of Congress . . . until that lifestyle is threatened. Then look out: Rouda will come at you with zingers and power plays, giving the coldhearted widow her veil of opportunity, proving repeatedly that it is the political spouse who wields the *real* power on the Hill, and she has no intention of letting go."

—Lisa Barr, *New York Times* bestselling author of *Woman on Fire*

"Gripping and brimming with insider intrigue, *The Widow* delivers with each scandalous, suspenseful page! With a main character I loved to hate, this story has all the twists and turns readers have come to expect from Kaira Rouda. Grab your copy and get ready to tear through *The Widow* faster than a pile of unmarked bills."

—Elle Marr, Amazon Charts bestselling author of *Strangers We Know*

"I tore through this book in two breathless sittings. With *The Widow*, Kaira Rouda has given us a political thriller that's ingeniously structured and packed full of razor-sharp observations about the machinations of Washington power couples. It's smart, timely, and wickedly fun. You won't be able to put it down."

—Grant Ginder, author of *Let's Not Do That Again* and
The People We Hate at the Wedding

"In *The Widow*, Kaira Rouda perfectly captures the experience of being a congressional spouse and all the complicated intricacies of that lifestyle and then adds her signature flair to make it a riveting story that only she could tell. It is impossible to put down."

—Lacey Schwartz Delgado, filmmaker, former congressional spouse, and Second Lady of New York

Somebody's Home

Listed in "Best Thrillers Coming in 2022" by She Reads

"Whatever the opposite of family values is, Rouda seems intent on perfecting a genre that enshrines it."

—*Kirkus Reviews*

"Suspense and thriller readers will be on the edge of their seats for this novel that exposes the dark underbelly of human nature."

—*Library Journal*

"There are great characters moving the story along, that sweep away the reader in this story of families, revenge, and secrets."

—*News and Sentinel*

"A truly unputdownable novel that had me gripped—and anxious— from the first sentence! Captivating, fast paced, and unsettling, *Somebody's Home* is astonishingly good. I gulped it down."

—Sally Hepworth, *New York Times* bestselling author of *The Good Sister*

"*Somebody's Home* kept me riveted from the first page to the last. A gripping psychological thriller you don't want to miss!"

—Lucinda Berry, bestselling author of *The Perfect Child*

"*Somebody's Home* starts like a hurricane out at sea: some wind, some waves, a sense of approaching danger. But the story moves fast, gains velocity, and suddenly you are turning the pages, unable to stop, heart in your throat, knowing that something terrible is going to happen and nothing will stop it. The threats come from all sides, and it's so hard to know who to trust. The characters are wonderful and complex; the setting feels like the house next door, which makes it all the more terrifying; and the ending nearly killed me. Kaira Rouda has written a terrific, gripping thriller."

—Luanne Rice, bestselling author of *The Shadow Box*

"With an intriguing cast of characters and a killer premise, *Somebody's Home* is a thriller worth staying up all night for. Fast paced and relentless, Kaira Rouda cranks up the tension with every turn of the page. With unexpected twists and jaw-dropping revelations, Rouda knows how to draw readers close and keep them entranced."

—Heather Gudenkauf, *New York Times* bestselling author of *The Overnight Guest*

"Privilege, social disenchantment, and extreme family tensions are the threads running through this tense novel. Kaira Rouda lets us into the lives of two families and what happens when their paths cross. Gripping and fast paced with an explosive conclusion!"

—Gilly Macmillan, *New York Times* bestselling author

"Taut with foreboding from the first page, Kaira Rouda's *Somebody's Home* is an unsettling portrait of an antisocial man, a master of the universe, and the women caught between them. The rotating points of view and incisive, clear writing are sure to keep you flipping the pages until you reach the shocking conclusion!"

—Katherine St. John, author of *The Siren*

"Trust your instincts and grab a copy of Kaira Rouda's *Somebody's Home*. In Rouda's latest thriller, a mother trusts her instincts when she knows the person on her property is threatening her family. But what if the threat is coming at her from all sides and more than one person is hiding a dark secret? A compulsive, fast read, *Somebody's Home* reveals what people will do to protect not only their homes but the families within those four walls. A captivating read."

—Georgina Cross, bestselling author of *The Stepdaughter*

The Next Wife

"Rouda hits the ground running and never stops . . . [*The Next Wife*] is so much fun that you'll be sorry to see it end with a final pair of zingers. The guiltiest of guilty pleasures."

—*Kirkus Reviews*

"This gripping psychological thriller from Rouda (*The Favorite Daughter*) offers a refreshing setup . . . Rouda keeps the reader guessing as the plot takes plenty of twists and turns. Suspense fans will get their money's worth."

—*Publishers Weekly*

"In *The Next Wife*, two women go ruthlessly head-to-head. Kaira Rouda knows how to create the perfect diabolical characters that we love to hate. Equally smart and savage, this is a lightning-fast read."

—Mary Kubica, *New York Times* bestselling author of *The Other Mrs.*

"Rouda's talent for making readers question everything and everyone shines through on every page of her propulsive new thriller, *The Next Wife*. Her narrators are sharp and unpredictable, each one with a tangle of secrets to unravel. *The Next Wife* will leave you tense and gasping, with a chilling twist you won't see coming."

—Julie Clark, *New York Times* bestselling author of *The Last Flight*

"One of the most insidious, compulsive books I've read recently. Kaira Rouda has a way of drawing you in with great characters, fast-paced writing, and a story that won't let you go. Brilliant, dark, and dazzling."

—Samantha Downing, *USA Today* bestselling author of *My Lovely Wife* and *He Started It*

"One man. Two wives. Kaira Rouda has masterfully created cunning twists and sharp narration that take you on an unexpected and delicious journey and will leave you with a gasp. Devious and fun, *The Next Wife* should be the next book you read!"

—Wendy Walker, bestselling author of *Don't Look for Me*

"I absolutely inhaled *The Next Wife*. Nail-biting suspense, dark humor, and family intrigue. I savored every page and now have the worst book hangover. Loved it!"

—Michele Campbell, internationally bestselling author of *The Wife Who Knew Too Much*

"No one writes deliciously devious narcissists like Kaira Rouda. *The Next Wife* showcases her remarkable talent for making unlikable characters alluring. With twisted egos, lavish wealth, and three women vying for power, this compelling, compulsive thriller is sharp, fun, and shocking. I was riveted by every word."

—Samantha M. Bailey, *USA Today* and #1 national bestselling author of *Woman on the Edge*

BENEATH
THE
SURFACE

OTHER TITLES BY KAIRA ROUDA

Suspense

All the Difference

Best Day Ever

The Favorite Daughter

The Next Wife

Somebody's Home

The Widow

Women's Fiction

Here, Home, Hope

A Mother's Day: A Short Story

In the Mirror

The Goodbye Year

Romance

The Indigo Island Series

Weekend with the Tycoon

Her Forbidden Love

The Trouble with Christmas

The Billionaire's Bid

Nonfiction

Real You Incorporated: 8 Essentials for Women
Entrepreneurs

BENEATH THE SURFACE

A Novel

KAIRA ROUDA

Published by Thomas & Mercer, Seattle

www.apub.com

Amazon, the Amazon logo, and Thomas & Mercer are trademarks of Amazon.com, Inc., or its affiliates.

ISBN-13: 9781662511929 (paperback)
ISBN-13: 9781662511912 (digital)

Cover design by Kimberly Glyder
Cover images: © Susann Guenther, © Michael Duva / Getty Images; © Balkonsky, © Andrea Berg / Shutterstock

Printed in the United States of America

To my friends, who cheer me on, inspire me,
and love me unconditionally.
The feeling is mutual.

In one drop of water are found all the secrets of all the oceans.

—*Khalil Gibran*

You are cordially invited to an overnight voyage on the Splendid Seas.

Departure from Newport Beach Yacht Club at noon on Friday, July 15, for an over-night journey to Catalina Island, with a return on Saturday evening, July 16.

Attire: yacht fabulous.
RSVP at your earliest convenience to Mrs. Serena Kingsley.

FRIDAY, JULY 15

NEWPORT BEACH, CALIFORNIA

1

PAIGE

My heart fills with a sinking feeling, a weight I can't shake. That's the only way I can describe it to my husband, Ted. He's driving and I'm trying to be calm. It's not working.

"I suppose that's apropos of something, sweetie, given we'll be boating this weekend." Ted grins. In front of us, the light changes. He pounds the steering wheel in frustration. "Seriously? Another red light? We're going to be late now, for sure."

Most of the reason for our tardiness lies with me. I hate leaving the kids. Even now. They're teenage twins, just graduated high school, and they're fine without me for one night, I know. It's an irrational, deep-seated-control thing called *motherhood*. As I think about it, I swallow a lump in my throat. This has been our goodbye year. They are off to college in the fall. I'm not ready for the empty nest they'll leave in their wake. Sure, I help run Orange County's food bank—one of the largest and, in fundraising terms, most successful in the nation. But it's as a volunteer. I told them years ago when they offered me the CEO position—and every year since—Ted and I decided I'd be a mom full-time. And I have been.

I glance at Ted and push down the sorrow. It's not like I will be empty-nesting alone. Ted and I will reconnect, have date nights. We'll have a real relationship again. It will be wonderful, I tell myself. I hope this trip will bring us closer.

But I'm still worried about being away from the girls, no matter how much Ted and I do need some alone time. For some reason, he is unaffected by any such tension or worry. I believe that may be called *fatherhood*. Still, if he touches me again—like a wife instead of a roommate of sorts—well, I'll forgive him for the months of distance and sexual disinterest. I can't seem desperate for his attention, his affection; I know that much about my husband. Instead of bringing up our lack of romance, I'll focus on my very real fear of this boating trip. That way, Ted can be my knight in shining armor and we'll be partners again, in everything. That's my dream, at least.

"Maybe all these red lights are a sign we should stay home? Did you know that the water between here and Catalina Island forms one of the deepest saltwater channels in the world? We'll be crossing over four thousand feet of deep, dark ocean," I say and grip the passenger armrest of Ted's Tesla. I'm not an ocean person, despite growing up in Southern California. Give me a nice pool, and I'm happy. I'll walk the beach, too, with the best of them. But swim in the sea? Never.

Likely, it was a bad idea to spend so much time on the website I found, reading about all the tragic deaths that have happened on Catalina Island. I may have become addicted to the stories, and now I've scared myself over all the things that could possibly go wrong during this weekend. On land or at sea.

"Good thing we're not swimming to Catalina," Ted says, punching the accelerator, as the car shoots from zero to sixty, leaving the other cars idling at the now-green light. Ted enjoys his emission-free power. "You don't have a thing to worry about, anyway. I haven't seen you go in the ocean for years."

True. Despite his cajoling, I haven't been in the ocean past my knees since the girls were young. *The girls.* I swallow. I should have been fixating on stories about leaving teen girls at home alone rather than reading newspaper articles about tragic deaths on Catalina Island. Oh God. My heart thumps in my chest.

"I'm just worried about Emily. What if she has a party?" Our oldest by a minute is a good girl, I know, but she is seventeen. She is also our social twin. Amy is serious, and more of a bookworm—like me, truth be told. Amy will run a company someday and, for now, keep Emily in line this weekend. I hope. We are terrible parents to have done this, I've decided. Ted says we're empowering the kids to make good decisions.

"Amy will tell on her. We have a built-in narc. It's great," Ted says. "We'll have phone service on the yacht. Honey, relax—please. For me. I feel like we're due for a vacation. Teenagers are draining but they're almost adults. They're fine. I'm trusting them to take care of Peanut."

"Your dog will be fine. It's the girls I'm worried about," I say. Peanut, a small rescue mutt Ted brought home for the girls two years ago, is completely bonded to him. It's cute, their connection. But he should be worried about our daughters, not his dog.

"Come on. Let's focus on us. Let me see your smile, gorgeous. Remember how you always close the deal, no matter what? That's the Paige I need to see this weekend. Oh, and try to have fun for once," he says, grinning.

And there it is. The perennial judgment: Ted is fun. I am boring. Ted is spontaneous. I am a worrying planner. Ted is a gregarious salesperson. I'm a skilled fundraiser who knows how to go in for the kill. I hear myself sigh as I glance at my husband in the driver's seat.

Ted has a trendy movie-star haircut and in-vogue facial stubble. He's completely into personal grooming and looks almost as handsome—perhaps *more* handsome—than the day we met, when I was a college senior interning for his family's company. He strolled into the marketing office, full of confidence, and all the women in the department paused, watching him. He'd walked over to my desk, stuck out his hand, and said, "Ted Kingsley. You're new?"

I could barely speak, he was so handsome. "Yes, Paige, nice to meet you." I tucked my blonde hair nervously behind my ears, feeling the heat on my face.

"The pleasure is all mine," he said. "Can I help you with those?"

He pointed to the stack of presentation binders I was assembling for an important business pitch that afternoon. My heart raced in my chest. "Uh, I think I have everything under control. But thank you."

"Wait, did you go to USC? You look familiar," Ted said.

"I'm still there, yes," I said.

"I just graduated. I knew I recognized you." He grinned. "If you need anything, just let me know. It's hard to be the new kid on the block." I was stunned by his kindness, his courtesy, his warmth. Of course I knew who he was. Ted Kingsley was one of those big men on campus. College famous.

"Thank you. That means so much. I need to get back to work, you know. Don't want to let anyone down on my first day," I said. "Nice to meet you."

"Oh, I'm sure you're doing a great job already. I can tell. Say, how about I take you to lunch today?" he asked. "A welcome-to-the-team lunch of sorts."

"Sure, that would be great," I managed to answer, simultaneously wondering if he invited all new staffers to lunch. Something told me he didn't. He likely wasn't part of the official welcome-to-Kingsley committee, so I was flattered. Even if it was just lunch.

"I'll swing by around noon," Ted said. "I'll be looking forward to it."

And from that moment on, I was smitten. I knew he was the one. He says he did, too, and I believed him, back then. For a long time, we were that connected, that in love. Sometime along the way, we lost our spark. At least, he did.

I've done my best to stay attractive for Ted, I really have. I pull down the passenger visor and peek in the mirror. My shoulder-length blonde hair is too blonde, a by-product of playing team tennis in the constant California sunshine. My blue eyes shine through my sunglasses. I'm always watching. I'm trying not to seem desperate for his attention. But I am. When the girls leave for college this fall, I'll be devastated. I need my husband to love me again.

I side-eye Ted before closing the visor and pasting on a smile. "See, I'm smiling," I say. I'm trying—I am. I can be fun again. Maybe I'll take the CEO position at the food bank once the girls leave for college. The board has begged me to take the leap, and I'm considering it. I've raised the profile of the organization, as well as revenues, and I know I can do more. That would give my life more purpose, and I will have plenty of time with the girls away at college. I think about the marketing and development campaigns I created, targeting the top one hundred largest companies in the region. I met with every CEO personally and closed the deal with almost all of them. Food insecurity is a major issue, in Orange County and across the country. I just needed these important CEOs to understand the mission, and once they did, they opened their checkbooks.

I fold my arms across my chest and stare out the window. I'm dreading this weekend, and it's my own fault. I have anxiety, and this trip has triggered it big-time. It's been hard to sleep ever since Ted accepted his dad's invitation to join him on his new toy: a 185-foot yacht, the *Splendid Seas*. I know it's irrational. But I come from a long line of worriers.

"It's going to be the time of our lives, Paige! Imagine. We've never been to Catalina Island. Our first time, and we're going in style," he says, driving through a yellow light as I grip the armrest. "Dad and Serena only invited us. That means big things for us. Big things for you and me. We're the perfect team. We're going to take over Kingsley Global Enterprises. You and me, sweetie."

My husband's eternal optimism is cute, and I love that he called us a team. I really want us to be a team, in everything, again. But the truth is, Ted has no idea why Richard has invited us on the trip this weekend. It could be just to toy with us, make us squirm under his all-powerful eye for a weekend. I wouldn't put it past him. I feel sorry for my husband when it comes to his father. He keeps looking for love that's often not returned—not at all. He does have it better than his siblings; from what I can tell, Ted is the golden son. But that's not saying much when it comes to Richard. That's probably one of the reasons I put up with Ted's shenanigans. He needs unconditional love from someone, and that someone, for the longest time, has been me.

"You want me back at the office? You and me, like the beginning?" I ask. Back when I was vice president of marketing and Ted was vice president of sales, we were unstoppable. We repositioned what was once a mature, stagnant company and turned Kingsley into a powerhouse. I'd like to think my quick adaptation of emerging technology played a big role. I know it did.

"Yes. Dad can't resist you—and, by extension, you and me as the face of Kingsley. It will be great," he says. "Remember those pitches we did together? We doubled Kingsley's land acquisitions in four years, record expansion for the company at the time. We can do it again."

As he continues his excited proclamation, I try to absorb what he's saying. We'll work together again. I want to pinch myself, but then reality sets in. I worked my way up to vice president of marketing at Kingsley before deciding to stay home and raise our twins. Does a seventeen-year employment gap disqualify me? Maybe they'd consider my volunteer experience with the food bank. I know they should.

"Would Richard value my experience with the food bank since I'm essentially their de facto volunteer CEO?" I ask.

"Sure, of course. Marketing is at the heart of everything we do," he says.

"I do a lot more than marketing. I've raised revenue tenfold, led us through a huge capital campaign that funded our new facility—and I'm good at what I do," I say.

"I know. Besides, I'll be by your side," Ted says, a twinkle in his blue eyes. "Just follow my lead. And relax already."

I take a deep breath and try not to obsess over crossing the ocean in my father-in-law's new yacht. I remind myself he can buy anything he wants, of course, and does. He's Richard Kingsley, scion of the Kingsley family and a rather terrifying control freak. I tell myself he will also purchase or hire the best yacht crew money can buy. We'll be safe— we will be. But still, the seemingly beautiful Pacific Ocean is actually menacing and cold, waiting to grab anyone who innocently challenges her authority.

"Did you know there have been a lot of deaths in the water around Catalina Island? I found a list of all of them. I can't stop reading the stories." I pull up the Deaths on Catalina site. "Like this one. Tony the Greek. Back in 1908. He was a renowned captain, and then he just disappeared one night when he was taking a family around the island on his boat named *Zeus*. These people wake up in the morning, and they're drifting in a storm without a captain. They have two kids. They were adrift for two days with no food or water. Can you imagine? Oh my God."

Ted rolls his eyes. "Look at that. We made it right on time," he says, turning in to the Newport Beach Yacht Club marina.

I attempt to meet his words with a happy face even as a shudder rolls through me. I can't shake the dread this weekend has created in my heart. Is it because of all the scary stories I've read about the waters around Catalina, or is it because my life is about to be crushingly lonely and empty unless I can reconnect with my husband? Ted must want our relationship back on track, too. He keeps talking about being partners, so that's a step in the right direction. I tell myself to enjoy the moment.

"Yes, this is going to be fun," I say. "I love you, Ted."

"We are a great team. Richard knows that. I can't wait to see you in a business suit again," Ted says with a wink. He pulls to a stop and stares out the window. "Look at the size of that boat! This is going to be great. Smooth sailing from here on out."

2

JOHN

I may have miscalculated the departure time from our house, because we're now at the marina half an hour early. I clench the steering wheel, already frustrated by this little weekend on my dad's ridiculously expensive new toy. Beside me, I feel Rachel's anger pulsing in my direction, although I am not sure she feels mine. I am good at masking it. During childhood, my mom taught me to stuff my emotions away. All that stuffed anger is still inside me.

"What are we supposed to do? Stay here, sitting in the car?" Rachel asks with a huff, her forehead wrinkled above her oversize, black-rimmed sunglasses. My wife is displeased, to say the least.

"Early bird catches the worm, dear," I say. I squeeze the steering wheel tighter and imagine snapping it from the car, hurling it at something. "I guess we could go on over."

"Early bird looks like an idiot in front of bird's father," Rachel says. "Richard will ridicule you if you look too eager. We sit."

I glance at my wife. She's right, of course, and that's the problem in most of our fights lately. She's become more powerful in our relationship, shorter with me as her career has soared. I don't blame her, I guess. My job as the CFO basically means catering to every one of Richard's whims, and it has become something of a bore. She tells me

I should make a change; I tell her I'm waiting to take over the family business. She says I'm lazy; her snippy self-righteousness is beginning to fray my nerves and fuel my restless discontent. She's always pushing me to achieve more, be more. Her expectations are unbearable. It is out of my hands.

Although she is correct. I am being lazy, biding my time, but it's more complicated than that. I've given my all to the family business through the years, done everything my father asked. Lately, perhaps, I've been less engaged. Dad's slowing down—ergo, I am. That said, I'm not going to give Rachel the satisfaction of agreeing with her. Soon, I'll have plenty to do at Kingsley Global Enterprises. I'll be the one in charge.

I have parked the car as far away from the behemoth boat as possible. *Splendid Seas* bobs in the distance like a gleaming mirage. I cannot believe Dad bought that showy thing, but I'm also beyond excited to see it. My wife is right: I shouldn't look too eager. Dad would mock me.

"OK, you're right. We'll wait. It's just that I'm impatient. You know this weekend could change everything," I tell her. When I close my eyes, I still imagine us happy together. We aren't that far away from happy. She says if I had a fulfilling job like hers, we'd be equals again. It's her version of a gentle nudge—smashing me over the head with her opinions. I can't wait to show her how equal I am when I take over Dad's company. Heck, when I'm CEO of Kingsley, I'll be more than her equal. That thought alone makes me happy.

"Did you just agree with me?" Rachel says, and she's smiling, too. "I do hope you're right about Richard. I really do want you to have the company and a challenge, a change. Being in charge will look good on you. After everything you've been through, everything you've done— you deserve it."

"Thanks," I say, and we lock eyes for a moment before she turns away and looks toward the huge boat. She has no idea all the things I've done, but I appreciate the sentiment. "You're a trouper for coming along. I know you hate this."

"What, the forced family fun or being out in the elements? It's almost eighty degrees, and it's only nine a.m.," she says as she smooths the white linen pants of her summer business suit. The way she's dressed, she could be heading into the office. She's an attorney—a shark, I'm told. She's the brains in this family.

"I told you to wear shorts," I say.

She laughs. "As if. You know I'm a rugged outdoorswoman—*not*. And I will not dress down for comfort when we have your dad and Serena to impress."

"Ha! You and me both." I glance down at my pressed khakis, my crisp navy button-down fitted by the best tailor in Orange County. This is how we dress for dinners out or any other social event we happen to be asked to attend. To be honest, I'm an accountant and she's an attorney. Outside of our respective offices, the most adventure we have in life is trying a new restaurant. We're both out of our comfort zones here. I don't tell her that the forecast calls for huge southern swells and a chance of rain. I focus on the positive.

"Look at that yacht. There's plenty of indoor space, air-conditioning, and a chef. What more could you want?" I ask.

She doesn't answer as we both stare at the boat. You couldn't help but catch sight of the yacht when turning in to the Newport Beach marina parking lot. It's the biggest vessel in the marina by far. Despite its outsize proportions, I must admit it's gorgeous. Stunning, or whatever yacht terms you want to use, that's it. Its silver-gray hull and polished chrome accents gleam in the bright sunshine. I cannot wait to get on board and have my father to myself for the weekend. I tap a beat on the steering wheel.

"This is going to be so great," I say, watching a group of midwesterners flaunting college football teams on their T-shirts tour the marina from the sidewalk, as close as any of them will get to a yacht. "Look, Rachel, it's a beautiful Southern California day. The sun is shining, the seagulls are squawking, the tourists are gawking. What could be better?"

"They'll definitely be gawking at us on that thing. I sort of wish the managing partner could see me on board," Rachel says. "He's very into the trappings of extreme wealth."

Rachel pulls out her phone and takes a photo. My wife works for the top white-collar criminal-defense law firm in the state; she's a partner now, gunning for senior partner. Rachel is intense. And good at what she does. She vacillates between hating her boss, her clients, and then me on any given day. But she wins cases, so it works for her, this angst. Most days, I'm just in awe that she's stayed by my side. I'm what most would describe as a slice of white bread: boring, predictable, better with something—someone else—as garnish. But looks can be deceiving, I'm told.

"He'll have a stroke when he sees this," she says.

Does she want to kill the managing partner? I guess that is one way to move up the corporate ladder.

"Lovely thought. Let's focus on our weekend. You promised to be on your best, sunniest behavior, remember?" I ask. I pull my sunglasses off and turn to look at her.

"I'll be good. As long as you show me the money, honey," Rachel says with a sharp cackle. She brings home the bacon—but I do, too, of course. Dad pays me a hefty salary, but I suppose she'd like me to have a windfall. A life-changing windfall. We both would but for different reasons.

I turn up the air-conditioning in the car as sweat trickles down my back. It's going to be a scorcher. I'm in the hot seat in more ways than one now. What if Dad doesn't give me the company? What if this isn't what this is about? I need to set expectations, for my wife and myself.

"You know it's a process. This is the first step. Clearly, Dad is considering me—and me alone—for the promotion or position or whatever his succession plan entails. With Richard, though, you never know exactly the timing, details," I say, thinking of my dad's sneaky eyes and his cold heart. He is the devil, but he's all mine. Well, mostly. There's the brother to contend with, and my sister, but she's been out of the mix for years.

"Richard's going to toy with you. You should expect that," Rachel says. Now she's serious. She pushes her sunglasses on top of her head. In her eyes I see a little glimmer of concern, a bit of compassion. She touches my hand; I pull away. I don't need her pity—I need her respect. I deserve it.

"I know that. I'm used to Dad's games," I say. I hate it, but I *am* used to them. I pull my sunglasses back on my face. Whatever my dad wants, I do without question. I am the protector of him and the company.

"You stood by me for all my career hassles, the good old boys and all. I'll be here for you this weekend because I know how important it is to you. OK?" she says.

Despite myself, my throat tightens. I swallow. I've never been good at displays of affection. "Thanks," I manage. "Look at that. It's time to grab our stuff and climb aboard. Ready?"

"As ready as I'll ever be," Rachel says, opening the car door. She scans the parking lot. The yacht sparkles like a pot of gold at the far end. "Good thing we packed light."

I pop the trunk and pull out our two matching roller-board suit-cases, and we set off across the hot black pavement. The lot is half-full, leaving us plenty of space to roll between parked cars. We make it to dock twelve in no time. My heart thumps with excitement as I punch in the code Dad gave me. I feel like a little kid on Christmas morning as the metal gate clicks open.

"After you, dear," I say. I'm grinning from ear to ear because I'm excited and because I know they are probably watching, my dad and his wife. I look up at a security camera and smile as we make our way down the dock. The air smells like salt and metal. I step to my right to avoid fresh seagull poop.

As I roll down the gangway behind Rachel, I admire the smaller boats on either side of us. Any one of these would be a prized posses-sion. A dozen of them could fit inside Richard's extravagant purchase.

Rachel comes to an abrupt stop, and I stub my toe on her suitcase. "What are you doing?"

"Look," Rachel says, pointing to two people at the end of the dock.

"It can't be," I say. "No."

Rachel yanks on her suitcase. "It's them. Come on. Straighten up. Don't slump. Shoulders back, John. Don't act like you're afraid of your own brother. And do not act disappointed—do you understand?"

"I'm not afraid; I'm furious." I square my shoulders as we close the distance between us and Ted and Paige.

"Hi!" Paige says, waving unenthusiastically.

"Good to see you," Rachel mumbles in response.

The two women manage a quick hug.

Ted makes a limp effort to shake hands with me, and I return the gesture before wiping my hand on my khakis.

"I take it Dad told you guys you'd be the only ones on the boat this weekend?" I ask, knowing the answer. "Us too."

"This is a classic Dad move," Ted says, pushing his hand through his full head of hair. I covet that head of hair, although I know that's a sin. I'll likely have a list of sins to take with me to confession next Sunday. It's fine. I got the brains of the offspring; Ted got the looks. I'd rather have the brains—of course I would. Brains lead to taking over companies. Looks fade, and quickly. Everyone knows that, even my dad. Besides, no one takes Ted seriously. Not anymore.

"Maybe we can tell your dad that we'd rather yacht on separate weekends. We arrived first, so we'll go this weekend and you all can have the next," Paige says with her signature Perfect Paige smug smirk. She's infuriating me already, and she hasn't even insulted us yet.

"We got here half an hour ago, so we were actually here first," Rachel says.

Ted rolls his eyes. He's wearing shorts. They both are, like children. Ted is a child, a Peter Pan of sorts. He'll never change.

Paige says, "Look, it's just not as easy for us as it is for you. We've already arranged for the kids, the dog, and all that. It's tougher for parents. You don't have any of those responsibilities to deal with. You're more flexible." Paige looks to Ted for support.

"She's right," Ted says. "Think of Peanut. Think of our girls."

I shake my head. I'm not stepping down, not for a dog or their twins. It's unfortunate Paige wants to go there. Ted too. I brace for Rachel's response.

"You chose to have children. I chose not to," Rachel says, and I can see her hands shaking in fury. We are all easily triggered by each other at this point in our lives. Buttons pushed might as well be pins pulled from a grenade. "Your problems are your own creation. All of them. But they'll be gone soon, right? Off to college. Hope they get in someplace good. Have they?"

Here we go. Rachel believes their daughters are entitled brats.

"Amy will be attending Chapman University, and Emily is going to USC. They'll be close by. We're thrilled," Paige says.

"Didn't they want to go someplace else, explore a new part of the country? I thought you'd mentioned the East Coast, some Ivy Leagues?" Rachel asks.

I watch Paige's hands clench into fists as Ted puts his hand on her shoulder. It's clear they didn't receive any Ivy League acceptance letters to brag about.

Behind them, I see my dad's latest wife, Serena, appear on deck above us like a mirage in gauzy white fabric. "Hello, everyone!" she says, her red lips glistening. "Welcome to the *Splendid Seas*!"

This is anything but splendid. I paste a neutral look on my face and nudge Rachel. I whisper, "Be nice, remember?"

"Likely not possible," she whispers through a clenched-teeth smile.

I agree, it's tough to fake it. I've dealt with this most of my life. I'm the oldest, the only child until my golden-boy brother appeared when I least expected it. Since then, his bulging muscles and athletic prowess, his perfect model face and full head of hair have mocked me. I'm the competent one and he's the charming one. I feel like kicking his shin.

But that's childish, and my sweet mother, Mary's, face pops into my head. *What would Jesus do?* she whispers.

I'm not sure what He would do, but what I need to do is help Dad finally—and clearly—see the difference between Ted and me: his weakness and my strength. I take a deep breath and realize this weekend will be even more challenging than I imagined. My enemy will be on board. I wipe the sweat from my brow as a huge wave rolls under the dock. Ropes strain and metal groans. The wave crests against the side of the yacht, spraying us all with cold salt water, soaking my pants and shoes.

Rachel gasps. Paige looks terrified, eyes huge, her white shorts and striped T-shirt dotted with water.

I look up at Serena, the cherry on top of the shit sundae this family yachting excursion has become, and she's laughing.

God help us.

OC SCOOP

MEGA-YACHTS AND BILLIONAIRES:

THE NEW MUST-HAVE TOY

Kingsley Global Enterprises Chairman and CEO Richard Kingsley, one of our favorite local billionaires, has acquired a new toy, OC Scoop has learned. Kingsley, who's worth more than $1.2 billion, bought the 185-foot *Splendid Seas*—said to be one of the highest spec yachts ever built—for about $67 million. The yacht has been spotted docked in Newport Beach marina, although OC Scoop hasn't noted any guests or voyages until this afternoon when, we're told, Kingsley's sons, John and Ted, were seen boarding with their wives. Could be an interesting trip for them, given the younger son left the company a few years back under hushed-up circumstances. We wonder if the boys enjoy the company of their sexy stepmother, who sources say greeted the family members in a tight-fitting, revealing dress. If you spot the *Splendid Seas*, give us a call. We'd love to report on its journey and, of course, anything Kingsley.

3

SERENA

I laugh as a wave douses Richard's boys and their spouses. It soaks one of them—John—and sprays the others. Poor John. It's hard to believe those two are brothers, even without the drenching.

Seems a fitting welcome, as I know none of them really want to spend time with us or each other. Might as well pour some cold water on them early on, dampen those expectations—literally.

The captain hurries down to greet them, handing out fresh white towels and helping them with their luggage. Bill is his name. He's cute and he's my age, but we will not become friendly. He is staff. I am the owner. It's a clear line of demarcation.

I used my intuition to hire Bill—the same intuition that got me in a position to be able to hire a captain for my yacht in the first place. It's true I may have pursued Richard Kingsley for his money, gotten myself invited into the right circles to come into his orbit. But I've stayed with him because I fell in love, with him and this lifestyle. I followed my survival instincts, and they've brought me here, to this luxurious weekend on the *Splendid Seas*.

Not bad, Serena, I tell myself constantly. *Not bad at all.*

I turn my attention to myself and my carefully selected wardrobe for this weekend. At the moment, I'm wearing what I like to think of as my welcome outfit. If it were simply Richard and me yachting for the weekend, I'd be wearing a bikini and a thin silk cover-up. Pink, all of it—his favorite color on me. He says it makes my eyes shine, but I know he likes it because the color gives him energy. He needs energy. He's fading into old age like a man who has consumed too much red meat and spent too much time at Javier's, his favorite bar. He is guilty of both.

Richard hasn't joined me to welcome his sons, which I'm sure they'll inquire about soon. Earlier this morning, he was called away for an important phone call and told me not to disturb him in the stateroom. He left me at the table, in a rush, but only after finishing an early lunch prepared by our onboard chef, delivered to him on a silver tray adorned with a gleaming china plate bearing our yacht's logo—two S's intertwined—engraved in gold along the edge. My husband is hungry, always hungry these days, and he still makes unhealthy food choices. When the chef removed the silver topper from the plate, she revealed a bacon cheeseburger.

"Richard, honestly?" I said. "The family will arrive any moment. We have lunch plans for the crossing."

My husband looked up at me like a boy who had been caught with his hand in the cookie jar, or some other childhood analogy. We don't have children—not yet. He is the father of three, each with a different one of his wives. Ridiculous, isn't it? I will be his last wife, and our child, his final heir. He is running out of time to find a sixth wife. I will make sure he does not.

Richard is a lot to deal with, truth be told. But even so, I needed a child of my own. For security, for comfort when he's gone. Richard's ex-wives have all signed confidentiality agreements. At least, the ones who are still alive have. Ann-Marie, Ted's mom, didn't have to. There is nothing she could say now, not from the grave. She died in childbirth. Terrifying.

"I'm hungry, and so I'm eating. They're late, aren't they?" Richard asked, then stuffed a ridiculously large bite of cheeseburger in his mouth.

"No, your guests are not late. Your manners, Richard," I said and watched as grease dripped from either side of his mouth and onto his *Splendid Seas* crew polo, leaving an oily stain on the dark-blue fabric just below the logo embroidered on the chest pocket.

"Oops. Can someone bring me something to clean up this mess?" Richard said.

I watched as the crewmembers scrambled to get paper towels and soda water, wondering, *Can someone bring* me *something to clean up* this *mess?*

Captain Bill appeared and announced, "Your guests will be arriving soon. I see them in the marina parking lot."

"Well, let me get out of here, then," Richard said, somehow finishing his meal in the time I was distracted by Bill. "Sisi, please tell the guests I'll join you all as soon as possible."

"Wonderful," I said and pushed a smile on my face. I glanced at the huge diamond ring on my left finger. I take a deep breath. He used his term of endearment for me because he knows I'm angry at being left alone to welcome the motley crew of offspring he's invited. "Can't wait to greet the dysfunctional family baggage on the dock."

"Serena, behave," Richard said, but he was chuckling. He likes my dry wit and my lack of any interest in common courtesy and social appropriateness. Although, between the two of us—him with grease splatter on his shirt and me in a pristine, tightly fitting white welcome dress—I'd say I'm the appropriate one.

"Never," I answered and held out my hand to help him out of the deck chair. "You behave, old man. And don't be gone too long. The boys will get restless."

"What fun is there in that?" Richard asked. "I'll be finished with the call and out here to entertain as soon as I can. Remember, the kids likely haven't been on a boat like this before. Be humble and helpful." He pinched my butt for emphasis, a habit I hate but tolerate, as it began on one of our first dates. Don't judge.

"Of course, dear," I said. "Do you want me to do the history first or the rules?"

"History, then the shoe thing," he answered as he turned and made his way toward our stateroom. As I watched him walk away, I wondered what he was up to and why he didn't want to greet his guests. Richard has a lot of secrets, and that's how he likes it. I find it best to not ask questions. That way, I can keep secrets of my own.

"Your guests are at the dock," Bill told me, and we walked together to greet them. And there they were, clustered grumpily on the dock below us. "You look lovely this morning, Mrs. Kingsley."

Ooh. He was flirting with me. That will make things more fun. "Why, thank you, Captain. This little cruise is going to be so much fun." For me—not necessarily Richard's offspring.

I know for a fact Richard's two sons each believed they were the chosen one, the only one who was invited on this adventure with us this weekend. I wish I had seen their faces when they spotted each other on the dock. *Surprise, boys.*

At fifty-two, John is the oldest, a product of Richard's first marriage. That one lasted the longest, fifteen years. Mary, John's mom—a rather homely looking woman—divorced Richard when she found out about his affair with Viki, who became wife number two. Theirs was meant to remain an affair; Richard's second marriage lasted less than a month. But Mary refused to take him back. As a devoted Catholic, she couldn't forgive.

Richard moved on, finally, to Ann-Marie, his third wife and the mother of his son, Ted. They were married five blissful years before she became pregnant. Her premature demise occurred from postpartum bleeding only six hours after Ted's birth. If I had to guess, Ted's mom was Richard's true love. Perhaps because she died giving him what he wanted. Look where that got her. I shake my head to push the images of poor, lovely Ann-Marie aside. Richard's fourth wife, Cassie, was an exotic dancer who swept Richard off his feet and only married him when she became pregnant. That relationship barely lasted a year and resulted in Richard's only daughter.

All I can say is, he's lucky I came along.

"Hello, everyone," I say. "Welcome to the *Splendid Seas*. Your father apologizes for not being here to welcome you. He had urgent business to attend to and is not to be disturbed. He promises he will join us as soon as possible."

Ted shakes his head, and John kicks the dock with the toe of his shoe—a shoe he will soon remove like everyone else before climbing aboard. I stare down at Richard's spoiled offspring and remind myself of my position in this family. They should be grateful I'm here to greet them on their father's behalf, even though, quite obviously, they are not. *Too bad, boys.*

"Thank you for being here to welcome us, Serena," Ted says. Which was nice of him, I decide, and so I give him a smile.

"Anyway, I'm sorry if you all thought you were the only one invited on this trip. But your father decided to mix it up. Have a sort of family reunion this weekend. Fun, right? So . . . surprise!"

I watch as the two brothers share an awkward silence. Perfect. Make them completely uncomfortable from the get-go. I clear my throat.

"I know you all enjoy seeing Catalina Island from the mainland," I say. "It's going to be so fun to be there in person. I, for one, can't wait."

"We can't see the island from Irvine," Rachel says. She is John's wife, and she looks sour. Such a Debbie Downer. She always has a dark cloud over her head, or maybe that's only when she sees me. She's attractive, sure, in that women-who-mean-business way. Corporate, I'd call it. Every time I see the couple, they look the same: suit for her, khakis and a button-down for him. Today is no exception, except John is soaking wet. Ha.

"I always forget you choose to live inland. What a shame." I smile and push my chest forward just a bit; I'm wearing a low-cut dress, on purpose. I catch Captain Bill checking out my cleavage. He winks and takes a step back. I love some harmless flirting, and it seems the captain does, too.

"I don't like the ocean," Rachel says, reminding me of her boring presence. "Shady Canyon speaks to me."

I don't want to know what the canyon says to her beyond her love of golf, so I decide to ignore her as much as possible this weekend. We are like oil and water.

"Everyone, welcome to my little home away from home. Your father purchased her just for us. We're excited to share her with you for a night. Please remove your shoes and come aboard."

I notice hesitation on their faces.

"You all *do* realize everyone removes their shoes on yachts? It's protocol, to protect the decks and such." I watch with satisfaction as they awkwardly comply, a seemingly complex task on the bobbing marina dock. I enjoy the show.

Ted and Paige are the first to shed their shoes and join us, each of them kissing me lightly on the cheek. I like them better—always have. They've made an effort to look like they're spending the weekend on a yacht. Ted wears a white linen button-down and navy shorts—very handsome—while Paige sports white-striped shorts with blue anchors embroidered on them. Cute. They're like a J.Crew ad.

"How is the cell service on the boat? The girls are home alone," Paige asks, eyes wide.

"It's great, no problems," I say. I want to add *Your girls are women about to start their own lives*, but I know Paige's only role in life is mom. And that's about to come to an end. I do feel a bit sorry for her.

"Oh, good," Paige says. "Thanks. I know, I worry too much. I'm trying to change that, for Ted's sake. It's going to be just the two of us starting next year." Paige looks adoringly at Ted.

I smile at Ted and watch as his cheeks flush. I say to Paige, "That sounds like a lot of fun. Very romantic."

Ted says, "Paige, you deserve a vacation. It's one night. The girls will be fine. And they know to call your mom for anything at all. Did you tell them to feed Peanut?"

How sweet. How husbandly of him.

Paige shakes her head. "I'm texting them that I'll have spotty service—you know, just in case. And they know how to feed your dog, but I'll remind them."

"*Our* dog. Thanks," Ted says.

Paige does seem a little jumpy, like a scared rabbit. It must be a little grating, dealing with that all the time. Poor Ted.

"Hope you guys are hungry. Lunch will be served on the top deck in an hour." I nod to Talley, the young, blonde crewmember standing next to me. "Take them to cabin one, please," I say. "It's the best."

"Sweet," Ted says with a gleam in his eye. "Thanks, Serena!"

"Of course," I answer. "Only the finest for you."

"Right this way, please," Talley says, leading Ted and Paige away.

Finally, John and Rachel climb aboard. Despite the towels the captain provided, John is dripping wet. He shakes my hand awkwardly, his lack of social skills shining through as usual. Rachel hangs back and gives me a wave from a distance, like I have an illness she could catch.

"Where do we go now?" Rachel asks.

I don't say what I'd like to. "You head to your cabin to freshen up and change, obviously."

"Right. Good. Say, I'm on a case; I need to be accessible," Rachel says, hands on hips. "Do we have phone service on the yacht?"

"Of course we do," I answer. She is so annoying. "We have the finest of everything on board."

"Rach, honey, it's just until tomorrow night," John says. "It would be good for you to disconnect for a bit."

"The managing partner will kill me if he can't get in touch with me," Rachel says.

I really cannot imagine working with her. But I don't have to. No need for me to work—not anymore. "Lunch will be served on the top deck in an hour, so you have plenty of time to change out of those wet clothes, John." I nod to the other crewmember, Halley, who is equally as blonde and cute. "Take them to cabin three."

She knows what that means. The yacht is four stories of livable luxury. The top level is the captain's bridge and the sun deck, complete with a small pool and an outdoor dining area. The next level down is our stateroom, which is huge and elegant, as well as the library. The floor below ours contains two very nice staterooms and one that is a bit smaller—cabin three—the kitchen, an indoor dining room and living room, and an outdoor seating area. The bottom floor holds the crew rooms and the engine room. A few more steps down, and you arrive at the marina, where we keep the ocean toys: rafts, Jet Skis, a water trampoline, and the dinghy.

The layout is straightforward once you figure out your way around. I have no doubt Rachel and John will realize their cabin is not quite up to the same level as Ted and Paige's, but that's where the fun is for me—when these little discrepancies create opportunities these spoiled siblings will blow out of proportion.

I wonder if they'll complain. For their sakes, I hope they remember Richard hates whiners.

4

PAIGE

"This isn't bad, right, honey?" Ted says once the cute, uniformed crew-member exits our cabin. The girl can't be much older than our twins, I swear. "Honey? Are you OK?"

I try to clear my mind of all the articles I read about terrible trag-edies that happened on the water around Catalina Island and attempt to smile at Ted. I can't help it; I'm on edge. There is some sort of under-current on board in addition to all my other fears. I suppose it's the appearance of John and Rachel, but it seems like something more. Ted's waiting for a response.

"It's a nice room, that's for sure." I touch the soft throw on the end of the king-size bed. It's a white cloud of luxury. The stateroom is something you'd see in *Architectural Digest*: white fabrics, mahogany cabinetry, and a big bathroom with a real bathtub and a double vanity. It's nicer than our master bedroom at home. My heart pounds when I look out the window to the harbor. "So now that your brother is here, too, do you have a plan?"

"I do. All you need to do is relax, enjoy yourself. This is supposed to feel like a vacation, and it's a chance for you to work your charm on Richard. He's always liked you. And he likes our whole family—or at least, the appearance of it. He always makes a big deal over you and the girls, how cute you three are. And you and me, we're a great team. I haven't had a marketing person since who understood commercial sales channels and the art of the deal. Your insights were always on target and cutting edge. I know he'll choose the two of us to take over the company. I mean, he'd be crazy not to. We are the future, personally and professionally. Together we'll make Kingsley into a cool family company; we'll make the brand sleek and beautiful. You can oversee marketing and sales and technology, and I'll take over Dad's role. It's going to be perfect. Like us," Ted says. "You do look gorgeous. Right at home on this yacht."

"I would love going back to work full-time, in an official corporate role. I've missed it—the mental stimulation, the travel, the client pitches. It means a lot that you see that in me. We need to be sure to tell your dad about all I've accomplished for the food bank," I say, not quite believing what he's saying but loving every minute. I was good. I'm still good.

"Sure. Of course. Whatever. You have a great marketing brain. I mean, you got promoted all the time, remember? I need you by my side at the office," Ted says. A big grin leaps onto his face. "I love this yacht. We deserve to be on a yacht. I feel right at home."

This thing is the opposite of homey. "You know, all this luxury doesn't mean we're safe," I say. "Bad things can happen, even on a boat like this. Look at this article I found." I hold my phone out for Ted, but he won't take it. Fine. I'll read it to him. "Listen to this: Once, a new yacht exploded right over there in Avalon Harbor, killed a woman and a two-year-old. All because of a rope getting caught in the engine."

"Paige, stop it," Ted says and wraps his arms around me. It feels nice to be in his embrace, but it's short-lived. He walks to the window across the room. "Please don't read any more of those sad stories. We're safe. The girls are fine. The only dampers on this day are John and Rachel. I can't believe he invited them, too. Dad knows we can't stand each other. I suppose that's the point."

Poor Ted thought he would get that father-son bonding time alone. His dad has been pitting his two sons against each other almost since Ted was born. Ted the golden boy, who excels at everything; and John, who is more of a worker bee, just going about his job in a predictable and mediocre fashion—or at least, that's what Ted tells me. I could count on two hands the time we've spent with Richard that weren't big family holiday gatherings. Even this yacht excursion is a small group, by Richard's standards. Which puts Ted in an unwanted spotlight: it's a lot of pressure, living up to his dad's standard of perfection.

The pressure, the incessant competition, would get to anyone. I'm surprised Ted isn't more stressed out.

"Sorry about John, but it's a small group, so you'll still get to spend time with Richard, and that's what's important," I say. "But as for your stepmom, I don't know what to say or what to think about her, as usual. I mean, what's with Serena dressing like a hooker around us? And she was flirting with the captain. I know your dad likes it when she dresses that way, but we're family. It's gross. I don't need to see that. I'm glad the girls aren't here."

"I suppose if you've got it, flaunt it, or so they say," Ted says, a twinkle coming back to his gorgeous eyes as I swat at him. "OK, let's make a deal: I'll try to ignore John's presence, and you try to stop worrying about everything and everyone, including Serena. Look at this cabin. Fit for royalty. It's over the top. Still cannot believe Dad spent so much money on a yacht. We begged him to buy one when we were kids, but he always said boats were a stupid investment. I'm glad he's lightening up. I guess Serena helped him see the fun in yachting."

"She is good at spending his money, that's for sure. And maybe he is more open to sharing some of his fortune? Maybe," I say, patting him on the shoulder. I, for one, hope it is true. I need money for the girls' college education. Ted is too proud to ask for Richard's help, but I will do it. For all of us. Ted will never need to know.

And now Ted wants me to work with him, leading Kingsley. I'll have a paycheck again, and a purpose. "Thanks for including me in your plans for the company. I'm really honored."

"Of course. I can't imagine taking the reins without you by my side. I bet Richard will love this idea. A package deal. Our perfect family taking the company into the future. You, me, and the girls can be in the company's advertising, give Kingsley a squeaky-clean image," Ted says. "We'll have everything, honey."

Of course, I realize Ted is cashing in on the family image, using me and the girls, to a certain extent, to create an appealing package for Richard. I'm happy to go along if I get a position in the company, too. I'm ready to go back to work, at Kingsley or the food bank. But I'd love to work with Ted again. And I'd love to get a paycheck again. When I married Ted, I thought we would be set for life. And to be honest, I was raised that the man of the family controls the finances, so I didn't give it much thought. Besides, Ted was a Kingsley.

But there is no turning back—just looking forward. I'm going to borrow money from Richard to replenish the college fund he generously set up for us when the twins were born. I will explain we needed to use the money for living expenses, and hopefully, he will believe that. And if he hasn't decided the time is right to make Ted and me the co-CEOs yet, I'll ask for my old job in marketing to pay him back. In my day-dreams, I imagine Ted and me walking to lunch across the street from the office complex every day, holding hands, talking about our days, solving the problems that arise, growing the company together to even bigger market shares. It's what we did when we first met. Thinking about it makes my heart happy.

Ted's current company's office is in the tower next door to Kingsley Global Enterprises' corporate home office. Even though he left Kingsley a few years ago, Ted's new job is impressive, and he makes a good salary. But we're always behind on our bills. It doesn't help that we live in Laguna Beach, one of the most expensive places to live in Orange County. I knew we'd been struggling financially. But when I went online to check on the college fund a few weeks ago, I was speechless. I'm certain Ted wouldn't have drained those accounts unless it was absolutely necessary.

Of course, I've asked him for explanations. But he's embarrassed, I know. He refuses to talk about it and reassures me at every turn that we'll be fine financially. I want to believe him; I always want to believe him. But it's come to a point where I must put my children first. And I will. I'm tired of asking Ted for answers, tired of being stonewalled in the name of getting along and trusting him.

He's a good man who sometimes makes some bad investments. I get it. He's only trying to help our family—that's what it has been about. He took a job outside his family's business to better himself and prove his value. He's done his best with our finances, and I know it stresses him out even more than me when he looks at our bank accounts. He's had such bad luck investing over the years, no matter how hard he tries. Poor guy. Every time I've put my foot down and demanded explanations, he has perfectly reasonable reasons for the things he did, and I in turn feel guilty for stressing him out about things he likely has under control.

I do trust Ted, and I don't want to step on his toes, especially now that he sees us working together again—but that might not happen soon enough. It's time for me to help financially, lighten the load of stress he must be feeling, and this weekend, I will have the chance. I take a breath and tell my shoulders to drop away from my ears. Sunshine pours through the floor-to-ceiling sliding glass doors. The cabin is beautiful, adorned with fresh flowers in crystal vases and soft contemporary chic furniture. There is no cheesy nautical theme on this boat; everything is white and cream, mother of pearl, Lucite, and elegance.

Ted walks across the stateroom and stands next to me. He is so handsome, despite the fact he's terrible with money. I mean, if the girls only knew . . . But they won't. I'm going to fix it.

I smile at the thought. "I must admit, I could get used to this," I say.

"Me too," Ted answers.

I slide the door open to our gorgeous deck. On the horizon, I see Catalina Island shimmering in the distance. My heart races despite the grandeur. Ted joins me on the deck as I try to forget all the newspaper articles I've read. But I can't.

"Did you know a lot of people drown over there? I was reading about a group of Utah tourists who were out in a glass-bottom boat, floating over the marine gardens, when, on the bottom—in twenty-five feet of water—they saw the body of a man. The magnifying effect of the water made the body appear to be a giant, and some of the ladies in the party fainted."

"Paige, please. You're safe. There won't be giants floating below us. It's cute that you read about all this stuff, but I think you should try to forget about it," Ted says. He's bothered by my death obsession, but I can't help myself. I'm a nervous wreck.

I push the image of the dead man out of my mind, take a deep breath, and focus on Ted. He's distracted again.

"Look, I know why you're disappointed John is here, and I get it," I say.

Ted says, "I know. But here's the thing: we will use this to our advantage. Or rather, I will. I just need you by my side, following my lead. John is a micromanaging bore. Rachel is an overly opinionated know-it-all. Maybe, despite all the games he plays, Dad will see that even more clearly over the next two days. I'm not too worried."

"You never are," I say and lean into him as he wraps his arms around my waist. "Should we call the girls? Say goodbye?"

He sighs. "We haven't been gone an hour yet. Take a deep breath," he says. "They'll be fine. I need you to focus on your one job here: convincing Dad we're the future of Kingsley Global Enterprises."

The yacht shudders, and I reach for the polished wood railing of the deck. "Oh my God, we're moving," I say, noticing the shift of the land as the ocean slaps the hull of the boat. I hang on for dear life.

"We are," Ted says. "Looks like our weekend has officially begun."

"I hope one of those freak storms doesn't hit," I say. "Gales happen all the time."

Ted chuckles. "It never even rains in Southern California."

That's not true. It's twenty-two miles from here to there. That's a lot of deep, dark water to cross. Things go wrong all the time. Ted wraps his arm around my shoulders as the yacht slowly plows through the harbor. We're the largest boat around, which gives me both comfort and the creeps.

The sparkling ocean doesn't look menacing—not here in the harbor, where tiny Duffy boats dot the water and sailboats glide by. This yacht must be incredible, even for other boaters accustomed to mega-yachts. I notice a lot of people staring up at us from their little boats. Some take photos or maybe even videos. I know the gossip column OC Scoop loves to cover Richard and his wealth. I wouldn't be surprised if they write about this weekend.

I wave shyly, feeling a bit self-conscious about this overt display of wealth, as Ted scans the water and gives the fellow boaters in the harbor big grins.

He shakes his head and kisses my cheek. "This is great, isn't it? I feel like I'm king of the world. Let's go socialize. I need you to bring your A game, sweetie. Dad brought us all here for a reason, and whatever game he's playing, let's plan on winning. I hope this is the weekend he will announce, finally, that he's ready to retire. Give up the helm at Kingsley Global Enterprises."

"It's exciting to think about," I say.

"I'd be CEO, and you'd be president. We should give you time to get your feet wet, so to speak. Get back into the groove at the office, hit your stride. You'll be a figurehead of sorts at first, but it won't take you long to grow into the job," Ted says. "Sound OK?"

"Sure, yes. I get it. President sounds great," I say. And it does. I like that Ted is excited about all this. Ted left Kingsley three years ago to get experience outside the family business so he could return more valuable than ever. He was convinced he could vault over John and become CEO if he had broader business exposure than John could ever have inside the company. I'm so proud of him for making such a bold, strategic move. I'm not so sure, though, that John is going to allow this to happen.

Imagine me vaulting over John to get the president's job. I want to see it—I do. Ted seems to believe it. I know I'd do a great job. Sure, I'll need to learn a lot of new things—technology has changed everything since I was last in the Kingsley office—but that's exciting. My food bank experience has kept me on my marketing toes. And Ted says he'll give me the support and time to get acclimated. Besides, everybody knows if you want something done right, you hire a busy mom . . . or a formerly busy mom whose nest is about to be empty.

Ted is the best option. Ted and me. I don't trust John—never have. I think he'd do anything to make Ted look bad in Richard's eyes. Then again, Richard is known to be a real jerk to his family, so maybe Richard was behind Ted's exit. I don't know the whole story, of course. Ted said it was best left in the past, that he'd moved on and I should, too. At least until it's time for him to make his triumphant return. Even though he doesn't work for the company anymore, he is still the favorite son. I know that, and so does Ted. I take a deep breath and see the hope in Ted's eyes. Maybe this boat trip is the start of something more, for all of us. Ted deserves it. Maybe when I ask Richard for the college money and a job, I'll have a chance to talk him into giving Ted what he wants, too.

"Keep that sparkle in your eye. The future is ours; the future is us," Ted says, pulling my thoughts to the present.

I smile at him.

He stares off into the horizon. "The only person in my way is John. He's the loyal foot soldier—taking all of Dad's shit, never causing waves. But John could never be a leader, right?" he says, pushing off the railing and walking inside before I can answer.

The problem is that none of us know what Richard is up to. Not yet. I touch the seasickness bracelets I slipped on before boarding, making sure the raised dots are aligned with my pulse points as directed. Ted wears the ones I bought for him, too. The forecast calls for mostly sunny skies with a risk of pop-up thunderstorms and big southern swells, whatever that means. I remember hearing something about the wind picking up, but I figured that didn't matter since we aren't sailing.

I step inside the cabin and close the sliding door. "OK, Ted. Let's wow your dad. It's the least I can do on my last day on Earth."

"Very funny," Ted says, then kisses me on the cheek as we reluctantly exit our beautiful cabin.

The boat lurches as the engines roar to full power. We are cruising out of the harbor and into the big open ocean. I grab Ted's arm, and we make it down the hallway to the stairs. I hope for the best, fighting the urge to run off this boat as fast as I can. I realize, though, as I stare out at the endless sea surrounding us, it's much too late to change plans now.

And besides, I've decided today marks a fresh start. It's the first day of the rest of our married life together. Ted and I are a package deal. Always have been, always will be. I try to tell myself not to get too excited about the future. We haven't seen or heard from Richard yet.

And Richard always has plans of his own.

5

RICHARD

I sit in our huge stateroom and enjoy my final moments of peace before I reveal myself to the kids. Yes, family is wonderful, in theory. In practice, I find all this quite draining. I walk to the sliding glass doors and take in the busy marina. It's nice having the largest yacht around. Serena convinced me it was the one thing I had never owned, and we have been enjoying it since.

I think about my grandfather and wonder if he'd approve. Likely not. But I deserve it. I built a huge company, a multinational success story, on the back of what my grandfather had started. I cleaned up our act, refocused on the real estate and investment portions of the business, and I've been successful beyond my wildest dreams.

But none of that really matters in the long run. No, it's not about the money, because you can't take that with you. It's about your legacy, your family—no matter how annoying they can be. The puppets on my board support my every move, and they are well compensated for doing so. I know they, too, are awaiting my decision for the future of Kingsley, and they will have an answer soon. I have of course hinted that my succession will be a family matter, but I have made no promises.

My kids. I still don't know who to trust. Not really. This trip is important. I will watch them all closely, try to get to know them better. Nothing like family togetherness to bring out the worst—I mean, the *real*—character in a kid.

I turn back and walk through the stateroom, touching a favorite sculpture that Serena and I bought on a quick trip to Europe. It's a lion—gold with a fierce, roaring face framed by a huge mane. Strong and ferocious. I like to think it's my self-portrait. Ha.

I walk to the door and step into the library, another favorite room. None of our guests are here yet. I take a seat in one of the white leather chairs and remember my wife's reaction when I told her I'd be in our stateroom and was not to be disturbed when our guests arrived. I doubt she believed my business excuse.

"They should be here any moment," my wife said with a smirk. "This is your plan. You invited them. You should be here, in person, to greet them. Champagne?"

Serena doesn't realize I'd arrived at the yacht at sunrise. The things I needed to take care of have been handled.

"I'll reappear as soon as I can," I told her. "You drink champagne, but keep your wits about you. You are the host until I return."

"Don't worry. I can handle your boys," she said, pouring herself a glass.

When she kissed my cheek, all I thought about was what a beautiful baby we'll have together. If I'm not mistaken, my newest bride is pregnant. It's the tiniest of clues: a paler-than-usual complexion and slight but detectable weight gain around her waist and those fabulous breasts. I'm sure she is waiting for the perfect time to make the announcement, or she's in denial. Some women don't even know the happy news for months. I'm also hoping she'll moderate her champagne consumption for Junior's sake, but how can I judge her if she doesn't even know she's carrying my child? I bite my tongue, for now.

Maybe I'm the first to know. I'm often the first to know things other people keep hidden.

6

JOHN

Even though this is a nice room, I think they stuck us in the worst guest cabin. I don't tell Rachel that, though, because she'd be furious. I'll keep my suspicions to myself. I'm known for keeping my cards close. That's why my dad trusts me with his dirty secrets. I wonder what mess he's gotten himself into this time. Maybe he needs my help with one of the executives at Kingsley Global Enterprises again.

That would be an easier task than taking down my perfect brother, Ted. Man, was I angry when I saw him and his wife on the dock. I can still feel the fire burning in the pit of my stomach. I thought it would just be me and Dad, palling around, making plans for the future. Ted always ruins everything for me.

"Should we go back upstairs? I'm claustrophobic in here," Rachel says. "I want to see Ted and Paige's cabin. Where's a picture of the floor plan of this boat? We're getting screwed, I'm sure of it."

And I'm sure she's right. She usually is. From what I can tell, we *are* screwed. There are three cabins on this level, according to the evacuation chart framed in the hallway. Ours is at the end. I'm not sure why Serena didn't give us cabin number two, across the hall from the golden couple. Or cabin number one because I am the oldest. But she didn't. Our cabin is nicely decorated, all whites and creams and sleekness. I appreciate the king-size bed, but it almost fills the space. Our bathroom is acceptable, and the small balcony adds a feeling of spaciousness to the setup. But compared to the other two cabins, which are double the size, we are being sent a message that we're not equal to Ted and Paige. I just don't know who is sending the message—my dad, Serena, or both.

Our suitcases are open in the small closet. We'll be fine here, but I do want to see the other staterooms. As I change into dry khakis and a navy polo, I watch Rachel. She looks disappointed, and I feel terrible. It seems I've let her down again, me and this measly cabin. It's like I can't catch a break. And every time Rachel points out the inequities, it cuts me like a knife. I'm sure Ted and Paige's cabin is superior, and I'll hear about it for the rest of the trip. My jaw clenches. I decide we'll spend as little time in here as possible, much like what I've read passengers on cruise ships do.

"The good news is, we don't have to spend much time in here other than sleeping. I'm sure we'll enjoy the common areas. We'll make the most of it! It's got to be lunchtime by now," I say and yank open the cabin door. "Come on, honey." We make our way down the hall, past cabins one and two.

I see Rachel shoot a dirty glance at cabin two but ignore it.

As we continue to walk, I try to release my jaw. I must admit, my anger bubbles up a little, sometimes at the worst-possible moment and at the smallest little slight by my father. I do my best to keep it down—I do. I come from a long line of Kingsley men who have allowed their tempers to ruin them. My dad wrestles with it himself. He's never laid a hand on a woman, but his anger can lead to some nasty verbal abuse. Some of the men in our family tree hit their wives to blow off steam; others went to bars and picked fights; most had heart attacks and died young, filled with adrenaline and hate. And of course, the Kingsley affairs are legendary, with my father taking the grand prize.

I am an accountant. I deal with facts and numbers, not emotions. I do not have a temper. That's not true. I will not *allow* a temper.

My wife climbs the stairs in front of me. I notice how quickly she ascends, while I take my time. I don't have much choice, given the excess weight I've accumulated in midlife. Rachel is in far better shape than I am, and she works at it with a personal trainer. Although she's also gained weight through our years together, she carries it well—far better than I do. I know she's more attractive than I am. But that's fine. We are soft around the edges but strong in our careers. We are where we are supposed to be in life: middle-aged and successful.

She's right. We should be in cabin one. I'm the firstborn. Cabin two, at least. It's empty. I'll demand to be relocated.

We make it to the main floor of the boat, and Serena appears. My mom, Mary, was Dad's first and only true love. I'm convinced of it. And she reminds me of that whenever I visit her in the nursing home. Serena is the voluptuous fifth wife. Seldom seen. Short-lived, I'm sure. I've placed a bet with my assistant that the next wife will appear before the end of this year.

Unlike Ted, I never lose bets.

"Hope you two are all settled," Serena says. She's made a wardrobe change, too, I notice, and now wears a tight red dress and a big straw hat with a red scarf tied around the brim. Her huge hat barely fits through the door. "Come up to the top deck. Lunch is served. How's your cabin? Settling in well, I hope, even though the quarters are a bit tight?"

Beside me, Rachel stiffens. We both know Serena made a dig, but that's not important at the moment. What is important to my wife is a cabin upgrade. She is about to complain; I can feel it. I grab her hand.

Serena spins, the bottom of her red silk dress floating in the air, showing off her impressively long legs. "Follow me."

Rachel glares at me, and I shrug.

"I'll take it up with Dad. Not now, not with her," I mumble.

"Fine," she says and hurries after sexy Serena. Despite myself—and my own bets regarding her exit—I do admit she's fun to look at. Dear old Dad sure knows how to choose them, that's for sure.

We step outside and I fumble for my sunglasses. It's a spectacular day. Not a cloud in the sky and no clue as to what is churning beneath, creating the waves. The water is iridescent blue, almost Caribbean Sea light blue on the surface. Looking at it, you'd want to jump in for a swim to get away from the heat. But I know better. The Pacific is twenty degrees colder than the Caribbean on its hottest August day, and unlike those calm and peaceful waters, the Pacific Ocean is a menace. A beautiful, dangerous illusion.

"There they are finally," Ted says. He's seated at the head of a large table in the center of the upper deck. The table is shaded by white awning and draped in more white. Two silver buckets hold bottles of wine and champagne. Paige sits next to him, smiling. They are already drinking champagne. Not a good play, if you want to win. Alcohol makes you soft, pliable, easy to manipulate. Hopefully, they'll drink a lot.

My heart pounds in my chest. "I don't know if I can do this," I whisper to Rachel. She squeezes my hand.

"Stay calm. We will stick to our plan, despite these interlopers. You will be Richard's heir. You are the only choice," she hisses. "He's not even part of the company anymore."

"Join us, you guys. Have some champagne," Ted yells across the deck, attempting to orchestrate harmony with alcohol.

Paige has changed outfits and now wears a light-blue linen dress. I look at Rachel in her navy suit and me in my khaki pants. We look like we're at a corporate retreat, not on vacation. We will need to step up our game, it appears. This is going to be a long weekend.

"I'll stick to iced tea," Rachel says, yanking out the chair next to Ted as he stands to help her.

Paige grins. "How's your cabin?"

Now she's taunting us, too. I watch Rachel as Serena takes her seat at the other end of the table. Ted's power play—taking Dad's seat—is bothering me. I hope Rachel doesn't mention the cabin. Not now.

"It's fine," Rachel says. "Great. Perfect."

I pull out the chair next to Perfect Paige and sit down. "It's a lovely cabin. I'm sure it's the same as yours. We're all on the guest-stateroom floor, right?"

"Yes, you're all on the same floor. I'm so glad you're all settled in," Serena says. "Have some champagne, John, Rachel. I insist! It's a family celebration!"

I don't know what we're celebrating, but when Paige hands me a bottle of champagne dripping with water from the bucket, my plate is swamped, my napkin soaked, my second pair of khaki pants drenched in the short time since arriving for this excursion. Frustrated, I grab the bottle and pour myself a glass before realizing my mistake of pouring for myself first. What is wrong with me? Ted jumps up, grabs another bottle, wraps his napkin around it, and fills Rachel's glass.

"Well done, Ted. Paige, you should learn how to pass a champagne bottle," Serena says, but she's laughing. At me. "John is doused again. Cheers!"

That's when I realize I was right: this is going to be a long trip. I finish my glass of champagne in one chug as the two young, gorgeous female crewmembers appear.

Serena stands and clinks the side of her champagne flute with a spoon in an unnecessary bid to get our attention. She already had it, and she knows it.

"Welcome again, everyone. Talley and Halley will now serve lunch prepared by Chef Jean. Bon appétit!" Serena says.

Rachel stares at me, and I gulp down another glass of champagne despite telling myself not to drink, not to be weak. I can't help it. Dad's demented sense of fun means bringing us all together here, trapping us on his yacht, and waiting for the explosion to happen. Just when I thought he was inviting only me and Rachel to spend some quality time with him. Just when I believed he might harbor some sort of feelings for me, his least favorite son, he proves I was right all along.

But I know things Ted hasn't a clue about. I've been around ten years longer, and I'm the first son. Dad may be disappointed in me: In my career choice. In my wife. In my girth. In my boring life. But he needs me. He's needed me in the past. I'm Mary's only child. And he still loves her, I'm sure of it.

I'm not the obvious favorite, but I am the obvious choice for whatever he's planning. He's always planning something. He's choosing between the two of us, Ted and me. I'm certain that's what this little excursion is all about.

And in the end, one way or another, it will be me. He turns to me to protect what is his—always has.

"So what exactly do you have planned for us this weekend?" I ask Serena because someone needs to say it aloud.

"No plans, really. Your father just wants a fun family trip on the new yacht," Serena says. "Quality time together."

She's lying, whether she knows it or not. There's always an underlying plan, a scheme.

"Come on. We all know he's up to something. We don't get together as a family often, and not without a lot of other people around for buffers. So tell us. It's about the family business, isn't it?" I know I'm pushing, but I need answers.

Serena shakes her head as one of the beautiful crewmembers deposits a plate overflowing with food in front of me. "I'm afraid you'll just have to wait until your father appears to find out. For now, we eat lunch."

Across the table from me, Rachel sighs. I look toward Ted. He's staring at me, a huge smile on his face. "We're on vacation, big brother. You need to relax a little. Chill out."

I look down at the huge plate of seafood in front of me. I crack the pink shell open, pick up a gleaming knife, and stab it into the soft flesh of a lobster claw.

I'll relax when I get what I want, Teddy. And what I want is you out of the way, one way or another. Once and for all.

7

PAIGE

Ted is still smiling at his older brother, but all I can feel is hate lurking behind his pasted-on grin.

"Ted," I whisper. "Stop that. Eat your lunch." This tension between the two of them is stressing me out—more than I already was. I left my phone in the stateroom, at Ted's insistence. I can't check in on the girls, and now Ted and John are having some sort of silent war with each other. I'm surprised by John's boldness, peppering Serena with all those questions.

I quickly gulp my champagne as Talley or Halley—I'm not sure who is who—places a silver bowl next to my lunch plate.

"For shells," she says helpfully. I don't even know where to begin with this extravagant meal, one in line with Richard's proclivities and taste, I assume, even though he is not here to dine with us. The plate in front of me is laden with seafood: fresh, chilled lobster tail; four huge prawns; and a salad with what appears to be french dressing, hard-boiled egg slices, and blue cheese crumbles peeking out from under the dark-green lettuce.

"Enjoy your seafood salad," the crewmember waitress says. "Pepper?"

"No, thank you," I say as I feel someone staring at me. Serena.

"Paige, are you feeling all right?" she asks.

I nod. "Yes, wonderful. This is amazing. Thank you. I'm just a little nervous—you know, about the girls. We've never left them home alone before." And then there's the emptied college fund. The prospect of empty-nesting. Trying to help Ted position us to take over the company somehow. And, to top it off, all this tension at the table. But I don't say any of that.

"The girls are fine, relax. Enjoy," Ted says. His tone is sharp, even though I know he means well. And I'm not the one he's angry with; I know that. Fortunately, my sunglasses hide the hurt in my eyes. Meanwhile, Ted's furrowed brow tells me he's anything but enjoying himself. "Look, John, why don't we agree to keep this little voyage light, friendly. Do you think you can do that?"

John laughs. "I hardly think I'm the one who needs a lecture on decorum, Teddy."

These two are ridiculous. I take a deep breath and tell myself to relax and enjoy, as Ted said. I touch his thigh with what I hope is a calm, loving gesture. He takes my hand. We're a team.

"You always do have a plan, Johnny boy," Ted says. He takes a sip of champagne, but he still hasn't touched his lunch. "I'm certainly proof of that. Am I right?"

John finishes chewing the bite in his mouth as silence descends on the table. I close my eyes and imagine I am anywhere but here. What is Ted talking about, with John and *plans*? What did John plan for Ted? I stare at my husband, who has a look on his face I don't recognize, and wonder what is going on.

"Teddy, lighten up," John says. "Eat your lunch. When Dad gets here, you can whine to him like always. This lobster is superb, Serena."

"Thank you, but it's all the chef's doing. Oh, and your dad's; he planned all the menus," Serena says.

I notice she has barely eaten her meal. I'm the only one, it seems, who can eat while stressing. And Rachel, who's tucking into her lobster now. I should change the subject.

"Serena, how many times have you been on the yacht?" I ask.

Beside me, Ted gestures for the crewmember and motions for pepper. I watch as tiny black flecks fly around his plate. What kind of game does he think he's playing here? Because this talk between the brothers is anything but productive. It looks like Rachel agrees, too. She's silent, eating her salad, but clearly upset by the conversation. If we all pretend to get along for one night . . . well, then we're a happy little family yachting to Catalina Island like it's supposed to be.

Correction: it's *supposed* to be me and Ted, Richard, and Serena on this little voyage. Older brother John was never in the discussion, never part of the plans, as far as I knew. But now they're here—we're all here—and the bigger issue has become why did Ted really leave the family business? He told me it was his choice, that he wanted to pump up his résumé to appear more ready to take over the company. But was there something more? Was it something to do with John? The realization that I may not know the real story is adding to the knot in my stomach. Richard must be tough to work for, and Ted said as much when he left the company. He needed to get away from his dad to get more power in their relationship. It made sense, but was that the truth?

All I know is I kept all my promises in our marriage. Raising the girls; not taking a job even though several positions have been offered over the years, including at the food bank; being the homemaker so Ted could be the breadwinner. I don't have any secrets . . . but now I think he does.

I remember I asked Serena a question, and I try to pay attention to her even though I'm tired of her smugness.

"Just a few times—never overnight. I really love it, this boating life, and I think I look good on it, too, right at home," Serena says, grinning. "You feel like you're getting away from it all."

"It is a lovely escape," I say, trying to focus on the conversation I started, not the one running through my mind. "It's always nice to get away from it all."

Unless you bring it all with you, I think but don't say. I take another bite of the salad. It's superb, of course. I look around the table and notice John and Ted still locked in a staring contest like third graders. Rachel and Serena are chatting about the weather.

"Look, John," Ted says, catching my eye like he needs my help. I squeeze his hand under the table. It's cold, clammy. "Paige and I are so thankful to be invited on Dad's yacht. It's a dream come true, of course. Let's put the past in the past. We're all just one big happy family, right?"

"Oh, just get to the point, Teddy. All this mucking around. You know it's what I don't like about you—your slick-salesman routine," John says.

Ted looks wounded as his hands clench into fists preparing for a fight. John is a temperamental bully. That's why Ted has always been the favorite son. His poor mom was Richard's favorite before she died. I know Richard still has a photo of Ann-Marie on his wall at home, the only one of his wives to have that honor aside from the current one. My stomach can't handle the growing tension, and a small burp escapes my lips.

I jump in. "I think what Ted is saying is that we all should feel lucky to be here, and we need to treat each other with kindness. Serena, thank you again for inviting us. It couldn't be more perfect. And you're a wonderful hostess. Cheers."

Ted shakes his head but joins in the toast. After everyone clinks glasses, I turn back to my salad. *It's fine,* I tell myself. And no more mucking around—whatever that means. Teddy doesn't muck, not that I know of. No muck. Never another muck. Ever. And why can't John and Ted run the company together, if that is what they're fighting about? Actually, I don't think that would work; they despise each other. I take another bite of this extraordinary salad. It's been quiet at the table too long. I decide to engage Serena again.

"Serena, the girls would love to go shopping with you again some-time," I say, and everyone freezes, including me. I shouldn't have men-tioned the girls in front of Rachel. Darn it. I know Rachel thinks they are my attempt to one-up her with Serena, which is, of course, the furthest thing from the truth. Rachel chose work over having a family; I made the opposite choice. So if we get a little extra cash from Richard because he loves his granddaughters, that's not my fault.

Serena's lack of enthusiasm for her husband's family doesn't extend to my daughters. Sometimes, she even takes them shopping, and when she does, she spends a small fortune on each of them. I'm not sucking up—I'm not. Well, at least not a lot.

Serena smiles. "They are nice girls. I'll take them again soon. Tell them hi for me when you can."

I say, "Thank you. I will."

"Oh my God," Rachel mumbles. "Enough about shopping already."

"You should try it sometime. It's fun. And you learn what's fashionable," I say before I can stop myself.

"All right, you two. Let's change the subject. Richard has so many surprises planned for you all. The first one was Richard's lovely sons seeing each other on the dock. Surprise!" Serena laughs and then applies lipstick to her very full bottom lip. Once finished, it glistens as if she's just eaten a rare steak.

"How fun. Sure, surprises are great," Rachel jumps in, her tone of voice indicating she thinks this is all the opposite of fun, "if you're five and you want a pony. And you get a pony. That's great. But no one ever gets a pony."

"Ha! Funny," Serena says. "No ponies, Rachel. Sorry. But you might find that something even better is on the table. Does that help?"

Rachel has sunglasses on, so I can't see her eyes. But her lips are puckered, as if she just sucked on a lemon.

"We will play along, of course. It's Dad's weekend. Assuming he makes an appearance," John says. "When do you think his meeting will be over? Did he say? I mean, I know it must be an important call for him to miss welcoming us on board."

What a suck-up. I mean, it takes one to know one. I can see how he gets on Ted's nerves.

I'm full. I place my knife and fork at four o'clock and look to Ted to do the same. He does. Unfortunately, John and Rachel continue to plow bites of food into their mouths like it's the last meal until we get off the boat. Did they forget breakfast or something?

Beside me, Serena motions for more champagne. "Fill the glasses all around. What a beautiful day. I feel like a queen when I'm on this thing."

Richard pretty much *is* king of the world by Southern California standards. He inherited a commercial holding company from his father, a company started by his grandfather, and grew it until he owned most of Orange County and billions in real estate assets around the world. As for Ted, he is a senior vice president of sales at a marketing firm in Irvine. He has a great family, if I do say so myself, and a lovely home in north Laguna Beach. As far as I'm concerned, we have a wonderful life. A very nice, very boring kid-focused life.

Ted didn't tell me the full story about leaving Kingsley—that's becoming clear—but he always seems to have the perfect explanation for things. Like leaving his dad's company. Of course I believed him, although it did seem abrupt at the time.

I look across the table, and John finally indicates he's finished eating. Beside me, Rachel cuts a slice of hard-boiled egg in half. She slowly raises her fork to her mouth, slips the egg in, and chews. I think she's drawing out this tense lunch on purpose.

Everyone else's plates have been cleared. What is she doing?

"Aren't you full yet?" I say.

"What did you just say to my wife?" John raises his eyebrows, leaning forward.

"Nothing," I say. I shake my head. I do try, but I can never find common ground with Rachel. She's used to being in charge—that much is clear. And I'm sure she's a great attorney. It's sad that we've never gotten along. I guess with the decades-old tension between John and Ted, we never had a chance.

"Paige, let's go stretch our legs while Rachel finishes eating," Ted says, standing up. "Come on. It's gorgeous out here."

"Excuse me." I push back from the table, happy to be away from John's stares and Rachel's chewing. Serena seems content to relax and drink champagne. The boat is rocking, and I grab the chair to keep from falling over.

"Don't start more fun without us. We'll be right over there," Ted says, giving Serena's shoulder a friendly squeeze as he passes by.

Serena gives us a quick smile and nods.

Somehow my legs snap to attention, and I make my way to where Ted stands at the railing. I look down at the rolling, white-topped waves and feel sick.

"Stare at the horizon line. Toward Catalina Island. I read that's what helps," he says. "Do you want to tell me about another death on Catalina Island?"

"Not right now," I say and glare at Ted as he turns back to the view.

I can't be seasick. I need a distraction. "OK, fine," I say. "In 1919 a man was showing off his boat to perspective buyers on the bow when the boat lurched and threw them all into the water. The bodies were never found."

"Creepy, for sure," Ted says, but I can tell he's distracted. Whatever is going on with his brother is to blame.

"Do you want to tell me what happened—what *really* happened—at the company?" I ask.

"What does that mean, exactly?" he asks. "I told you what happened. I needed space from the family and to bulk up my résumé. It's not good being so close to Richard all the time. He tends to stop appreciating you when you're too readily available. Nothing really happened; there's nothing I'm keeping from you."

"It seems like you blame John, and I suppose I always have thought he had something to do with it," I say. "Did John have anything to do with you wanting to leave?"

"Paige, please drop it," he says with an edge. I notice the color has drained from his face. I wonder if he's suffering from seasickness, too.

I take a step back. "I think I have a right to know, Ted."

"Honey, sorry to be so harsh. Look, I just hoped this trip would give us time to reconnect—you know, like you keep telling me. Without the girls and all that real-life stuff. And we have a common goal now: running the company together," he says as another wave rolls through. "I'll ignore John from now on. Promise." He wraps his arm around my shoulders. It feels good, like the early days.

"Oh, OK," I say, although part of me loathes myself for letting Ted's warm touch and future plans derail me from the conversation. But after so many months of distance, I'm loving the attention from Ted. I'll drop this for now and question him again when we get home at the end of the weekend. I need to know the truth—but right now, I need my husband's attention more. I wink. "Just when I thought this trip was all about business and Kingsley Global Enterprises, you're telling me it's a romantic weekend? That's even better. It's been a long time. I miss you." We're both busy, of course. It happens to all couples, my friends tell me. A lull, a lack of romance. Our intimacy hiatus has been a bit of a long one.

"I'm so lucky to have you. You're so loyal, and dependable, stable, not to mention gorgeous and sexy," Ted says. "I love our girls. Why do I seem to forget how great I have it sometimes? Because I'm an idiot."

"What do you mean?" I ask him. "What did you forget?"

"Nothing, honey, nothing," he says. "We're here now. There's nothing for you to worry about."

Goose bumps cover my arms as I hold tight to the railing. I believe Ted and believe in him. I must if I want to get our relationship back in shape. I want us to enjoy this trip as a couple. I look into his eyes, and he smiles, kissing me on the forehead. I take a deep breath and reach for his hand.

The yacht plows through the deep ocean. Ahead of us, Catalina Island looms like a sea monster, white cliffs that look like teeth on the left, the safety of Avalon's harbor somewhere in the middle of its serpent belly. I take another deep breath. Ted stands next to me, gripping the railing. What does he mean by forgetting how lucky he is?

Ted's color has returned, thankfully. He looked as ill as I felt when we started talking.

"I need you to focus on our future. It's going to be great. I still don't know what Richard's up to, bringing us all here together," Ted says. "But don't worry; we'll come out on top."

"Of course we will," I say.

I lean against his arm, soaking up the warmth of the sun and the misty spray of the ocean on our faces. He's dragged me into a lot of things since we married twenty years ago. It has been quite an adventure staying by his side, but for the most part, I wouldn't trade anything. We've built a life to be proud of despite the weight of the Kingsley name. We're in debt, sure—but who isn't? We have the important things in life. Ted makes me laugh, and his daughters adore him. He's the perfect complement to my overly worried, overly serious demeanor. We are meant to be together. Everyone tells us that—*has* told us that since we met.

A thought races into my mind. "You are his favorite. You must be. John is so mean and grumpy. Right?" I ask, then swallow fast and attempt to slow the pounding of my heart. Ted needs to stay in Richard's good graces no matter what. Would there ever be a scenario in which Ted might be disinherited? No, that can't be a choice. Sure, I thought this weekend meant he'd picked us for big things, but it's OK. There's enough to go around. That's something we've been counting on. It's the only path forward for our family. We're Kingsleys. Our daughters shouldn't be saddled with student loan debt. I look at my husband and almost get the nerve to ask him about the tuition account. It's not the right time.

Ted leans closer. "Have you seen the way Serena sneers at John? She's on my side. I can tell. But Dad has all the power here; we all know it."

"Oh, there you two are," Serena says, gliding to a stop next to Ted. For some reason, I feel like she floats around everywhere on the yacht. She doesn't make a sound but rather appears, like a slinky, silky, sexy big-breasted ghost with all but her nipples exposed.

"Here we are," Ted says with enthusiasm. "Is it time for the next surprise?"

Serena grins. "It is. I do hope you enjoy all that your dad has planned."

"I'm sure we will. You played a big part in it all, I bet?" I ask, although I'm certain she's speaking only to Ted.

"Yes, I've been very involved," Serena says.

"Say, since you must be on our side, can you give us a clue about what to expect for the next two days? I mean, we'd be happy for any assistance," Ted says.

"You're not asking me to ruin the surprises, are you, Ted? I would never do that. Richard would kill me. He's been working on this weekend for months. He's so proud of what he's come up with," Serena says.

"We're excited to be here," I say. "Thank you for all of your hard work."

Serena smiles. "That's the spirit. You're welcome. We'll meet Richard in the library. That will be the official start of all the fun."

"Great! When did Dad's meeting end?" Ted asks.

"Just wrapped up now," she says. Serena pecks Ted on the cheek, nods at me, and floats away. Her bloodred lipstick leaves its mark on his cheek.

I stare out at the ocean, searching for the coastline. But I can't see it. It's too late; it's already gone.

8

RICHARD

I love the library. It sounds pompous and rich, like me. Ha. Who knows what this room really is called? And obviously, there aren't very many books in here. Mostly fluff left by the interior decorator. Big photo books of boats, oceans, rich people, and vacations. But still, it's my yacht, and I'll call the rooms whatever I like.

I sit on my white leather chair, Gucci loafer–covered feet crossed on my ottoman, and wait for my subjects. I'm certain they'll be here any moment; I have summoned them through Serena.

John and Rachel walk into my lair first, faces flushed from the effort of hurrying here, I suppose. They look as they always do: Rachel could spring into action, defending a client in her business suit, and John looks like he does every single day at work—navy shirt, khaki pants. My son is predictably routine, let's say.

"Ah, son, Rachel. Glad you made it! What do you think of the *Splendid Seas*? And this room, my library, it's my favorite," I say. "It's a hidden treasure, and it's all mine."

"The whole yacht is yours, Dad, and it definitely lives up to its name," John says, shaking my hand before he plunks down on the couch across from me. Rachel kisses my cheek before joining him on the couch. I remain seated, watching.

"Richard, this is amazing. Thank you so much for inviting us here," Rachel says. She tucks her hair behind her ears, and diamond studs flash in the light. Good for her; a little bling is good for business. "Before the others arrive, could we ask you about possibly moving to a different stateroom?"

Serena walks into the room from the back, a special passageway only we use.

"Oh, yes, Richard. I'm afraid Rachel informed me at the end of lunch that her cabin wasn't quite up to par. They're in cabin three," Serena says. She winks at me. "We're looking into a move for them. Don't worry."

She won't look into anything, of course. They'll stay where we put them. I have this uncontrollable need to undermine John and his wife's smug entitlement for some reason. John's mother is a saint; he only pretends to be one.

"Well, Rachel, John, I'll leave this in my lovely wife's capable hands, but I imagine you're where you're meant to be," I answer with a smile as Ted and Paige walk into the room. "And here they are. Join us!"

Now I'm energized. I stand up and wrap an arm around Paige. I've always liked the girl. After I give Ted a quick hug, I tell them all, "Be seated, please. Ted, John, I know you both came to the yacht thinking I had invited only you to join me. I confess, I wasn't sure you both would come if I told you the truth from the beginning. I hope you'll forgive your father for the little white lie, particularly when I had the best of intentions." I steeple my fingers and stare at them. I'm a kind dictator—I really am.

"The thing is, sons, I need to spend time with both of you, and here we are, all together. It's been years since we've talked—*really* talked— and I know that's mostly my fault. I've been busy, with the company and keeping up with this one," I say, then kiss Serena on the cheek.

Ted's face is pale; he looks nervous. John wipes a bead of sweat from his brow. Both wives look annoyed. This is fun already. I needed to see them together, side by side, to really make my decision. We've only begun our journey, and yet I have seen so much already.

"Dad, you and I have worked together for more than a decade. Speaking for myself, I think we spend a lot of time together. You know everything about me, and I feel the same way about you. It's been an honor being your right-hand man at the company all these years."

I realize this is John's way of noting that Ted is not at the company anymore. I watch Ted's face flush.

"Not really, son. People change, grow. Some aren't what they seem, and others—well, they surprise you in a good way," I say. "Can a father ever know his sons too much? I think not. And their lovely wives. We never get to spend quality time together."

"I think it's a wonderful gesture. And to spend time together on this boat . . . It's a once-in-a-lifetime opportunity. It really is," Paige says. She has a cute smile. Always has had such a wholesome demeanor. Something that's rare in the land of *Real Housewives*.

"Thank you, my dear," I answer. I stare at my boys. From the serious looks on their faces, they already know this weekend is about their inheritance and my succession plan. I didn't raise fools, I'll say that much for them. That doesn't mean I'm going to make things too easy.

I stand as the boat rolls to the right, and I drop back into my seat. I need to talk to the captain and have him find calmer seas. It is not good when the king of the ship can't stand up. "The thing is, you all showed up for this trip. You're here. That's so good. The first step."

John manages to stand despite the waves. "Paige is right. It was a nice idea. And you couldn't have picked a more gorgeous setting. Thanks, Dad. It would have been perfect if it had just been Rachel and me getting to spend some alone time with you. But at least I have that chance at the office."

"That's the spirit, John," I say. "Say, while we're on board, maybe you and Ted can reach some sort of understanding, some sort of truce?" The notion is ludicrous, of course.

"No way in hell that will ever work, Dad," Ted says. "But we're happy to be here, Paige and I. Thank you for inviting us. This library really is exceptional. Have you read all of these books?"

"Suck-up," John says.

I swear they are children, spatting like this. I do realize this situation is my doing. I've pitted my sons against each other almost from the start. But I'm tiring of it all. I am.

"Oh, that's classic Johnny. I'm the suck-up?" Ted looks like he's about to be sick.

"Are you seasick, son?" I ask Ted.

"Excuse me," he says, then races out of the room.

"Um, yes, we think this is just the best way to spend a weekend, Richard," Paige says. "Should I go after him? Or stay?" A wave rocks the boat, and Paige drops back into her seat.

"Sit, relax. I'm sure Ted will be back soon. Never could keep that boy down for long. I believe we've almost reached our mooring," I say. "It should be much calmer soon."

"Thank goodness," Paige says. "Will we be going onshore?"

"Not tonight, dear. We'll be dining on board," I say.

Paige nods, trying to appear brave, I suppose. "I'm going to go find Ted, see if he's OK."

"Of course, go ahead. We will see you for drinks back here in the library before dinner," I tell her. "John, Rachel, see you then." I love dismissing people. Once they've left the room, Serena walks to my side, careful to slide onto the couch before the next wave hits.

"I've been meaning to ask you something, darling," I say when we're alone. I reflect on the fact that my children each have a different mother. That makes for interesting family dynamics, that's for sure. Most of the time, I was a reluctant father, agreeing to offspring because my wife at the time demanded it. Something has shifted in me lately, just over the past couple of months. I cannot wait to meet this baby. I must confirm my suspicions.

I want legacy. History. I want to be remembered. I want another son. One who can be raised right.

"What is it, Richard?" Serena asks.

I take both her hands in mine. She has soft, young hands. Perfect hands for holding a baby, for holding my son. She's only thirty-eight, and although I'm almost eighty, I'm virile. I've been tested. I know these things, mind you.

I look into her eyes and ask, "Are you pregnant?"

Serena tilts her head. She looks down. I squeeze her hands.

"It's OK, actually. It's wonderful to know I'm going to have another heir. Tell me I'm right," I say.

She meets my eyes. "Yes. I'm pregnant. I was waiting to tell you when I reached the second trimester. I hope you aren't upset."

"Upset? No! I knew it. It's the perfect time for you to have our baby." The boat lurches over a wave, and we tumble together on the couch.

"This isn't in my contract," Serena says once we're stable. "I'm not sure how it happened, but it did." .

I stare at her. Of course it isn't in her prenup; I just decided this would be what would happen. It's easy to tamper with birth control pills, especially if you know people. Geez. I see the look in her eye and decide to soften my approach.

"Oh, of course it wasn't in the prenup. But don't worry. I'm so excited about this, and our son will be added to my will and to all my plans," I say pulling her close to me. "This is great, Sisi."

"I'm glad you're happy with the news. I was worried." She grins and says, "Son, huh?" She walks to the corner of the room, opens the mini fridge, and pulls out a bottle of Veuve Clicquot.

I watch as my wife expertly uncorks the bottle of champagne without spilling a drop and realize we are speaking almost like this baby is a business deal. But of course, it's not. She was only worried about my reaction, and that's sweet.

I remind myself to relax as she brings me a flute. I'm happy about this development. In a sense, my baby-to-be is now a new contestant in this game my existing children don't even fully know they're playing, and he hasn't even been born yet. How wonderful to have options.

9

PAIGE

I race down the hall to our cabin and yank on the door. It's locked. Ted has the only key. I bang on the door. "Ted! Ted! Let me in!"

My husband pulls the door open, and I stare at him. "Are you feeling OK? Why didn't you come back to the library?"

"I'm sick of them: Dad. John. Both of them. My stomach is in a knot. I needed a break. I needed to think," he says.

"So you just left me there alone." I push past him and walk to the sliding doors, managing to keep my balance as the boat lumbers over a huge wave. This is typical Ted. Whenever things get tough, I realize, Ted disappears. And this after he told me he would stop taking me for granted. I think about the early years, with twins. There were so many nights when Ted had to work late, so many business trips. A thought flashes through my mind, a doubt—but I push it aside. I love Ted and he loves me and the girls. He's stressed, that's all.

"I just need to get to Dad alone," he says. "I need to talk to him. Tell him my side of the story."

What *is* Ted's side of the story, exactly? I drop onto our bed. I feel sorry for him. I wish he would tell me what he's feeling, but I know he won't. Ted is the stoic, manly type who likes to be the provider and doesn't want his family to ever worry about anything. That's a lot of pressure; I know it, and I will try to help alleviate it this trip.

Ted walks to the bed and sits beside me. "Hey, look, there's Catalina Island." He hops off the bed and stands in front of the sliding doors to the deck. Another tragedy I read about pops into my head.

"You know, if you fall overboard from a big boat like this, you can die. Think of what happened to poor Natalie Wood. She drowned over there, just off Catalina Island. Fell out of the yacht or the dinghy, or was pushed. Nobody knows." I shudder.

Ted turns around. "Well, let's make sure we don't fall out. Am I right?"

"Good plan," I say.

"Focus on getting Richard to see John and Rachel are not the face of Kingsley, that they are too small-minded to lead into the future," he says. "We are the only choice."

"I'm not sure that's the right approach. I think we should talk about our positives. Tearing people apart makes you look bad. When they go low, we go high and all of that," I say. A huge wave rolls under us, and I feel my stomach turn. I am starting to realize he may have lied again. "You weren't really seasick, were you?"

"No," Ted says.

"Convincing. Quite an act. Your dad bought it and so did I," I say, trying not to be bothered by the fact that Ted is so good at it—the deception, the acting. "But it didn't really get us anywhere. And it left John and Rachel alone with Richard as soon as I came to check on you."

"I had to get out of there. I think I may actually hate John," Ted says.

A chill sweeps over me. Ted is acting so dark, so strange. I've never heard him go that far in terms of John. "*Hate*'s a strong word. Remember, we don't use it in our family."

"What?" Ted asks. He's looking outside, focused on something I can't see. Once again, it's hard for me to read him. Something is going on, something he hasn't told me. It's easy to ignore his little idiosyncrasies and half-truths when we're going about our normal lives. Somehow, just having a handsome, charming husband who loves his daughters is enough for me most days. Here—around his family on this yacht—I can't help but face the truth of my life. Do I really know my husband? Does anyone, though? My mom thought she knew my dad, but the reality was worse than she imagined.

I push my seasickness band into the inside of my wrist. I've never been seasick in my life, and I didn't like that feeling earlier. I wish now that I hadn't had so much champagne. "I'm going to open the balcony door. Get us some fresh air in here. OK?" I ask, holding on to the handle.

"I don't think that's a good idea with all the sea spray. Those huge waves will likely soak us and the cabin," Ted says. "You don't want to look like an ass like John did when that wave drenched him at the dock. That was hilarious."

I decide I won't risk it. I find a thermostat and turn the air-conditioning on high. I study the tumultuous waters outside the cabin windows and try to pretend I'm not crossing one of the deepest channels in the Pacific. I try to forget about all the tragic tales of lives lost in this very water, people who took their last breaths in roiling seas just like this. I imagine Ted and me in a large client presentation, leading the management team, inspiring them with our latest development and marketing plan, just like we used to do. Ted and I alternating speaking as the presentation picks up steam. I can see it so clearly. It makes me happy. In fact, these days, I may be even more prepared than I was then, more so than Ted or Richard.

"That's better," Ted says. "I like to see you smile. And it feels like it's getting calmer."

"It feels like it's getting rougher," I say. On cue, we roll over a huge wave.

Ted is a minimizer, and I'm a maximizer. The truth is usually somewhere in the middle. I let him get away with sweeping things under the rug, mostly because life is easier that way. But I do know one thing for certain: Things change. Things always change. My heart lurches, and I think of Emily and Amy. I miss them. It's crazy how you complain about your kids all the time when you're stuck at home and raising them but then miss them as soon as they're out of sight, with an ache so present and persistent it hurts. I can't imagine what I'll be like once they are off to college. Actually, I can. I'll be devastated. This is the last year of our family being under one roof together. I bite my lip to keep the tears at bay.

And then I remember Ted's plan. We are going to work together, re-create Kingsley Global Enterprises into a friendly, community-focused company, something that has been missing since my internship days. Some companies engage with the community through donations and events. They encourage their employees to volunteer. Kingsley never has. We can change that, Ted and me. And in the process, we'll literally work our way back to each other, to how it was when we first met.

My heart skips a beat. Will our ability to be Richard's chosen couple determine the rest of our lives? Could this decision of his be the one thing that brings Ted and me back together? What if Richard doesn't pick him? What does that mean for us?

I stare out the window of our stateroom at the violent ocean passing by and try not to think of the blackness below us.

"It's all going to work out just fine, sweetie. Don't worry. We're smarter than Rachel and John," Ted says.

I'm certain neither of us believe that.

10

SERENA

Something is wrong with Richard, but he is not confiding in me. He's distracted, antsy. It's hard to get him engaged in any sort of real conversation. I am the mother of his next child. He needs to tell me what is going on. At least he seems happy about the baby. We had agreed we wouldn't have children. Ever. One of the reasons we were drawn to each other was because of this fact. But obviously, things have changed for both of us. I touch my almost-flat belly. It was a surprise, this child of mine—but a welcome one, once I'd gotten over the shock. I knew the pill wasn't 100 percent effective, and I sometimes forgot to take it. So this is what happens, I guess.

I'm still shocked Richard noticed I'm pregnant. I'm barely showing. I thought it would be months before I told him the big news.

Maybe Richard is distracted simply because he's drunk—on his own power if not on actual adult beverages. He's on his own yacht, with a captive audience of his children. The fact that he could summon his boys here and hold them and their wives at rapt attention, leaning in to his every word, has gotten to his head as usual. He loves the power he has over his kids, his entire family. It's a lot, what he's asking of his sons—to hang out together, especially when he's been mostly absent all the years of their childhood and has pitted them against each other during adulthood. And now he's reconstituting a family he's turned his back on. It's all a bit macabre, and sad.

They're so desperate to please him they'll do almost anything.

I am not so inclined. I am happy with the way things are, including this baby, if he is. And besides, I have leverage. I know the rules of the game and how it is played: the game with his children and the game with his wives. I do not go into these things blindly.

I am the last and final Mrs. Kingsley. All of this is true. Most everything else about me is false, but that's our little secret.

"Serena!" Richard bellows, walking into our opulent stateroom. "Where did you disappear to?"

"Oh, darling, I just came up to change for dinner," I say. He rounds the corner to our dressing area and stops. A smile spreads across his face.

"You really are a gorgeous creature," he says.

I've changed into a silk slip dress, champagne colored, that hugs my body in all the right places. Even my little baby bump looks good in this dress, like perhaps I indulged in too much bread at lunch. I look voluptuous—yes, that's me. I tossed on a diamond-heart necklace Richard picked up for me a couple of weeks ago on one of his business trips. I look the part of the adored, spoiled fifth wife.

"When we are close to the mooring, Captain Bill will ring our stateroom. Talley and Halley will open the cabin doors at the same moment, and we will proceed into the library. Anything I'm missing?" I ask.

"No. You're perfect," Richard says. "And you'll be even more perfect when your baby bump proves what a stud I am."

I don't roll my eyes, although it takes all my willpower. Instead, I pivot and look out the stateroom window to the island in front of us that looms larger by the moment.

"Who do you think you'll pick to be your heir? John or Ted?" I ask, hoping to distract him from his baby ponderings.

"It's too early to be sure, but I know it's past time to talk about it. I need to decide, and I will on this trip," he says.

"I like Ted," I say. I hold a new flute of champagne and take a sip. It's important to moderate—a constant, light flow all day is the safest, I've found. To the casual observer, of course, it appears as if I'm drinking bottles of the stuff. I'm thinking about me and the baby. Don't worry.

"Of course you like Ted. Seems you have since you two met," Richard says. "He's the obvious choice, despite leaving the company so abruptly a few years ago. He's a natural-born leader, and people are drawn to him. Handsome, charismatic, fun to be around, and a family man, too. He had a great eye for the art of the deal. We haven't had a big one since he left, as a matter of fact. And Paige—well, she is a great presenter. Brilliant closer. They were quite the team at the office back in the day."

"Yes. Is there a *but* in there somewhere?" I ask.

"Astute, as always, my darling. *But* you just never know if what you're seeing is what you should be believing. That's all," Richard says as a wave tips us violently. "Christ. I'm ready to get off this boat, aren't you?"

"Dinner is on board tonight," I say. I've planned everything to the minute. He better not change it now, although I'm used to that.

"Fine. We'll eat on board, but let's you and I go into Avalon, walk around for a bit before dinner."

"Darling. Look at me. I'm dressed for a formal dinner with your family, not a walk on a pier. Put on your tux. Stick to the plan. We'll go onshore tomorrow, OK?" I am speaking to a toddler. A billionaire toddler.

"Bossy, aren't you? Fine, I don't really feel like a walk on the pier anyway. I'll go get dressed," he says and walks away.

Taking care of him and a baby is going to be a lot. It will take patience and a lot more money. The older he gets, the more he'll regress. In no time, he'll be an infant. I've been watching him over the past year—the memory slips, the searches for his car keys, the exhaustion. Everything is getting worse. He doesn't seem well to me, yet much to my dismay, he's kept up a rigorous global-travel schedule that would exhaust a young man. I beg to go with him on these trips, but he declines, tells me I'd be bored. In Switzerland? I doubt it. He did bring me home lovely gifts, assuring me that there was no next wife gallivanting around the globe with him. Just business.

Maybe he was telling the truth. Maybe that's all it is. Maybe he just needs to relax.

I watch as Richard shuffles into our stateroom's large closet and bathroom area like a drunken sailor. The waves are incredible today. I could be tempted to change plans and take everyone onshore. But I won't. There is nothing like eating a formal dinner on the yacht. The sky is clear despite the swells. The stars will be beautiful tonight.

"What's with these waves? It's a gorgeous day. It should be calm, as calm as the Pacific Ocean can ever be. But it's not. I've never felt anything like this, have you?" I call to him.

"No. I asked the captain if there was a better mooring, but he says we're in the best place. It's just a huge south swell." Richard makes it to the bed and sits down. "Maybe we'll cruise around the island, head to the other side, try to find some relief."

I can only stand up in the bathroom by leaning on the counter. The swells don't stop. I'm brushing my teeth when I hear the whooshing of a helicopter, one that must be incredibly close to the yacht to be heard over the sound of the waves. I've seen the company, some charter that tourists can hire for a one-way trip to Catalina from Long Beach for only $175. I'm terrified of helicopters, but it's a faster, smoother way to get to the island than by boat. The sound of the chopper blades is even louder now, as if it's right over our yacht. I hope it's not some prying eyes trying to get more photos of the *Splendid Seas*. I hear there are hundreds of photos on the internet as it is, despite Richard's strict security detail. There are entire websites devoted to tracking the world's largest yachts, spilling the beans about who owns them, what they cost, where in the world they are located on a particular day. And what it's like to be inside. But those sites can't replicate an experience like this. It's the pinnacle of luxury, except for these waves.

I drop my toothbrush on the counter. I need to find out what that helicopter is doing. I make it to where Richard stands at the master bedroom deck. He's opened the sliding doors, and he's laughing. All I can see is the belly of the chopper—the words *Catalina Express* painted on the bottom—menacingly close to us. I feel like I'm in an action-movie stunt as the wind buffets us.

"Looks like she found us!" Richard yells. "Well, the more the merrier."

I jump behind Richard as the helicopter drops down to the level of our stateroom. That's when Sibley comes into view. She's sitting in the passenger seat, laughing like her father.

She waves, and the hairs on the back of my neck bristle, but it's not because of the wind from the helicopter.

"Should be interesting," Richard yells as the helicopter lifts away into the sky. "I wonder how she found our mooring. Smart girl."

We walk back inside. I push on the sliding door, trapping us in the quiet but rolling comfort of our plush stateroom once again. Who would have told Sibley we were all together on the yacht this weekend? I doubt either of her brothers would mention it, selfish as they are. And they're both estranged from their youngest and wildest sibling. Even if they had somehow contacted her, there is no way she could have been able to get here so fast.

"You didn't invite her?" I ask Richard even though he seems quite surprised. It could be an act. I never know anything for certain with him.

"Of course I did," he says and makes his way to the sitting area, the closest spot to sit. "But I never thought she'd show up. This will be fun."

"'Fun'? How? She's been nothing but a nightmare for you. I cannot believe you invited her here," I note, sitting down on the chair matching his. "Is her mother alive? Did you find her?" Sibley's mother, Cassie, was my predecessor. By the time we met, Cassie had become a bad memory and a big regret.

His only daughter, a problem child who struggled in school, was kicked out of two boarding schools and one college before giving up on the whole idea. I have no clue what Sibley is doing now. Well, I guess I do—she's in a helicopter hovering over us.

She must be planning to come aboard.

"My daughter is here. How wonderful. We'll welcome her, naturally. If she wants to stay, we'll give her a room. It will be great, and you will be gracious. She's my only daughter, and I do think she loves me, in her own way," Richard says. "She'll shake things up, that's for sure."

The understatement of the year, I know—even if he doesn't. One thing is good about Sibley hovering around, quite literally: Richard seems more energized already.

"OK, I'll let the crew know we may have another guest joining us." I stand up. "I'm assuming she's who you were saving cabin two for, just in case?"

Richard grins at me. "That's what I love about you, Sisi. You're always so quick on the uptake."

Richard has kept me in the dark about elements of this trip. First, his closed-door business meeting this morning, now his daughter's arrival. I don't like it—not at all. But it's fine. I am used to his games. And I have some secrets of my own.

11

JOHN

I don't even know where to begin. Dad kept dodging my requests for a meeting, even after Ted left the library. Paige lurked around for a while but finally left, too. I lost my nerve in front of Serena—that's what happened.

"John, what are you doing?" Rachel says. She's on her knees next to our bed, where she's landed after a wave dumped her from the mattress to the floor. "And yes, I'm fine. Thanks for asking."

"Sorry. I'm just thinking," I say and rush to help her stand up before another wave strikes. My mind flashes to the straight edge of a knife. Dark, yes, but that's what comes to mind. Dad is always in hunting mode. He acquires land, property, wives, children. Maybe that's it? Maybe it's about the hunt? I imagine my dad holding a sharp knife, waiting to strike the son who disappoints him the most. That is Ted. Always will be. He always messes up. In my mind, I watch as Dad comes up behind Ted and slices his throat.

"John, it's time to dress for dinner so we can get up there first," she says as she manages to stand up with my help.

I shake my head to eliminate the dark thoughts. We all have them— all of us. Even the most seemingly happy, well-adjusted folks have a dark side. It's just that few of us can make our thoughts a reality. I remember once, when my mom and I had stopped by the office, hoping to spend time with my dad. We had an appointment, my mom told me, smiling. But things changed, and he was busy in a meeting, not to be disturbed. So instead, his assistant stuck us in a conference room to wait. That's where we met a motivational speaker who was setting up his presentation, getting ready to inspire the company's employees. I remember what he repeated over and over to my ten-year-old self, the little boy pouting in the corner who just wanted to spend time with his dad.

Son, it's up to you to make your dreams come true. I did it. You can, too.

Bet the motivational speaker wouldn't be saying that to some of us if he could see our dreams. The fact is, I just want control of his company, and I want Ted out. One way or another.

"OK, that's it. What are you daydreaming about? While you're doing that, Ted is likely talking to your father, getting alone time, making his case for Son of the Year," Rachel says, huffing and sighing.

"I'm focused, don't worry." I walk to the mini fridge wedged in the corner of our room, between the trash can and the dresser. Opening it, I'm impressed; even in steerage, they stock Veuve Clicquot.

As I work on the cork, I think about my dear old dad. When I was growing up, he was an absent, often angry ghost of a person who was either working or wooing and getting married to the next woman in his life. My mom was my rock. Since I was her only kid, she didn't know any better and loved me unconditionally. She still needs me, and I try to visit her at least once a week. She's a saint.

And she happened to fall in love with one of Southern California's biggest sinners. Despite my mom's crippling feelings of loss and betrayal when she discovered Dad's affair, and my dad's absence when he moved on to his next wife and family, I was determined to do what the life coach had told me and make my dreams come true. So I grew up, went to college, graduated top of my class in forensic accounting, and got a job at the number one national accounting firm. I enjoyed the autonomy from the family business, not that Richard had asked me to join Kingsley back then. I guess he felt one son in the business was enough, and Ted was it. Besides, I was happy. I was making a good salary, planned on working my way up the ladder at the accounting firm. I met Rachel, and we fell in love. Life was good, stable. And we had a safety net. My mom always told me I'd be rich one day. That there was a trust with my name on it, no matter how many women my dad slept with and/or married.

The only scar on my perfect future was my younger brother, Ted. His presence has been a threat since the day he was born. I was the Kingsley son—just me. Then he came along to challenge my dreams, to make me seem inferior somehow. That was a nightmare. I admit, I used to have very dark dreams about him. About getting rid of him. Turns out, there was a less violent way.

As for Richard, it seemed as if we'd all had our role in life, one that was separate from him for the most part. Ted was inside the company, and I was the outsider, working at the accounting firm. Our fates seemed sealed until the day Dad called me. The moment Dad decided to steal the company from his brother, Walter, I became his invaluable assistant. Our close working relationship lasted for months, and I loved it. And the fact is, without me, he'd be the one ousted from the company, living in Florida, pretending to be filthy rich. He needed me then, for a moment in time.

I'd just started at the accounting firm, no more than six months under my belt, when King Richard—as I'd thought of him growing up—summoned me to the Kingsley Global Enterprises office building and up to his executive suite. Kingsley Senior, his dad and my grandpa, had died of a heart attack. He left the real estate empire to Richard and his brother, Walter—fifty-fifty partners. Everyone knew that wouldn't work; the brothers hated each other. I guess history just keeps repeating itself.

"Hello, son. Thank you so much for coming. You look good," Richard said, holding the door for me and closing it once I entered. "I have some sad news to share: Your grandfather died. This morning."

"Sorry for your loss," I said because that's what you do, and I didn't really know my grandpa.

"It was bound to happen. He didn't take care of himself. Who smokes these days? No one," Richard said. "I need your help, John. Your expertise, so to speak. I've watched you grow up. You're a straight shooter who keeps his eye on the prize and doesn't let anyone take advantage of him. You're my kind of man."

Flattered and surprised—I didn't even realize he thought about me—I grinned like an idiot.

"Sit down, please," he commanded, and I did. "John, I'm going to let you in on a secret, and I trust you'll keep it to yourself for the time being. Can you do that for me?" When I nodded mutely, he acted like he'd had no doubt I'd give him the answer he wanted. "I believe it's time for me to wrest control of this company away from my younger brother. Walter can't run a business. Hell, he can barely run his life."

This from a man who was, at that point, an Orange County celebrity due to his womanizing and who already was on his third wife, but I didn't point that out.

"And you think I can help you?" I asked.

"I know you can. Find a way to get him out. You'll be rewarded handsomely," he said. "Dig into his background, his finances, his love life. I know he has some shady friends. Find them. Threaten to expose him. Start with the money. I've cleared an office for you right down the hall. Welcome to Kingsley."

My office was next to Ted's, and larger, as if I'd instantly vaulted over him in prominence. Secretly, I'd always wanted to work for my dad but thought he'd never ask. As for Dad's brother, taking him down was easier than I thought with my forensic-accounting background. Walter was sloppy with expense reports and eager to play favorites with vendors who gave him kickbacks of all types. And then I found the mother lode: an entire account set up in Walter's name with more than three million dollars squirreled away. I was so excited I hurried to tell my dad what

I'd found. He called Walter into his office immediately and confronted him with all I'd discovered.

Walter denied knowing anything about a secret account, but he folded, quit the company on the spot, and left for Florida the next day. It took an entire month for me to realize my father had set up the account to frame his brother. And now I was an accomplice. My dad valued my help, and I loved his attention. His ruthlessness made me uncomfortable, of course. And I started documenting my deeds, just so I could remember a time when I wasn't in so deep. A time when I was just a valued employee and a tolerated son. A time when I wasn't just Richard's enforcer.

"This means the world to me, son. I won't forget it. Not ever," Richard had said to me once his brother departed. But now he seems to have forgotten his pledge. I pop the cork, and champagne spews out over the bed.

"John! Really? Twist the bottle, not the cork!"

I smile at my wife. "Sorry. I'll pour you a glass. And then we should probably get ready for dinner."

Rachel is correct. I shouldn't be playing games; I should be seated in the office that once belonged to Uncle Walter. Richard has kept it empty all these years, but every time I pass by, I dream of my desk being in there, my name on the gold plate on the door.

She stands in our closet, pulling out a fancy dress for dinner, and I follow, yanking a fresh suit out of my luggage. A huge wave rolls the ship, and I crash into her. "So sorry. Are you OK?"

Rachel looks defeated. "I hate this stupid boat. I hate that we thought this weekend could possibly be anything other than one of your father's twisted mind games pitting you against Ted. I hate your dad for making us act like idiots."

"We might get the company," I say to cheer her up. To cheer me up. "I've handled Ted once, got him out of the way—I can do it again."

She looks up at me with fire in her eyes. "You're the only possible choice. He must know that. They all must."

At least she didn't say I'm idiotic, although that's likely what she's thinking. I remember when we first met. It wasn't lust but intellect that drew us together. We'd stay up for hours discussing our latest reads, the headlines, our wanderlust list of travel destinations. Since then, we've traveled to many, solidified our own likes and dislikes, and fallen into a routine. It's compatible—not always passionless, but our relationship could use an infusion of care, from both of us. We'll get there; I know we will. We're both in it for the long haul—at least, I am. But right now, I wonder if any two people are worse at being a team than Rachel and me.

One can only hope Ted and Paige are.

After dressing, we hurry upstairs together but find the library doors closed. Before I can stop her, Rachel bangs on the door.

I hear motion from inside. "Come in!" It's my dad's voice. We open the doors slowly, uncertain of his mood.

"Oh, hey, you two," he says, swiveling his chair back and forth. "Come on in. Have a drink. We'll be mooring soon, and the boat should level out nicely in the marina."

This is our chance. We join my dad at the table. "Can we speak to you in private, Dad?" I say.

Rachel grabs my arm and holds on. It feels nice. "Yes, if that would be possible. We'd appreciate it."

Richard shakes his head. "Not tonight. Let me just bask in the glow of having my family all around me tonight. You know what a rare treat that is. And speaking of treats, I do believe we are going to have another guest for dinner tonight."

I take a deep breath. I should have realized my dad believes he is the sun, the moon, and the stars. It's always only about him. And now, another surprise. I hate surprises.

"Who is it?" I ask. "Do I know him?"

"Why, yes, son, you do know *her*," Richard says. "It's your favorite sister, Sibley."

I feel like the floor has dropped out from beneath me, and it's not because of the waves. He knows Sibley. We all know she's trouble. I've never been more frustrated in my life.

"Great, the little monster is here to wreak havoc," I say. "Why would you do this, Dad?"

"Because I can, son. Because I can."

12

PAIGE

It's nice to have this time before cocktail hour for just Ted and me. Sitting on our private deck, it's almost like we're on vacation, just the two of us. I reach out and hold his hand. It's wonderful to feel this connection, this intimacy. It's been so long. I ache for his touch. I swallow the sadness and focus on the future, working together at Kingsley, and the spectacular setting before us.

I watch people onshore point and stare at the yacht. I feel special, important. It's funny how easily you can go from being embarrassed because you are standing on this huge display of too much wealth to really enjoying being a part of it. Luxury is captivating, and I'm trying to enjoy this moment now that we've reached Catalina. The sea is calmer here and closer to shore, but it's still turbulent, still hard to walk.

Ted squeezes my hand. We're connected.

"It's a beautiful evening," I say.

"It is. We're on our mooring, so the sea feels calmer; we have a perfect view of Avalon; and we don't have to deal with Richard's whims for another hour. Life's good, sweetie."

I must agree. I want to suggest a little romance, but I don't know where to start. I look into Ted's blue eyes. "We are good together, handsome," I say.

"Your hand is cold and sweaty. What's up?" he asks. "Are you sick?"

"I guess I'm a little nervous," I say, my heart thudding in my chest. I can't tell him I'm worried about trying to kiss him, about instigating things. No, I can't admit that. He's my husband. I'm being ridiculous. So I make up a little fib. "I'm worried about sitting out here. It's so exposed. What if a rogue wave hits, washes us over?"

"You aren't kidding, are you, my little tragedy monger?" Ted says, stifling a laugh. "You've read way too much about bad things that can happen on a boat. You're safe, on a massive yacht, in a harbor. Look, that's Descanso Beach. You could swim to it from here."

"That's what Natalie Wood thought," I say. "She was just having a fun weekend with her husband and Christopher Walken. Oh, and that creepy captain who keeps changing his story, even now."

Ted begins pacing back and forth on our deck. "You're not Natalie Wood, and I'm certainly not Robert Wagner. And God knows John is no Christopher Walken. Now, can we talk about something less morbid? I can't wait for dinner. I bet it will be great, like lunch. Over the top, even."

If he wants to change the subject, I can think of a few others that are almost as pressing. He doesn't appear to be open to a loving kiss, so I pivot to the issue that's been bothering me since John mentioned it at lunch. "Can you tell me, truthfully, why you left your dad's company?"

Ted's face becomes unreadable again. "I just need to convince him he needs me back. You know, he told me all the time I was his favorite. Remember years ago, after I'd secured a huge land deal right out from under our biggest competitor? He said, 'You're going to go far, Ted. All of this could be yours one day.'"

"I remember," I say. I did.

Ted says, "I still remember grinning like a greedy bastard. 'Sounds good to me, sir,' I told him. And then he told me to be patient, that I needed some time, some grooming. Needed to make sure the executives all felt comfortable with me. And then he told me to send John in on my way out."

"So what really happened?" I ask, examining the empty champagne glass in my hand.

"Why does it matter all of a sudden?" Ted asks. "Can't you just drop it?"

"I have, all these years. But now, on the boat, I seem to be the only one who doesn't know the truth. I'm your wife," I say. "Tell me what happened."

Ted looks at me through narrowed blue eyes. His jaw clenches. He's trying to decide what to say, that's clear.

I join him next to the balcony railing. "You know I'll find out the truth. John is hinting at it. Don't make me the only one in the dark. I deserve better," I say. In fact, I thought Ted had left on his own. I was content to believe his version of the truth. I shouldn't have been so naive. I continue to stare at him.

He sighs. "I suppose you do deserve better. You have to understand: I'd been dangled a huge prize. Richard told me the company could be mine. And then I started acting like it was, padding my expense account from time to time. It's no big deal. Everyone does it. I was young and stupid, and John used it against me. He told Dad, and I was fired," Ted says. "It's fine. I've changed."

Ted is a thief? He stole money from his own dad? His own company? My mind flashes to the girls' college fund. He's done it again. To his own daughters.

"Why do you blame John when you're the one who did this?" I ask. I'm stunned he is admitting to this, shocked he's lied about the reason he left the company. He blamed John when the fault was his own.

"John blew it out of proportion. It was a small amount of money, it really was. But John poisoned Richard's mind. Turned him against me," Ted says. "He's always been out to get me, to take me down. The feeling is mutual."

The bitterness in his voice sends my stomach into a knot.

"Do you think Richard has forgiven you?" I wonder if I would. I wonder if I *should*. I wonder if I can. I think back to the get-togethers with Richard and Serena after Ted left Kingsley. I'd noticed an awkwardness about Ted, some sort of resentment I'd vaguely picked up on. But now I know the dynamics had changed profoundly.

"Of course. It was a small thing, a mistake. We wouldn't be here if he hadn't. Dad's way past it. You should just forget about it. If John hadn't been on a campaign to get me axed, I probably would've gotten a slap on the wrist from Richard. It's in the distant past, old news," Ted says. He turns to me with a frown, places a finger under my chin, and meets my eye. "I hope you'll forgive me, too. It was just a mistake. We all make them. I didn't tell you the truth because I didn't want you to stop loving me."

And there it is: Ted's fear of being abandoned, of being unlovable. Despite the anger I feel over his lie, my heart softens a bit. "Thank you for being honest with me."

He takes a deep breath, and there's a real smile back on his face. "Thank you for understanding me. For always being there, even when I mess up."

"That's what marriage is about," I say. "I'm still hurt you didn't confide in me. I still can't believe you lied to me."

"I know. It won't happen again," he says. He kisses me on the cheek. "It really was a tiny amount of money."

"OK, I believe you," I say. "You know I'm always on your side." For a moment, I consider bringing up the twins' college fund. Its value was up to almost $900,000, but I decide I can't handle any heavier truths tonight. I'm afraid of his answer. So I decide to first tackle getting the money from Richard somehow, without changing his opinion of Ted in the process, even if *my* opinion has changed. I'll blame myself for draining the funds, tell Richard I used it to make ends meet. I'll protect Ted. I must.

But the truth is glaring at me. Ted says he has changed, but he is clearly still up to some financial shenanigans. I'll become a liar to protect my girls. I'm beyond frustrated. But then I remember if Ted and

I are running the company, all this financial stress that provoked Ted's lies will be eliminated. I am determined to focus on that.

"How big of a party do you think Emily is planning for tonight? Just girls, or guys and girls?" Ted asks.

My heart drops.

"I'm kidding," Ted says. He leans forward for a kiss, and I turn my head so his kiss lands on my cheek. Of course the first time he tries to kiss me is the one time I'm not in the mood.

I say, "Likely hundreds of guys. Maybe only her and all guys."

Ted laughs. "Ha! Good one! I love the life we've built for the girls. They're happy, well balanced, smart. You did a great job with them. You really did. Can't wait to see what you can do with Kingsley."

I guess I can forgive him for not telling me about this one small event at work. He's embarrassed, and John used it against him, so that made it all the worse. I get it—I do. I look into his eyes. He looks sincere and contrite and worried.

"Thank you. You helped raise them, too," I say. He really is a good father, engaged with the girls, their sports, their lives. "I love you, Ted. But don't keep any more secrets from me, OK? Secrets undermine a marriage."

"Deal!" he says while gazing at the ocean.

"And truth be told, I'm already coming up with ideas to make the company more engaged with the community," I say. "There's so much we can change in that old, stodgy place. There's endless good we can do in the Orange County community."

"I know. It would be so great. We just need to get Richard to see it—see *us*—as the future," Ted says.

I push away the negative thought that he isn't telling me the whole truth. The future—that's what I should envision. My dark ocean knowledge is a good distraction for now.

"Did you know rogue waves are unpredictable and don't have a single distinct cause?" I ask. "They happen when high winds and strong currents cause waves to merge to create a single exceptionally large wave." I scan the harbor. "It's freaky. They can happen anywhere, anytime."

So can teenagers, parties, bad choices, and complete ruin. And then one day, your husband admits he's a thief. What did he do with the money he stole from the company, and why did he need it? And beneath all this, the fear that paralyzes me is this: I don't want to be alone. I don't know how to be alone. I look at Ted; I think about the girls' college accounts, our mounting debt.

"What did you do with the money you stole?" I ask him.

"Honey, it wasn't enough to do anything with. A few hundred dollars, that's all," he says, the tone of his voice filled with an angry warning. "Can we drop it, please?"

I can't believe he'd be fired over such a small amount, but I am going to force myself not to dwell on it right now. I look out to the harbor, the boats bobbing on buoys in the still, large swells. It's a scene from a postcard. But I hate it, and I cannot find a way to relax. I watch as a boat labeled *Water Taxi* pulls up to a catamaran moored a couple of spots down from us. I didn't know there were harbor taxis.

Ted says, "We should probably get ready for dinner and prepare to talk to Richard. I'm sorry I didn't tell you the truth until now. I was ashamed," he says. He kisses me on the cheek. "Can we move on? Forgive me?"

I sigh. "We'll need to talk about it some more, after this weekend. You lied to me, Ted. I can't process that right now."

Ted nods. "I understand it was a bit of a shock to find out why I left the company and that I should have told you. I'll make it up to you. I mean, we're here, so that's something. If Dad still held anything against me, we wouldn't be. We're on a yacht in a beautiful harbor. We're planning our future as leaders of a huge company. And remember, nothing bad can happen here."

"Um, remember Natalie Wood? She was moored here, too, just having fun and partying with her husband and their guest and their captain, when the next thing you know, she somehow slips into the water in the middle of the night, even though she's afraid of the ocean. And not one of the men on board hears her cries for help when she's just right there in the water, screaming." I stand up carefully, gripping the railing.

"Bad things happen when you least expect it. Even on a yacht," Ted says.

Especially when people lie to you, I think but don't add. I remind myself I am committed to Ted and our girls. We are a family, and we stick together, no matter what comes our way. We'll work through this, and we'll be better than ever. A loud sound bursts into the air above us. My heart skips a beat.

"What is that noise?"

I grip my chair as a big wave knocks into the ship's side. Ted's chair slams into me, and we slide on the tilting deck toward the sliding glass doors. It's like an amusement park ride gone wrong.

"Sorry, sorry," he says.

"Do you hear that sound?" I ask once our chairs stop sliding. "What is it?"

Ted holds my hand as we stand on our balcony. The roaring sound of a propeller thumps in the air, and the sea below us blows in choppy circles. As we watch, a helicopter drops low, at our balcony's height.

"What the . . . Holy shit. It's Sibley."

"She's going to crash into us," I say, darting behind him.

"No, she won't. But she will crash this party, that's for sure," Ted says, shaking his head in grim surprise.

Before I know it, the helicopter lifts into the sky and heads in Avalon's direction.

"What does she even want?" I ask, my fear transformed into dread. I have more reasons for my trepidation about Sibley than the fact she might be a contender for the company. A chill rolls down my spine. "Did Richard invite her, too?"

"Probably. Just to mess with all of us, I suppose," Ted answers. "She wants what she's always ever wanted: money."

"The last thing I needed tonight was another surprise from you and your family," I say, glancing at Ted before stomping inside our cabin and over to our bed. "I feel queasy."

"It's the waves. Can I get you anything?" Ted asks.

"No," I say, climbing under the covers and pulling them up over my head.

I feel Ted sit on the bed. "We need to find out what Sibley wants," Ted says. "I assume the kid is here for the company succession plan, too. She's a long shot with that temper. But Dad has a soft spot for her."

"No way. Richard would never invite Sibley into the company," I say. Ted's younger sister—the kid, her brothers call her—has had a tough life. She's beautiful. The daughter of Cassie, a pole dancer Richard fell for at a strip club one night—or so the story goes. She was the most beautiful woman he'd ever seen, and he had to have her. Ted didn't grow up with Sibley. They only started living together when Ted was a senior in high school and Sibley was just eight years old. Her mom dropped her off at Richard's, said she'd be back in two days, and left, never to be heard from again. Sibley has a way of showing up when least expected and least wanted. Sort of like how she started life, poor girl.

I think about Ted's mom, dying in childbirth because she wanted to have a child so fiercely, and compare that to Sibley's mom, who used pregnancy to snag Richard and then abandoned her daughter. I don't know what's worse for a child.

"Dad is unpredictable. He knows she's trouble, but she's also his only daughter. He can be a bit sentimental about her—her hard life and all that. I need to find him, remind him of all her antics over the years. Remind him that he can't trust her," Ted says. When I pull the covers down and look him in the eye, he adds, "I know. I wasn't the model of trust, once upon a time. But that is one incident, one mistake. Sibley's chalked up a million of them."

"So you're the lesser of two evils?" I ask and pull the covers back up over my head. This family is such a mess. And Ted has lied more than once, that much I know is true. I often wonder if he blames himself for his mom's death, if his quest to seem perfect to atone for his first minutes on Earth has led to his hidden darkness.

"I'm going to find Dad. Right now. Remind him I'm Ann-Marie's son, his perfect wife, and therefore his most trustworthy, honorable heir," Ted says. "But I need to tell him all of this without saying it so, um, directly. Come with me? Please? Just having you by my side softens Richard a bit. I've seen it in action."

Reluctantly, I climb out of bed, fix my hair and makeup in the bathroom. I still look seasick, there's no hiding that. Ted and I hurry to the main deck and spot Richard in the library with Rachel and John. They beat us to him. Again.

"Ted, Paige, you're just in time! Guess who's decided to join us? Your favorite sister, the favorite daughter. Isn't that delightful? I'm sure I don't have to remind you that Sibley is welcome here," he says as we approach. "Let's go say hello."

The four of us follow him outside to the railing. We look down.

The captain holds the rope to the harbor taxi. We all know Sibley's on board.

"Dad, you can't let her stay. She will somehow ruin everything," John says. "You do plenty for her as it is."

"Enough, John. I thought we'd already established that this weekend is about harmony. Togetherness. Unity. Sibley is part of our family and part of that unity. And I should hardly need to remind you that this is my boat. My decision. Carry on, Captain," Richard says and turns his back on the men below to face us.

"I'm assuming you saw your sister, Ted? Quite the dramatic arrival. Don't you agree, Paige?" Richard asks.

"Oh," I say. "I guess you could say that."

It's the least he could say. Sibley has a rap sheet, a body covered in rebellious tattoos, and who knows how many sexually transmitted diseases. She might have grown up with little-to-no parental guidance, but she's made her choices, and every time I tried to feel sorry for her in the past, she'd prove to me that I was wasting my sympathy. There are people who deserve affection because of their life story, and there are those whose destructive lives wreak havoc on anyone who tries to care. I've learned to stay far, far away from Ted's sister. It's the only safe choice. Likely, that's what I should have done with all the Kingsleys, but it's too late now. I'm in the den.

I still can't believe my husband is a thief. I've been so naive. So trusting. To survive this family, I need to toughen up. I need to surprise *them*, for a change.

"Poor girl. Sibley's reputation certainly precedes her," Richard says, walking back to the library. "But everyone deserves second chances—don't they, Paige? Ted? John? Rachel? I mean, nobody is perfect in this family, am I right?"

13

RICHARD

Life can be full of surprises. One night, you walk into a gentleman's club and fall for a stripper named Cassie, then marry her because she gets knocked up; next thing you know, she's left her kid on your doorstep and disappeared. I know what everyone's move is before they make it, usually, but I never saw that one coming from Sibley's mom. That was a monster move.

Families are all unique, and every member has his or her secrets—some more than others. I attribute our family's mountainous pile of secrets to the golden spoons and shovels that allow us to keep them buried.

I sit in the library with Rachel and John, Paige and Ted, waiting for Serena and my daughter. When I heard a motor approaching, I asked Serena to delay dinner and add a place setting. I looked out the window as the water taxi came into view and I saw her: long hair black as night; her big, watchful blue eyes hidden behind designer sunglasses. She was wearing a red bikini top and a pair of skimpy shorts. But she wasn't alone. Sibley was holding hands with some string bean–shaped guy with white hair; tattoos; and, from what I can already tell from here, a big attitude and big trouble.

My daughter is terrible at love, just like her mom.

And me.

"Hello, sir. Look who has arrived from Avalon," Captain Bill says as he escorts my daughter and the gangly-looking creep into the library. It seems Sibley and her guest have made fast friends with the captain, all hugs and fist pumps. Interesting.

"Sibley, welcome!" I say and manage to find a wave-free moment to stand up to greet her.

My daughter pushes her sunglasses up on her head and grins. She has an orange slice–shaped bright-white smile like her mom. Man, was Cassie a wild one. I shake off the memory of the last time I saw that particular bad decision. She showed up at my favorite Michelin-star restaurant and caused a scene, threatening to take Sibley back if I didn't give her more money.

Cassie is a piece of work. She's left me alone since then, and as far as I know, Sibley doesn't have anything to do with her mother, either. I know that seems sad, but in this case, it's all for the better. I stare at the tattooed creature standing behind Sibley and wonder if I should have my security guy, Luke, join the party.

"Daddy!" Sibley cries as she runs toward me now. "Surprise!" She throws her arms around my neck and squeezes tight as I continue to hold on to the bookshelves behind me. Her ribs poke into mine, and I pull away.

"Hi, honey. You look great. Thanks for coming. Did you have trouble finding the yacht?" I ask, still watching the creep. A big swell rolls through, and Sibley grabs the bookshelf next to me. "And who's that?"

"Oh, this is Colson, my boyfriend," Sibley says as the loser finally extends his hand for a shake. His fingernails are painted black; I don't even know what to make of that. He wraps a possessive arm around my daughter's waist. I notice the polish is chipped on his middle fingernail. I also notice the handle of a knife protruding from his front pocket.

"Hey," he says, bleached-white hair glistening in the sunshine. "Nice boat."

Charming. I don't say a word, just watch. I find out a lot about people by listening and watching in situations like this. The kid holds my eye contact—that's impressive. He also doesn't say another word, just holds tight to Sibley's waist like she's a prize he's not going to lose. I suppose from his perspective, she is. I am her father, and I do own this "nice boat." But he doesn't know what he doesn't know, I suppose.

Ted walks over and gives his sister a hug. "Welcome aboard, kid."

Paige waves from her seat, which is smart, as do John and Rachel. They don't look very happy.

"Daddy, I had to come check this boat out after I saw Emily's Instagram story," Sibley says.

"What?" I ask, still staring at the leech, whose arm has menacing-looking tattoos on it. Why would he bring a knife here, on board?

"Daddy, don't tell me you've forgotten the name of your own granddaughter. Emily! One of Ted's twins. She posted about her parents being on her grandpa's new yacht for the weekend. Gave her mommy photo credit. So sweet. #Catalina, #DescansoBeach, #BelowDeck," she says with a laugh. "I knew just where to find you. I know, I should have called and told you I was coming. But I wanted to surprise you! Thanks for being so welcoming. I was thrilled to be invited to this little whole-family shindig, even though I never RSVP'd. Sorry about that. But here I am. And wow, I mean, you even asked Ted and Paige? I thought he was out for good."

I smirk as she rolls her eyes.

"I did. I invited all my children—at least the ones I know about. Ha! No seriously, I'm glad you made it, honey. It was hard to find you," I say. No emotion. Sibley and I have made our peace. She receives a flat sum of money from me each year, and we stay out of each other's way. I wish it could be different. I love her, love her spunk and independence. But it's not reciprocated. Not in a way that feels right to me. And that's a shame.

My boys don't ask for anything—well, not until now, when they're circling like vultures around my company. They have done a good job biding their time. Sibley, on the other hand, couldn't care less about what I think of her. She's simply an open palm asking for more, always more. To be fair, though, I've given her too much of my money and not enough of my time. What should I expect?

"We were in Saint-Tropez," the creep says. "Had a blast. Didn't want to leave, but this boat is pretty rad."

Sibley wriggles free of his arm restraint. "Anyway, can we spend the night? We brought our stuff."

I look behind them and Captain Bill, still in the doorway, holds up two roller bags. Having this guy on my boat is an unsavory idea, but of course I want my daughter to stay with us. That's why I invited her, even though I am certain my overt display of wealth, this little *Splendid Seas* of mine, has her seeing bigger payouts in her future. But still, she is my daughter. It will be nice to have all my children together, even for just one night.

"How about you stay overnight, Sibley? Colson, I'm sure you're a fine young man, but I'm afraid this weekend was intended only for family. Fortunately, Avalon has many wonderful hotels. I'm sure you can find one to stay in," I say with force. He could be a criminal, for all I know. He looks like a criminal. I haven't run his background check. I will. I need to call Luke once he leaves.

"Captain, hand my daughter's suitcase to the crew so she can get settled, and please return her date to shore. Mr., um . . ."

"Kelly," he says. "Colson Kelly."

Never trust a man with two first names. Oh my God.

"Mr. Kelly won't be spending the night. End of discussion," I say.

"Daddy, we're a couple," Sibley says, touching my shoulder. "Of course he's spending the night. Don't be old-fashioned. Besides, we're going to be married, so he counts as family, too. He gave me this promise ring. See?"

She holds up her left hand, and I take note of something on her finger that could have been from the dollar store. What does my daughter see in him?

I know what I see: trouble. Colson grins and flexes his biceps. Whatever.

"You aren't married yet, so we'll stick to my original plan. No real ring, no bring. Nice meeting you, son. Captain, call the water taxi to fetch him. Sibley, after you say your goodbyes, one of the crewmembers will show you to your cabin. Please join us all back here in the library as soon as you're settled."

"If he can't stay, I won't, either," Sibley says, her voice turned to ice. Colson's hand is on the knife handle.

"I don't want any trouble," I say and look at both of them.

"Cool, great," Colson says. "I'm staying, then."

"I'm sure you will appreciate this hospitality," Captain Bill says.

"Yes, of course. Thank you, sir," Colson says to me.

"Thanks, Daddy," Sibley says. "We won't be any more trouble than the rest of these losers. Let's go get settled, babe."

As they walk out of the room, I hear Sibley speak to Colson. I'm sure she's apologizing for my behavior, promising him I'll be nice and that it will be more fun than Saint-Tropez. Colson Kelly is trouble. I can smell it on him. My daughter is drawn to drama, to the dark rather than the light. Colson is darkness personified, even if he's dyed his hair a shocking shade of white.

I will not have Sibley infect this yacht with that—not with so much at stake and so little time. But on the other hand, I need my whole family together, for one night. I wince as another wave rocks the vessel. I am too old for this nonsense. I will tell Captain Bill to watch Colson closely tonight. I need to call Luke, get him to run the background check. Maybe join us on board? But no, we're fine. The captain should be able to handle this. It's what I pay him the big bucks for. At the first sign of any trouble, he will be instructed to dispose of the white trash by returning him to Avalon. Or tossing him overboard, whichever is easier.

Where is Serena? I know I threw her off-balance with the baby comment, a surprise she was saving for who knows where, what, or when. I did it on purpose. A test. Planting the seed that I'm all-knowing. Oh, and that I *can* plant a seed. Ha. I know women. I know how to work with them and how to work them.

She thinks I don't know how desperate she was when we met. She thinks she hid it well, but I knew her credit cards were tapped out. I had Luke investigate everything, for once—a smart move since every one of my previous spouses was a spontaneous decision. Sure, except for Cassie, they all worked out. My first wife was my first true love, and I was in love with Ted's mom the minute I saw her. But Cassie was a big mistake, and ever since then, I try to get Luke involved before I get in too deep.

Luke's report detailed Serena's poverty, her real first name—Adela— and photos of her parents' modest home in a middle-of-nowhere flyover state. She didn't belong there; she belonged with me. She needed me, and I suppose I needed her, too. After we wed, she wanted her parents and her grandma and her sisters here, too, and I made sure that happened. They all live in nice homes in Orange County now. She doesn't know all I have done for her, including dealing with her younger sister's stalker. I have been there for her and her family.

And now she will have a baby.

I look at John and Rachel, Ted and Paige. They're all grumbling about Sibley. "Excuse me. I'm going to go check on Serena. You enjoy your drinks."

I make my way to the master bedroom, which commands the entire front half of the main floor of the yacht. It's the reason I bought the thing in the first place. I love the sleek polished teak and mahogany accents. The Italian designer worked his magic on the entire ship but spent the most time in this room and my library. It's a sparkling cocoon floating on emerald-green waters. Life really doesn't get much better than this.

I heard through the grapevine that my estranged brother, Walter, also has a yacht. But it could fit inside mine. Could that be one of the reasons I bought *Splendid Seas*? I'd say yes. I pull on the sliding glass door and step out onto my private deck. A hot tub gurgles expectantly on one side. All around the bow of my yacht, I see tiny pleasure boats and fishing boats circle, checking out my ship, probably wondering who could afford such luxury and if someone famous is on board.

I wave down at the minions. I'm not famous. No, what I am is much better. I can hide. I can do whatever I'd like, whenever I'd like. I'm a billionaire, and we have our own set of rules. Not rules, really; we just live on a whole different plane than the rest of the people on Earth. There are a little over two thousand of us in the world.

It typically takes one to know one. We are isolated in our luxury, cordoned off from the rest of humanity by a magical ability to travel, even when airports are shut down, because we have private planes. If one country faces, say, a pandemic, we go to our home in the least-impacted country, say, New Zealand. If we're angry at the homeowner's association in, say, Southern California, we zip up to our Northern California home. It's like magic, elevated living, hovering above the masses and reality. Want to go to Rome tomorrow? Of course I have a home inside the old city, a villa near the Spanish Steps. Pick the destination of your dreams; I own something there. And not just *something*—the finest of what that city has to offer: a home, a yacht, a condo in the newest tower. And they're fully staffed, waiting for my arrival at any time. I am everywhere and nowhere. I own the world.

It's like even though I'm standing on a solid teak deck, I'm floating here, up above everyone else. I wave to a gorgeous young woman standing below me on a speck of a sailboat on the mooring next to us. Her pink bikini is a perfect fit. She's trying to flirt with me, pointing to herself and then pointing to me and my yacht. She wants to be up here, with me, above the fray. It's impressive she can stand, given her tiny boat is being tossed around by the waves. She's something.

"There you are," Serena says, walking to my side. Large emerald-cut diamonds sparkle in her ears, and the silk slip dress she's wearing for dinner is simply stunning. "Am I interrupting?" She stares down at the sailboat girl and slides her arm through mine.

"No, darling, you haven't missed a thing. You look gorgeous," I tell her.

"Good." She turns her back to the water and stands in front of me, blocking my view of the sailboat girl, hands on her hips. "You need to get ready. The guests will be in the library in fifteen minutes."

"John and Rachel are already there," I say. "Paige and Ted arrived in time to watch Sibley climb on board with her boyfriend. He's horrible."

"Of course they're all assembled, eager little beavers," she says with a laugh. "Did you tell Sibley's boyfriend to leave?"

"Well, yes, but she wouldn't stay without him," I say. "So I had to agree. I need one night with all my kids, you understand?" I hope I haven't made a terrible mistake.

"Oh, goody," Serena answers.

"Hey, just be glad she's not as neurotic as her brothers." I chuckle, but I know the boys' one-upmanship is my fault. My dad promoted fierce competition between Walter and me over everything. There was no love, only winning and losing, on top or on the bottom. Am I following in his footsteps? Most likely.

"So a tux or just a suit tonight?" I ask. I could wear either to complement her dress.

"A suit. Save the tux for tomorrow night," she says. "I do love a formal dinner. This will be nice, even if it's with every one of your children." She holds her stomach, and I smile.

"Yes, all four of them," I answer and follow her inside. She slides the glass door closed and, once again, we're in our luxurious cocoon. The sailboat girl could never imagine this. My parents would have never spent this kind of money on themselves when they were alive, but I bet that feeling changed the instant before they died. As their private plane was going down, I imagine they turned to each other in terror and, as the fuselage began spiraling out of control, my father screamed, "We should have spent the money on us."

But they didn't. So here we are. I retreat to my dressing room and find my suits pressed and ready for me. Serena has made it a habit to have all my suits at all my homes pressed daily, whether I'm here or not. She thinks it keeps them fresh. She also instructs staff to iron the sheets on every bed, at every house, no matter if we're planning to be there this year or next. Or not for a few years. The Bermuda house staff had a mutiny over her policy, and we terminated them all. It's hard to find good help, but it's even harder to find a good wife. Trust me, I know.

Once dressed, I step back into the master bedroom as a large wave tilts the room. "Damn it. I thought it would be calm in the harbor."

"Me too," Serena says, gripping the back of a chair. "You look handsome."

"Thank you. Do you think we should ask the captain to take us somewhere else? I've never felt waves like this in a marina," I say and stare out the window. Below me, other vessels cling to moorings, yanking and bobbing like toy boats in a naughty toddler's bathtub. The bikini girl has gone inside her boat, I hope. I can't see her any longer.

"I'm sure the captain has done all he can. We can ask, but it seems like it's a fluke. Maybe it will calm down tomorrow?"

Maybe, I think, but I smile. "I can't believe you're having my child."

"I know, darling," she says before pulling open the door that connects our stateroom to my favorite space, exposing us to the library and our guests. Could they have heard me? They better not have. This is our little secret for now.

"Don't you all look lovely this evening," Serena says and sweeps into the room.

I give my children my biggest grin. I look at Ted and Paige, Rachel and John, and they all seem nervous. Sibley has rejoined the group, wearing a shiny white dress and silver bracelets up her arms. She is alone. I like that. I have a big announcement to make, and I need their undivided attention.

Some people might think this looks a lot like love, all of them gathered here for me.

I know better.

14

PAIGE

As I stand in this glamorous library, bedazzled by the elegance of it all, I watch my husband. Is he flirting with Serena? They lean close together, whispering. No, of course they aren't flirting. She's his dad's wife. But I do wonder what they're whispering about. Likely, Ted is lobbying her vote for him to be CEO; I'm sure that's all it is. I hope he's mentioning we are a package deal, because he's promised me that. The thought makes me relax a bit despite the reality of how big the job will be. I can handle it. I want it.

I turn and catch my reflection in the mirror on the wall behind me. I must admit, I look good. Not as good as Serena, of course, but great for me.

Even though Ted told me not to overdo it on this trip—I guess he's afraid I'll steal the show away from Serena and ruin our chance at impressing her and Richard—I like having the chance to get dressed up. And besides, we should look the part. We're on a mega-yacht. I mean, back home in Laguna Beach, dressy is something other than jeans, which is what I wear most days.

Sure, when I'm in fundraising or marketing mode for the food bank, taking meetings with the area's business executives, I look the part. Professional, polished in a business suit, but not this type of formal.

This is different, glamorous and fun. I'm glad I splurged. I glance at Ted, but he's still talking to Serena and isn't looking in my direction.

I smooth my new dress, admiring how the rich fabric feels under my fingertips. It's a daring pick for me: a plunging-neckline number that Mark, the owner of the boutique I hardly ever visit but always lust after when I drive by, helped me pick out.

"Paige, honey, you have a perfect figure. Why do you hide it?" he said as I swooped out of the dressing room in this dress. "The gray makes your blue eyes pop. Wait. Don't move." He hurried to the jewelry case and returned with a sparkling, long gold-chain necklace, then wrapped it around my neck and threaded it just so on my chest.

"Wow," I said, seeing myself and my potential in the mirror. "I think the girls would be OK with this." I can't help it; I'm conservative by nature. I was raised that way. And I want to set a good example of purity and modesty for the twins.

"Here," Mark said, draping a cashmere throw, one in a lighter shade of gray, over my shoulders. "Voilà. Warmth and modesty. *Chic* modesty."

I ended up buying the dress but not the necklace. It was too expensive. Lately, Ted's been receiving a notification each time I use the credit card. Once the notice hits, he'll text, "This you?" or "What's this for?" or worse, "Really, are you trying to bankrupt us?"

I never challenge his spending. Now that I know the truth, I wonder how he would dare challenge a little shopping excursion occasionally. I'm very frugal; he knows that. I think of the college fund and can't help feeling something in addition to disappointment. I stare at Ted and Serena. I feel anger—that's what I feel.

On the day I bought the dress, I received message number three and deleted it. That was me taking a stand, and now I am very glad I did. Once I'm back in the workforce, I'll have my own money, my own accounts, my own sense of freedom. And Ted will see me as an equal again, working side by side. Everything is going to be just fine.

"So what's new with you, Paige? Likely not much," Sibley says. "You never change, never really do anything, do you?"

"I'm a mom and wife—and that's something, not nothing," I say, reminding myself not to let her get to me. "And I'm planning on going back to work, now that the girls are graduating high school." I almost tell her I'm about to earn my MBA, but I'm saving that surprise for my family. For Ted and the girls. I don't need to justify myself in front of her. Besides, nobody in this family ever asks about my food bank work, my community awards. They don't ask me about anything other than the girls. That's fine. They're my biggest accomplishment.

"Wow. You, working again? I didn't see that coming," Sibley says.

"I have offers already," I say, despite the fact I don't want to reveal anything to her.

"Who hires an old person who hasn't worked in forever? Somebody might, I guess." Sibley is so smug.

I will not engage with her any further. I take a deep breath. It would be childish and stooping to her level to bring up her lack of a résumé. I decide to rise above. "Thanks."

"How much do you think all that jewelry Serena has on is worth? I'd guess five million. You?" She smiles but her eyes don't. We both turn to stare at Serena, who is still in a deep conversation with Ted. The jewelry can't be worth that much, can it?

"I have no idea. I never think like that," I say.

"Of course you don't, because you're boring. Serena has so many expensive things. I don't like it. My mom doesn't have anything. It sucks," Sibley says. "Look at her. She's too much. Over the top."

"I guess Richard likes to buy Serena things—and he's not in touch with your mom, right? That was a short fling, I heard," I say. I know I'm being petty, but she's pushing my buttons. I take a deep breath and try to keep calm.

"You don't know anything," she says. "Excuse me." I watch as Sibley crosses the library and walks out of the room. Part of me wants to follow her, find out what she's doing. I need to warn Ted she's up to something. But before I can reach him, Serena clinks her fork on a wineglass.

"Can I have your attention?"

Serena looks directly at me, with Ted standing next to her. I don't blink.

"Yes, Serena?" I smile. I am being patient, friendly, wifely, and powerful. I push my worries about Sibley and what she's up to out of my mind when Ted hurries to my side and squeezes my hand. Is it for support or to tamp my enthusiasm, to keep me quiet? Is it wrong to be worried about how well Ted could run a company that he once stole from? I look at John. He's staring at Richard. I know one thing for certain.

Ted and I would be better than John, no matter what.

"You look good tonight, Paige," Serena finally says.

I can't help but blush as all the Kingsleys turn and look at me as if seeing me for the first time.

"Thank you, Serena. You do, too. Stunning jewelry," I say, thinking of Sibley's words.

Serena touches the diamonds at her throat and says, "Richard, any words for the family before dinner?"

Richard dressed to impress tonight, I notice. Dark-navy suit, navy paisley tie, and elegant dress shoes. He looks the part, for sure. He could be Mr. Monopoly or Colonel Mustard in CLUE. I'm kidding. He looks good for a man his age.

Richard says, "It's so nice of you to all be here, pretending to be one big happy family for my sake. Shall we go eat? I'm starving."

If Serena expects some wonderful and warm welcome to us all from Richard, she must be as disappointed as I am.

"Yes, I'm starving, too," Rachel says and sweeps out of the room ahead of us all. She looks beautiful tonight in a fitted red sequin dress and heels. I assume she is accustomed to events like this in her world, powerful events filled with connected people like her.

Ted slips his arm around my waist. "Paige, shall we? Your dress is gorgeous tonight, by the way."

I must admit, I'm glad Ted seems to appreciate the effort and hasn't asked how much my outfit cost, although he likely received a notification when I used the card. "Thank you. You look handsome yourself.

I think Sibley's up to something. I bet she has another, more devious reason for being here."

"Don't worry about her. She's here for whatever she can get from Dad, as always," Ted says. "She's a spoiled brat, but she isn't dangerous. Don't give her another thought. I'm not going to."

I will; I can't help it. We follow Richard and Serena through the open-air deck and up a flight of stairs. The fresh air feels good. I turn and look behind me. Sibley has reappeared behind us, quiet, watching, following us up the stairs. I'll try to talk with her, try to help her feel welcome. It's only right. And I'll try to discover what she's up to.

The setting sun paints miraculous colors on the water, blues turning to lavender, greens turning to orange. I look at the surface of the water and imagine the fin of a great white shark slicing through. Sharks are shy and coy, only showing themselves if they choose to do so. Great whites make themselves seen when they're curious, when they've decided on their prey. I like that about them.

I consider sneaking to the bathroom, undetected like the sharks patrolling the waters below us, and waiting to confront Richard when he's alone. I'd ask him to forgive Ted for stealing and make him CEO of Kingsley. That way, the college money and my job will take care of itself. Maybe I won't have to tell Richard about the trust fund—not if he agrees to pick Ted.

No, that's not right. I'll ask him for the loan and for a job, but Ted must make amends for his own mistakes. He needs to ask for the position on his own. And I likely won't be able to grab Richard alone. Not tonight, not with Serena watching me.

I'm sure she's watching me. I can feel her staring now. I just don't know why. If I were her, I'd be watching Sibley. She's the real threat here, not me. Oh, and her creepy boyfriend, Colson. The two of them are up to no good, I'm sure of it.

15

JOHN

I tell myself to calm down. This is just the start of Richard's folly, as I've come to think of this trip. Of course he invited my wayward sister. Because he's Richard. It doesn't matter. She has never been a threat to me—more of a distraction, a theoretical sibling who crosses my mind once a month when her payments are due. She's neutralized and doesn't deserve another moment of my time. Besides, given her choice in men, she'll likely end up like her stripper mom: gone. No one will even miss her.

I watch as her boyfriend appears for dinner, dressed in what can only be described as biker garb: all black, lots of chains. Distracting and disgusting. I'm convinced he's a thug. Or worse.

As the yacht tilts and rights itself again, I remind myself to forget about Sibley and her latest mistake and pay attention to the over-the-top luxury before us. We're seated for dinner on the top deck, a round table under the cover of an awning. Heat lamps are at the ready, but the air remains unusually warm even as the sun sets. China, crystal, more champagne, silver forks and spoons—all the trappings of wealth and power displayed, as you will, on the table.

The two crewmembers arrive with the appetizers: chilled stone crab claws with mustard sauce, caviar on toast points, and a smoked sea-brine canapé. Who eats like this? This is fancy even by Dad's standards.

Serena has outdone herself. I cannot even imagine how much money this all cost. The thought of money wasted causes my heart to bang in my chest. I despise wretched excess, and I thought Richard did, too. From the looks of Serena's jewelry and the gowns she has showcased so far on this trip, Dad has gotten over his fear of spending.

Rachel is seated to my right. She's angry with me, I know, for not cornering Richard sooner, for not closing the deal, so to speak.

She leans toward me and whispers, "Are you feeling confident tonight?"

I nod before slipping a canapé in my mouth. I nod while chewing until I feel my hair blowing about and realize I forgot hairspray. When you do a comb-over like I do, you must lock it down.

Across the table, I think Sibley is laughing at me. She's making motions on the top of her head, and her seedy boyfriend is laughing. She really is a brat. I squint back, giving her my best stink eye.

"Nice hair, Johnny. Must be hard to get it to do that," Sibley says. Now everyone is looking at me. And this is reason 7,456 that she is a little brat.

"Excuse me. I'll be right back," I say, standing and bowing a little for some reason and then hurrying from the table. I make it to the stairs and realize there are three more floors to get down to our cabin.

I see the captain outside the bridge—a rarity. I debate whether to bother him and decide not to. He doesn't appear to be the helpful type. And then I see Halley or Talley.

"Excuse me?" I ask.

"Yes, sir, may I help?" she says.

"I wonder if you might be able to bring me some hairspray. My wife, she's asking, and we forgot." I keep eye contact somehow as her eyes dart to the unruly nature of my few precious follicles.

"Of course, sir. For your wife. I will be right back," she says.

I'm humiliated, sure. But did I have to clamber down all those stairs in my suit? No. So in the end, I win. Just as I will on this stupid mini cruise. Ted thinks he is so pure, so perfect, like a full head of hair. He's not. I know it. He knows I know it.

"Here you are, sir. Shall I tell her to come down?" Talley/Halley presents hairspray on a silver tray. She tilts her head.

"No, thank you. I'll handle everything," I say, snatching the canister from the tray.

I'm pleased by my staff-management skills just now. If I could, I'd show Dad how I can be a people person when I need to be, even if he doesn't believe it. For some reason, I always feel like Dad likes me one minute and wants to replace me the next. But I know everything. Every little skeleton in our corporate closet. Richard knows that, too.

I step around the corner to a hallway and spray the toxic mist into my hand and slather it on my hair. Take that.

Happy with the now-frozen state of my top, I trot up the stairs to the elegant feast at hand. I am no longer upset; I am driven. I am a winner.

I pull my chair out, put my napkin in my lap, and smile at the table. "Did I miss anything?"

"We're going to play a game after dinner, Johnny," Sibley says. "You guys are. Colson and I think that's lame, so we're going to make our own fun. I see you found something to glue your hair back down. It does look better."

"Sibley, you are so charming," I say to my annoying little sister. "I'm so glad you're here with us all. I'm sure you won't be staying long."

"We'll see, Johnny," she says. "Have you missed me?"

I think about that question. "Yes, actually, I have. It's strange not to have you in town. Florida seems like a whole other country away. Do you like it there?"

"I do. It's easy to travel from. And Uncle Walter is there, so I have a little bit of family," she says. "Sometimes it's good to have distance. Gives you a new perspective. But you're all in, aren't you, Johnny?"

"I am. Someone needs to be there for Dad. By his side, day in and day out," I say. "Dad needs me, and it's an honor."

"Don't be a suck-up, Johnny," Sibley says with a wink.

Richard chuckles. "Sib, be nice. Leave your eldest brother alone. He's doing the best he can."

What the hell is that supposed to mean?

Sibley smiles, clearly enjoying herself. "I'll try to be nice for you, Daddy! Say, have you talked to my mom lately?"

I watch Dad's smile drop into a frown. "No, and I don't plan to. Why?"

"She's having a tough time, and she and I have sort of reunited, made amends. I think she might like to hear from you," Sibley says.

I can't describe the look on Serena's face. It's something fiercer than hate.

"Richard will have nothing to do with your mother, Sibley. You're lucky he even lets you come around," she says with an edge to her voice.

"Watch yourself, whore," Sibley says.

Serena leaps out of her chair.

"Serena, sit down. Sibley, apologize. You have the mouth of a trucker," Richard bellows.

"Chill out, Sibs," Colson says, wrapping his arm around her shoulders. "You're making a scene."

Yes, yes, she is. As always, and forever.

"Why don't you two have dinner in your cabin?" I say, trying to get the menace out of here.

"Shut up, Johnny," she says. "Mind your own business."

"Sibley, Colson. I like the idea of you two eating in your cabin tonight," Richard says. Beside him, Serena is drumming her long fingernails on the table. Talley or Halley appears behind Sibley's chair. Sibley stands, hands on her hips, as the crewmember pulls out her chair. Captain Bill stands in the shadows, watching the show. I suppose, ultimately, he is the one in charge if push comes to shove. And it could, with these two on board. I guess he has more time to babysit now that we're on the mooring.

"We'll bring your meals to you right away," Talley says to Sibley.

Good riddance, I think, staring at my sister. She's so ungrateful, after all Richard has given her. She still wants more, and she wants more for the mom who abandoned her. I take a sip of my wine. I guess it's sad, really.

"Get going, Sibley. I can't believe how rude you just were to Serena," Ted says. "You heard Dad. You aren't welcome here."

"Oh, Teddy, you're always so uptight, trying to be so perfect, always coming up short," Sibley says, lurking at the edge of the table, wineglass in her hand. "I thought you might have chilled out in old age. But you've just gotten more desperate and more uptight, more of the same. You are a fake, Ted, and completely rotten. You're just wrapped in a pretty package. Come on, Colson. We don't need this kind of company anyway."

"Sibley, just go. I'll find you later for a nightcap," I say.

I know it's important to Dad to try to keep the peace. He wanted one night with all his kids.

"Yes, Sibley, John's right. Go cool off, eat your dinner. We'll let you know when it's time to join us," Richard says.

"You're sending me to my room because she talked bad about my mom? You should send her to *her* room," Sibley says, pointing a finger at Serena. "You know she is what I said she was."

"Sibley. Now," Richard says.

Sibley stares at Serena for a hard minute before saying, "Come on, Colson. Who needs them anyway?"

You need us, Sibley, you just don't realize how much you need us. You couldn't live without Dad's money, I think but don't say. I'm more focused on the fact my dad just said I'm right, which makes me beyond happy. Yes, this family is a mess. And yes, Richard is trying to make me go crazy. That's what he's up to. He's testing me, pushing me to the limit. The realization allows me to take a breath and calm down. He knows I'm the one to run the company.

I have two choices: I can stomp back down to our third-rate cabin and fume or I can meet this challenge and give it my best. That's all he's asking. I will do that. I will rise above like a leader.

With Sibley and Colson excused, Serena seems to have calmed down. Richard's smile is back, likely because he's enjoying the view of Serena's sparkling diamond necklace and her barely there dress. I feel like I'm dining with an almost-naked high-fashion model. It's all I can do to keep my eyes on hers.

"This is much better with the riffraff gone," Serena says. "Here comes our main course. I hope you all like fresh Pacific snapper."

"We have snapper all the time," Paige says. "But I like it, so yum!"

Perfect Paige is such a boring housewife. I imagine her every thought ending in a forced exclamation point. She's irrelevant. A pretty package with nothing inside. It's too bad she's even here. I layer a generous amount of butter onto the sourdough roll in front of me and look around the table. I will win. And to win, you must at least pretend to play the game. That's what my mom told me, still tells me to this day. That, and to pray every day. I try to remember both pieces of advice.

Once they had divorced, Mary always worried about Richard damaging me emotionally. She was right to worry, I suppose. I can hear her words now: "When it comes to your father," she'd say, "he expects nothing less than winning, no matter the cost. And he's never wrong, even though he often is. You better please him, or he will destroy you."

Amen to that. At this moment, I can't imagine how Sibley could outmaneuver me, nor do I think she would try to cross me—and of course, I have Ted right where I want him. I need to relax. I'm almost king of the world. I'm the prince; I'm nearest and dearest to the Kingsley throne. I exhale and try to breathe in happiness. But as I inhale, I feel my own desperation, mingled with anger and the ever-present desire to win at any cost.

16

SERENA

Even as I entertain our guests, Richard's ungrateful children and significant others, I'm seething at my husband. My frustration is below the surface, like a small wave building slowly into a tsunami—an analogy I should avoid, I decide, as another swell rocks our yacht.

But the problem is, I'm starting to realize, Sibley's presence. Just her being here is pushing all my buttons, and that's before she called me a whore. Am I jealous of Richard's daughter? Maybe. She gets all the money with none of the responsibilities. She's a spoiled brat and can't be trusted. But she's clearly jealous of me and all I have. That's obvious.

I'm in charge here. I enjoy being Mrs. Kingsley, with all its trappings, and I'm especially enjoying my baby secret. Sibley thinks she's the youngest and cutest, but she won't be for long. And thankfully, she and her boyfriend have been dismissed from dinner. Good riddance. I ignore her and focus my attention on Paige. She's so clueless. I enjoy watching her and the startled, wide-eyed face she makes every time she catches me doing it.

Richard clinks his knife against his crystal wineglass, and we all jump.

"Everyone . . . Family, loved ones, can I have your attention, please?" Richard says. A silence descends over the table as I watch Talley and Halley scurry away. I hope he isn't announcing our baby. He better not say a word about it. I stare at him—a warning. He ignores my look. There was no planned announcement slotted into this meal. I'm in charge of the program. This is not acceptable. I force a smile on my face.

"First, let me say how much I've enjoyed seeing the whole family back together for once. Days like this have been too few and far between, and I know that's my fault as much as anybody's."

We all lift our glasses and murmur, "Cheers," and "Hear, hear."

"Thanks so much, Dad, for bringing us all together on this fabulous yacht," Ted says. "Thank you, too, Serena, for being such a gracious host—not to mention a beautiful one."

I nod at him and then turn my attention to Paige. She's watching her husband with an expression on her face that I can't quite read. That's interesting, as Paige is usually so predictable. I'm intrigued.

"I speak for both John and myself," Rachel says. "We are thrilled to be here. Cheers." I'll give her an A for trying to sound sincere. Well, maybe she is. I wonder why John lets his wife do the talking, but then I look at his ridiculous comb-over and know the answer.

Beside me, Richard sets down his glass and looks more somber, the smile erased from his face. What's wrong? I reach for his hand, but he shakes his head.

"And now comes the news that's harder to share. There's no easy way to say it, so I'm just going to rip off the Band-Aid. I've brought us all together this weekend to let you know I've been dealt a bad hand in the heart department," Richard says. "I'm dying of heart failure, and I'm afraid there is nothing even the best doctors in the world can do for me. I know; I've visited them all."

"My God, Richard," I say, rushing from my seat to his side and wrapping my arms around him. My stomach sinks. I had no idea he was sick, just that he was showing signs of old age. "No, this can't be true."

Richard pats my hand. "I'm sorry, darling. I didn't know how to tell you. I didn't want to believe it, either. All those trips lately, well . . . they were to try to find a cure. I went all over Europe and Asia. Even Australia. A wild-goose chase, it turns out."

Stunned, I drop back into my chair. I cannot believe Richard didn't tell me first. I am his wife. Oh my gosh, I've been so annoyed at him for all the travel lately. He told me it was all business. Tears roll down my cheeks. I'm humiliated to have found out like this, and I'm shocked by his news. I feel awful. I doubted he was on business, but in a sense, I was right. He *did* betray me. He's kept the biggest secret of his life from me. I've never felt such a rush of emotions.

"Dad, how long have you known this?" Ted's face shows the love and fear he has for his father. He really is a handsome man. Beside him, Paige has her hand over her mouth.

"Let's just say it comes on slowly—like old age, like betrayal, like a lot of things. The next thing you know, you get winded climbing upstairs," Richard says. "But enough about this. I didn't tell you all this so you could throw me a pity party. I wanted you all to know, and now you do."

The table is abuzz. I lock eyes with John. He seems stunned, lost in thought. And sad, his head drooping. Then I look at Ted. He's clearly shocked—and something else, too. I wish I could give him a hug. He looks away, frowning with grief.

"Is there anything we can do for you, Dad? Anything?" John asks. "You know all you have to do is ask. I am sure everyone at the table feels the same way."

Richard grins. "Thank you, son. I knew I could count on you. Your presence here is enough for now. Keep eating, everyone. I'm still here, still alive. Eat. Oh, and I imagine it's not a surprise for any of you to learn that I brought you all here this weekend in part to discuss my succession plan."

"Oh, Dad, let's focus on saving your life and not worry what is going to happen to the company," John says, ignoring Richard's request to carry on with dinner.

"Well, son, the reality is, I need to find the right person to take it over," Richard says. "I mean, I'm not dropping dead tomorrow, but I do want a succession plan. I will discuss my plans with each of you, individually, tomorrow. For now, eat, damn it."

The table is abuzz again. Richard smiles and slowly makes eye contact with each of us, ending with me. My tears have dried, but my thoughts are running wild. He reaches for my hand. "Now, now, dear, stop with the tears. I've had a good run. Let's not be sad tonight. There is too much to celebrate. I suppose I should go tell that wayward daughter of mine."

"She'll learn of this soon enough," I say. "Stay here, with me. Please."

My husband is dying. I am going to be a widow soon. A pregnant widow, oh my God. There will be endless sympathy for my plight, of course. But first, for Richard's. Poor man. I take a breath of relief. He is not going to announce the baby; this news was more than enough. I think about my selfish suspicions that he had found his next wife since he'd been away so frequently lately. What he has been up to is seeing specialists, sneaking around to doctors around the globe, looking for answers—not other women. I'm ashamed I thought he was cheating. I need to be strong. I need to embrace my dying husband's wishes and host a memorable trip for his family. And I will. My anger with Richard dissolves as I wipe away my tears. He wants this to be the perfect weekend. I will try to make it so. Starting now.

"Let's all try to enjoy our dinner. For Richard, who deserves to enjoy a fabulous meal with his entire family around him," I say. I know everyone has lost their appetites, myself included. And I know each of us also are selfishly thinking about our own futures. Where does this leave me? In my case, I need to protect my baby, guarantee he or she gets a fair share of this family's wealth.

I look around the table and realize I am Richard's favorite person. His life partner. I will be by his side until death do us part. And when that happens, he should leave the company to me.

I can't believe I didn't think of this sooner.

I deserve it. More than Ted or John, that's for sure. Despite my current circumstances, I'm no stranger to hard work. My poor momma did her best, but she worked three jobs, as did my dad, so I had to raise myself and my sisters. It's time a woman was at the helm of Kingsley Global Enterprises. I'm a feminist. I know, you're wondering how I, a trophy wife, could claim that title, but I do. I'm all about stepping into my power, no matter who gets in my way. I worked hard for this role, shall we say. I kissed a lot of frogs before I found my prince.

You don't just waltz into the orbit of someone like Richard. No. You must land on the outer planets first, look at the whole constellation of characters who surround him, interact with him. And then, when the time is right, you strike like a meteor—all flames and fire, passion and sparks—and he doesn't know what hit him. The clock was ticking for me and my bank account. He was my last hope, and I owe him. I will make a wonderful figurehead for the company. I will be the public face and delegate the actual work to other people.

I watch as dessert is served, and all the guests pass on coffee. Richard announces he's tired and would like to take a little break, change clothes before meeting in the library for a nightcap en route to informing Sibley about his medical news. I won't let that happen, of course. He's too tired, too sick for Sibley's games. As we are all leaving for our state-rooms, Captain Bill appears, a stern expression locked on his usually gorgeous face.

"Pardon the interruption, ladies and gentlemen," he says. "I wanted to let you know that unfortunately, we are about to be engulfed in a fairly significant storm."

"Oh my God," Rachel says. "That's it. I need off this boat. I can't swim."

"Rachel, stop," John says. "Captain, is there a chance we could all take the tender to shore, perhaps stay at a hotel tonight?"

"Yes, I'd like that," Paige says, gripping Ted's arm like her life depends on it. I glance her way. I wonder why she is so scared all the time. So jumpy. It's too bad she's not more comfortable in her own skin, like I am.

"I checked, and unfortunately, the hotels are sold out. We will be fine on the yacht. We just need to be careful."

"Could we head back to Newport Beach?" Ted asks.

Captain Bill shakes his head as a gust of wind pushes us all into the railing. Rachel screams, "I'm going to get blown over!"

"Let's get inside," the captain says, helping Rachel to the door. Paige races inside behind them, and finally, Ted helps me inside, too. I take Richard's hand and help him walk behind us. As soon as we make it inside, the rain begins. Sheets of it.

"Oh my gosh," I say, trying to be brave. The sky fractures with lightning.

"As you can tell, it's a bad one. I'm needed on deck. I'm afraid we can't return to the marina. I wouldn't risk a crossing during a storm this strong. So we'll stay on our mooring. We'll be fine. When you're walking around, do hold on to something. And for your own safety, I'll request that you avoid going outside on deck. I'd suggest trying to get to sleep early. It's only going to get worse through the night," Captain Bill says. "Where are the other two passengers?"

"In their room," I say. Although by now, they could be anywhere on the boat.

"This is terrifying," Rachel says. "How am I supposed to sleep in this?"

"Everything will be calmer tomorrow. Oh, and you won't have any phone service. I'm afraid a lightning strike has taken out the tower." And then he's gone.

"I, for one, plan to change clothes and enjoy a nightcap. It's far too early to turn in for the evening," Richard says. "Serena, shall we?"

"Of course," I say, managing to join him. I brace myself against the wall to keep from falling over. "Good night to everyone who isn't joining us. Try to get some sleep."

Richard and I make it to our stateroom and sit with relief, side by side, on the bed, a safe respite before trying to change clothes. Walking on this boat tonight is like walking on a moving fun house walkway, minus the fun. Outside, it's dark, still raining. The boat lurches on occasion from rough waves, but I feel more at ease here, next to Richard. I know the island is there, just off our bow. I tell myself it's swimming distance, even if it's not.

"How are you feeling, darling?" Richard says, his hand lightly touching my lower back.

"Shouldn't I be asking you that?" I shake my head. I stand up quickly, slip off my dress, and slide on jeans and a sweatshirt. "Can I help you change?"

He sighs. "I'm not an invalid. Not yet," he says and ducks into the closet. He reappears in a *Splendid Seas* sweatshirt and sweatpants. "Look, I know I blindsided you with my news, but I've been thinking about this a lot. And there is no good way to announce one's death sentence. I just wanted to do it once, in front of everyone, and be done with it."

I turn to him. My initial anger at him for not giving me a heads-up first has melted away. All that is left is sadness. "I understand. I do wish you'd let me go with you to see the doctors. I would have done that with you. I'm your wife. Have they told you how long you have?" I say as gently as I can.

"Not long, I'm afraid. I hope you'll be able to tell him—or her—all about me," he says, putting his hand on my stomach.

"Of course," I say with a heavy heart. I take a deep breath. "Richard, who will you pick to run the company?"

"Oh, darling, I don't want to talk about that. Not tonight," he says.

"I understand completely. Of course I do. But now it's more important than ever, your decision. Because of the baby, I mean. If I could just ask, would you ever consider me?" I ask.

"Ha!" Richard says and begins to laugh. "One thing I'll say about you, Serena: you're always full of surprises. Let's go have a nightcap. Enough of this business talk. It doesn't suit you, dear. Join me?"

"Let me grab something in my closet," I say. As I walk away, I seethe. My anger is back. I don't like being laughed at, by Richard or anyone. Not at all. I walk into my closet to breathe, but I can't. I have the sense that someone has been here. Some things have been moved, but I can't be certain. I touch one of my gowns, calming myself by rubbing the elegant silk between my fingers.

I take a deep breath. I demand to be taken seriously. I am, of course, devastated over his death sentence, and I feel terrible I didn't pick up on it. But I need to worry about myself and my future, too. He should understand that. We come into this world alone, and that's how we leave. Along the way, some of us require significant funds for lifestyle maintenance. And I'll get even more if I'm his successor. This is all serious, nothing to laugh about. The stakes are too high. I am his last wife, and there will be no next wife.

I check the safe and it's locked, as I left it. I'm imagining things. The storm, the family, the diagnosis. All of this is too much. But I need to be strong. I'm strong. I step back into the room.

"Let's adjourn to the library," Richard says, and we walk slowly, holding on to the wall, to the library. He does need me. He'll be the first to admit that. He just needs a little reminder. And I would make a brilliant choice as his first female president. Imagine all the magazine covers I'd appear on, all the women-in-business groups who would adore me. I need a little time to help Richard see I'm the perfect choice.

There is a knock on the library door.

Who has the nerve to interrupt us? Even though Richard invited them, I thought they'd all have the good sense to leave us alone. I feel my hands clench into fists as Richard tells whoever it is to come in. If I didn't know any better, I'd think Richard welcomes the end of our alone time. But that can't be. Of course not. Richard is as infatuated with me as Paige is with Ted. It's nice to be the recipient of unconditional love.

It's so rare these days, especially in this family. You just don't know what people are hiding or capable of doing in the name of love, but I imagine on this trip, we'll find out.

17

RICHARD

When Sibley bursts into the library, I can tell by the look on her face someone has told her my news.

Bad news travels the fastest, I've found.

"Daddy," she says, running to my side. An impressive feat, given the massive waves and her state. Her eyes are shiny. I don't know what drugs she's doing, but she's on something. "You're dying!"

"We all are, Sib. Calm down," I say. Beside me, Serena is quiet, cold. "Have a seat. You owe my bride an apology."

"Sorry," she says. Serena shakes her head and looks away.

Colson walks through the door, looking like a creep in a scary movie. I swear he still has the knife on him.

"Son, could you leave your weapon in your stateroom from now on?" I say, pointing to his pocket. "You won't need that here—although apparently, you do wherever you're from."

"I'm from Tampa," Colson says. "I always carry my knife. Sorry you're dying, man. That's heavy."

Serena stands and makes her way to the bar. "Can I get you something, Richard?" I watch her pour champagne.

"Cognac, please," I say. "Sibley, stop staring at me. We all die sometime."

"True that," Colson says. "I'll try a cognac."

Serena shoots him a death stare. "Serve yourself."

Colson shrugs and walks to the bar. "I'll make you one, too, Sibs."

"Listen, Daddy, I know I've been behaving badly. I didn't know you were dying. I'll do better," she says.

She looks so innocent that it almost makes me want to believe her.

"And, Daddy, before you die you do need to make it right with Cassie," she says.

Serena places my drink in my hand and then turns to Sibley.

"I'll say what your dad can't or won't, Sibley: your mom was a mistake. Every moment with her. Every part of that relationship. Every part," Serena says. She takes her seat next to me and sips her champagne.

"How dare you," Sibley says.

"Now, Serena, that's not right. The best part of my time with Cassie is Sibley. But I will not be in touch with your mother. She is dead to me," I say. The girl needs to hear the truth.

"You have so much. You can take care of her. She's in bad shape," Sibley says. Colson hands her a drink.

"Maybe we should go," he says.

"I think that's a good idea," I say. It's the only thing I can imagine agreeing with the creep on. "I'm sorry about your mother, Sibley. But I'm done."

"No, you're not. I won't let you be. She needs help," Sibley says, her tone menacing, threatening. She frowns at me before turning and walking out the door.

I take a deep breath and consider my options. I suppose I could give Sibley's mom something in my will. I do have plenty.

"Don't waver, Richard. You don't owe Sibley or her mom anything," Serena says as if reading my mind. "Sibley's dangerous. Unstable."

"No, she's not. But her mom is, and her mom has likely gotten to her. She's an addict but very compelling when she wants to be; I know from firsthand experience," I say. "You know what? I can't put Cassie in my will. She'd only use any money she got from me for drugs. It is sort of sad."

"Whatever," Serena says. "As far as I'm concerned, that whole chapter of your life was a huge mistake."

"Seems sometimes I do choose poorly," I say. And as I admit that, I look at Serena and hope I haven't made a bad choice bringing us all together. It's too late now. I've set everything in motion, and what will be, will be.

18

PAIGE

Ted and I hold hands as we sit on the bed in our stateroom. My emotions are all over the place. I'm terrified by the raging storm outside, and I'm surprisingly sad about Richard's diagnosis. I can't say I love the man, but it's a cruel ending for someone so much larger than life. I thought he was indestructible.

Beside me, Ted has his head in his hands. "What do we do? My dad is dying."

"It's so awful. Your poor dad. But the fact is, we need to do what we came here to do, I suppose," I answer. "Tomorrow, as soon as possible, you need to get Richard alone and talk to him." *And so do I,* I think to myself.

I want off this boat. I want to stop moving. I want to hug my girls. I take a deep breath as another wave rolls under the boat. I'd like a hug from my husband, but he's too distracted. And I know I shouldn't even want his touch after he's admitted to lying to me. For years. I can't help my warring feelings of anger and suspicion and love and longing. Oh, Ted.

Ted says, "I need answers sooner. For both of us, darling, for the girls. I need him to understand what we offer for the future." He puts his arm around my shoulders. "You are what will convince him. You're normal, kind, and he knows he needs more of that to polish the Kingsley image. He's ruthless; you're not. The company employees respect Richard, but they'll love us. People in the company know what you've accomplished for numerous charities, the fact we will be a team. It all works in our favor."

"OK, then go find Richard tonight," I say. "I can come with you, if you'd like."

As we change into jeans and sweatshirts, I watch Ted's face. He's practicing his pitch, I can tell. Meanwhile, I'm oddly feeling pretty good despite the crazy movement of the ship. I realize that's because I'm drunk.

"You did look lovely tonight in that new dress," Ted says. He's changed into dark jeans and a light-blue cotton sweater. He looks as young as the day we met.

"Thanks, Teddy. You look good, too," I say. I'm surprised at the affection I feel for him, given the ups and downs of the day. A wave of nostalgia sweeps over me until I remember the new arrival on board.

"Do you think we need to worry about Sibley? I mean, should we worry about why she came?" I ask. Sibley and her boyfriend have added an uncomfortable edge to the evening.

"Nah. She barely said anything at dinner before she was banished to her room. It's clear she feels out of place, she hates Serena, and she's trying to pit Dad against his latest wife. It won't work," Ted says. "But it's fun to watch."

"She brought up her mom, too," I say. "I thought everybody hates her mom."

"That's a joke. Sibley and especially her mother are nothing to Richard, nothing more than an afterthought," he says. "A mistake that resulted in a lifelong dependent. That's it."

I know I'm drunk, but Sibley seems to be a lot more than an afterthought. I mean, she's here, on the boat, all the way from wherever she lives in Florida. I push Ted's sister out of my mind and focus on my husband. Sure, I'm still angry and confused, but Ted's looking hot. I reach over and kiss him on the lips. It's been so long since we've held each other, so long since we've made love.

"Wow, tiger," Ted says. "We have work to do tonight, no messing around. But I like it. I missed it. Save those thoughts."

I know I've been more of a mom than a lover, but I can change that. I can try, at least. It's just when the girls are around, well, they're old enough to pick up on things. It's safer just to not have sex than to have them walk in on us. Oh my Lord. I can't imagine it. But still, his rejection now stings. He has other things on his mind, I tell myself. Important things, like his father's impending death. I can hardly blame him for not being in the mood.

"OK, let's go find Richard," Ted says. "Focus on the task at hand."

"Sure," I say. "What?" He's looking at me funny.

"I want to be the man you think I am. I do, sweetie," Ted says. "I want to be the next CEO of Kingsley Global Enterprises, with you by my side as my president. I can do it. I can be a better person. I'm glad you're forgiving my little mess up. It's way in the past. Tonight, we grab our future."

They're the words I've been waiting to hear for so long, but I don't quite feel the elation I would have expected.

"I'd love that. I would," I say anyway. He's making me worried again, though. What else has he done that he hasn't confessed? I push the thoughts out of my mind and take a deep breath, following him out of the room. He is focused on our future, together, and that makes every problem solvable, doesn't it? We will talk through everything after this weekend. There will be no more secrets. Across the hall, I hear music. Sibley and Colson are partying in cabin two. They are blasting a song so loud the door of her cabin shakes. Fine, she can hide out in there with her spooky boyfriend, and we'll have a nightcap with Richard.

"Ted, go," I say as we hurry up to the library.

"The doors are closed. Maybe Dad and Serena want privacy?" he says.

Too bad. They're not going to get it. I knock on the door and open it when Richard yells, "Come in!"

"Sorry to bother you guys," Ted says.

Serena's eyes are puffy from crying. Richard seems tense.

"You aren't. Come on over. Are the others on their way?" he asks.

"No idea," Ted says.

"I'm glad you're here, Paige," Richard says. His eyes light up, and he grins at me.

It hasn't escaped my notice that he is acting extra kind to me. I do think it will help our cause.

We take our seats in the library just in time; a huge wave rolls under us. I'm not sure I can handle a whole night of this, let alone the fact that it's predicted to get much worse.

One of the crewmembers hands me an after-dinner drink of some sort.

Ted clears his throat.

John walks into the library in a hurry, rushing to stand by the bookshelf next to where Richard sits. "Good evening, everyone. How's everyone holding up in this crazy storm? Say, Dad, I'd like some time alone with you—if not tonight, first thing in the morning. Please."

I nudge Ted's leg, willing him to ask for the same thing, but before he can, Sibley appears.

"Here you all are," Sibley says, stumbling into the library. She's changed into purple tie-dyed sweatpants and a matching sweatshirt. "Are you all making plans without little ol' me?"

Richard laughs. "You're back. Come on in, honey. No, the boys are both trying to get me alone to chat, but they're going to have to wait until tomorrow, as I told you all at dinner. John, we'll meet first thing in the morning since I know you're not going to stop hyperventilating until you get that alone time you've been begging for."

I watch John's face flush. He's embarrassed, but he got the first meeting.

"Ted, you're next. And then my little girl sometime tomorrow afternoon. Sound good, everybody?" Richard says. "Besides, I'm not making any rash decisions tonight, in the middle of a storm. So cheer up, OK, gang? I'm not dead yet."

"Sure. Great," Ted says. His jaw is tight; he's frustrated. As usual, he's been outmaneuvered by John.

The library doors open, and Captain Bill stands in the doorway. "Sorry for another interruption, folks. It's worse than I thought. The storm. I'd strongly encourage you all to retire to your cabins, and absolutely no one outside on deck."

As if we'd even be tempted.

Sibley says, "Sleep is for losers. I'm having a dance party in my room if anyone wants to join."

I wonder if she's stoned. I don't know if Richard notices.

"A dance party. Funny, honey. All right, everyone. You heard the captain. Let's all turn in. Meet for breakfast at nine a.m.," Richard says. "We have more surprises planned—but not bad like tonight's surprise, so don't worry."

"What could be worse than the bombshell that you're dying, Dad?" John says.

"I can't think of anything worse," Richard says.

"Oh, good. More surprises," Ted says. He sounds angry. "Come on, Paige."

"Richard, I do hope you feel better," I say. I give him my best smile.

"Thank you, dear. I'm glad someone in this family is looking out for me and really cares," he says and winks. My heart breaks for him. "Good night, all."

I watch as Richard and Serena make their way out of the library, through the special doors to their stateroom, before we leave. As we walk out of the library, a flash of lightning illuminates the sky. I stop and watch as another bolt makes the roiling ocean glow. From where we are moored, the famous Catalina Casino beckons like a castle in the distance.

I imagine what it would be like to fall off this yacht and try to swim to shore. But then I look down to the cold, dark, churning water. I'm five stories up, at least.

It would be certain death.

"What are you doing, Paige? Come on, let's get some sleep. Or try to," Ted says, taking my hand and guiding me down the hall to our cabin.

Our evening is over, and so is the romantic connection I felt earlier. It's time to get down to business—the only thing Ted is interested in on this boat. So much for my romantic notions and my fancy new dress. Nothing matters but Ted getting the company. I see that now. And it matters to me, too. I think of the girls, of the money we need for them. I wonder what will happen if we don't get the money or the company.

Goose bumps dot my arms as another wave tilts the boat.

19

RICHARD

Serena walks into our stateroom with a grin on her face. "You're so strong, you know that? The way you command a room, even in the face of your devastating diagnosis. It's amazing."

True. I am nothing if not in control. "Thank you, Sisi."

"Did you see the look on John's face when you told him no business discussions until tomorrow?" She's changed clothes again—my little chameleon can pretend to be whoever she'd like—and now wears a robe and fuzzy slippers. The look is both sexy and cute at the same time, an elegant beauty who fits in perfectly with her luxurious surroundings. It's almost like all this—the cruise, the wife, the family, my life—is too good to be true.

"John's look was priceless, almost like the look on yours when I told you the same thing," I say and watch her pout. "Come on, you know I love a good competition, and that was embarrassing for Ted, too. The man never got a word out before John barged in. But whose fault is that? His own. All of his mistakes are his own fault, don't you agree?"

"I think you embarrassed them both by giving Sibley equal time. You'd never leave the company to her, though; we all know that. So when is my meeting?" she asks, then nestles on the bed next to me like a cat.

I shake my head but don't comment. Serena seems almost serious about this. It's absurd, of course. I didn't marry her for her business prowess. She'd be laughed out of the company, rejected by the board. It's a nonstarter. Besides, I've never considered leaving my company to anyone but my offspring. Sure, they are all far from perfect, but they're still Kingsleys. As for my wife, I know she likes Ted over John and Sibley—that much is clear. Does she find him attractive? I suppose so. But is that the only reason? I climb out of bed, suddenly restless.

"You think Ted is equipped to lead Kingsley Global Enterprises? He could replace me? He is a skilled salesman," I say. I pour vermouth into two crystal tumblers and carry one to Serena the cat. "Paige is great. I've been impressed by what she has been able to do for the food bank. I can't go to a YPO or United Way meeting without hearing how much positive impact Paige has had in the community."

"Paige is irrelevant. Ted is a good choice, although of course no one can replace you, darling," she says, taking the glass. "You're one of a kind."

"That's true." I clink my glass against hers and chug my drink, enjoying the taste of the digestif as much as the company.

Serena slips out of bed and walks away from me, perhaps drawn to the spectacular lightning show and the reflection dancing on the water. Lights twinkle from condos built into the side of the mountain, reminding me of the Amalfi Coast. The yacht glows blue underwater, luring schools of fish to the light. It's funny. I've loved women of all types through my life, and I imagined Serena would be my final, great love connection. In fact, her behavior has been disappointing of late, to say the least. The selfish little minx.

"Well, it's my decision alone, and I will make it," I say. I walk to the bar, careful to stay next to the wall of the cabin for stability's sake, and pour myself another drink. This time I pick something stronger. Scotch on the rocks will do.

Serena turns and strolls to the bed again, removing her robe and climbing beneath the sheets.

"Why yes, of course, it is your decision. I'm only trying to be helpful. I'm worried about you. I'm so sorry about your diagnosis," she says.

She seems sincere, and I hope she is. "Thank you, Sisi. We all die sometime, as they say. I just wasn't expecting it so soon," I say. "Cheers to making the most of the time I have left." I walk over to the bed, sit down. Maybe a little romance is what the doctor ordered. I touch Serena's thigh.

"I really do think you need your rest tonight," she says. "This day has been emotionally exhausting—for all of us but especially you. Let's just sleep tonight." She kisses me on the cheek before turning away, switching off her bedside lamp. "Good night, Richard. I love you."

Well, I wasn't expecting that. The bikini girl on the sailboat would have stayed up and talked to me. Gladly. She'd be set for life. I try to remember the last time I screwed my wife. It's been weeks, maybe months? I've been flying around the world to doctor's appointments, trying to save my life. And I've been caught up in a succession plan. Meeting with lawyers, doctors, and such.

I put my hand on my traitorous heart.

I have been cleared for exertion, so they say, as long as I'm able.

I remember the damn doctor's cocky face. "Make love to your wife. Enjoy yourself while you can."

I wanted to punch him but instead leaned forward in my chair. It was just the two of us, mano a mano, in his office plastered with degrees from famous universities.

"Look, dickhead, I know how to enjoy myself. OK? I don't need some over-credentialed doctor to tell me how to live my life. What I want to know is how long?" I said.

He leaned back, lightly tapped his fingers on his desk, and slipped on dark-rimmed reading glasses that made him at least look old enough to sit in that leather chair of his. But never my equal. No, never that, the pompous toad.

I might have come on a bit strong, but I didn't like his attitude. Not at all.

He cleared his throat and seemed to realize the error of his bedside manner. "Look, Mr. Kingsley, I know this is hard. But we can't give you a definitive life expectancy. I'm not trying to be flippant; I'm just telling the truth. Men with your condition, in their late seventies, with otherwise good health, I'd give you six months to two years. It's inoperable, untreatable. I'm sorry, sir, I really am."

I stared at him then, in a mix of shock and disdain. Disbelief, I suppose. How could a man who can afford anything not be able to fix himself? How can I die so young? My parents died in the plane crash when they were both in their sixties, but they were otherwise healthy, no heart conditions. When I'd asked the doctors that question, they all told me lifestyle choices are a big factor. I've made all the best choices, as far as I'm concerned. But what good has it done me?

"And there's nothing I can do? No other country has a treatment? I can afford anything," I said, standing up on now-wobbly legs.

"No. There's nothing. I wouldn't advise going on a wild-goose chase around the globe. We have the finest doctors in the United States. No one has been able to find a cure for heart failure, except for a transplant, and even then, as you know, you aren't a candidate. I am truly sorry, but there is nothing to do but live your life as much as you can for as long as you can."

Tonight, as I think back on that encounter, I realize it was the first time in my life I felt out of control. Completely. It's only a matter of time before I'll need an oxygen tank just to handle the strain of daily life. I'll need medicine just to function. It's stupid and unfair.

I will not allow my employees to see me that way. Sometimes I dream that I will live in one of my European homes with staff who do not speak English. In those dreams, it's a bonding time for us: Serena, our child, and me. But then I wake up, unsure of how I want to live the last months of my life.

I do know one thing: I will live to see my baby born. It is the only thing worth living for.

I watch Serena sleep and decide tomorrow night will be when I decide what to do with my company and the remainder of my life.

"Sleep tight, my darling. Tomorrow's going to be quite a day," I say as I climb into bed, the motion of the huge waves rocking the vessel. I make it to my side of the bed without spilling my scotch and arrange my pillows so I am mostly sitting up, a position I've grown accustomed to since my body became a traitor, a ticking time bomb of doom.

20

JOHN

It doesn't hit me, the fact that my father is dying, until we walk back to our stateroom. I sit on the bed, my emotions swinging rapidly from sorrow to disbelief to a restless and raw sense of even more urgency. I must be his successor. I feel like punching the wall of our cabin, repeatedly. But I don't. Rachel would kill me.

So instead, I put my hands together and said a prayer for Dad, for trying his best at being a father, for succeeding spectacularly in business. And I pray for God to save his soul and forgive his sins. There are many. I'll tell my mother the news and have her prayer circle jump into action. I do love my father, despite who he is. But I must admit, I hate him more for the things he has made me do in his name. There is no indifference, not when it comes to my dad.

Rachel sits next to me on the bed. She is green with seasickness. "Why won't this storm stop?"

I lean against her, pat her hand. "It will, eventually. We're safe."

"It doesn't feel like it," she says.

"There is a reason to be happy tonight," I say.

"Your father just announced he's dying. We're stuck on this boat in the middle of a crazy storm. Why would I be happy?"

"I got the first meeting," I say. "This meeting could change our lives."

Rachel is miserable, nauseous, and terrified. Meanwhile, I can't stop grinning at the thought of my meeting with the king, and I've never been prouder of myself. I walked into that library like a leader and demanded his time and attention. Tomorrow morning, I'm going to convince him I am his only choice. I take a moment and think about Dad's death sentence. I'm sure he's scared; anybody would be. I need to remember to be compassionate when I'm speaking with him, not desperate. Dad can smell desperate a mile away, no matter how sick he is.

But the truth is, I *am* desperate. And Dad fucking owes me. He has no idea all I've done for him, all I continue to do for him. It's because of him that I need cash. Desperately. They're giving me until the end of the weekend. I let out the breath I was holding and paste on a smile, but the angry anxiety courses through my body like a bolt of lightning.

"You know, we'd be fine if you just kept your position and Ted rejoined the business in some capacity," Rachel says. She's lying down on the bed, curled up in a ball. "It might make Richard's final days easier. It's not like you need the whole company. You make a great salary as is."

"No, that wouldn't work," I say, unable to tell my wife the real reason Ted can't come back into the company, unable to tell her I'm being blackmailed. I sound grumpy and evasive. I just need time to think and some sleep. "And we will be fine, Rachel. This is a state-of-the-art vessel. The best money can buy."

The entire boat shudders and groans as our stateroom seems to tilt on its side.

"I'm glad we aren't going to die," Rachel says. "I have a big case coming up."

"OK, let's try to rest. You should, honey. Just close your eyes," I tell her.

"I have to get ready first," Rachel says, lurching out of bed and clutching the wall to make it to the bathroom.

This is ridiculous. I feel like we're on a roller-coaster ride in the dark, never knowing when the next swell will take us. The boat never stops swaying, and it's a comforting and nauseating feeling all at the same time.

If my talk doesn't go well with Dad tomorrow, I must have a plan B. I suppose I would phone Richard's brother, Walter. He might be interested to know he's getting out of the company. Walter might want to make a run at it himself. He might even need the help of the guy who drove him out in the first place. But then I remember the cell service has been knocked out. We'll see how things go tomorrow. There is time. Walter will take my call, if my price is right.

Yes, this could work if my little talk with Dad doesn't. I wouldn't tell him, of course. If I'm pushed against a wall, though, I'm coming out swinging. I stand up. *Eureka!* I've come up with a plan.

"Why are you smiling?" Rachel asks. She's made it to the bathroom and is back, ready for bed. She's wearing her usual oversize T-shirt, mouthguard, and reading glasses. It's not sexy, but it's my wife. My badass, white-collar-criminal-defending wife. She climbs back into bed beside me.

"I have an idea."

"What?" she asks, rolling over. "Did you feel that wave?"

"Yes." I sit on the bed.

"I'm going to reach out to Dad's brother, Walter, if need be. Only if Dad won't agree to make me his successor."

"No, don't do that. They despise each other," Rachel says, stifling a yawn. "Richard would be furious. He's sick and dying. The last thing he needs is more family drama around him. You are going to get the company; I'm sure of it. Come on, it's late. You need to be your best tomorrow."

"I'm dreading tomorrow," I say, getting up and walking over to the tiny bathroom and finding my toothbrush. A wave rocks the boat, and I smash into the wall. Rachel doesn't understand why I might need Uncle Walter; she doesn't know what I'm facing daily. She doesn't know what

I'm capable of. Nobody does, and I like it that way. Oh, poor John, just a quiet, nerdy accountant. He's meek and weak, people think, until I strike. "Damn it. Why won't this yacht stop bouncing?"

"Try to calm down and pretend we aren't in a death trap—that's what you tell me," Rachel says. "Look at it this way: we can secure your place at the helm of Kingsley Global Enterprises by tomorrow, and by Monday, I can go back to my clients, who are infinitely more interesting and more devious than your family. Sorry to say."

She's not sorry to say that at all.

"You represent crooks. Of course your clients are more interesting than the Kingsleys," I say from the bathroom. I'm holding on to the sink so I don't fall over. I finally finish and hurry to the bed, flinging myself onto it like it's a lifeboat.

"Most successful businesses have some sort of crime taking place, either in this generation or previously. It's common. Kingsley Global Enterprises isn't as pure as it seems—I'm certain of that," Rachel says.

In the dark cabin, I can't see her face and she can't see mine. "What do you mean? We're just a regular old dysfunctional family. That's all we are."

"Nobody believes that, John. Nobody. And some people know who you all really are. At least, I do."

SATURDAY, JULY 16

CATALINA ISLAND

OC SCOOP

WHAT'S HAPPENING ON BOARD

The mega-yacht the *Splendid Seas* has been spotted in Avalon Harbor in Catalina Island by a helpful tipster. We hear there are rough seas, even in the harbor, and the yacht is bobbing up and down like a child's bath toy, along with the rest of the vessels on their moorings. Of course, the Kingsley yacht *is* a toy for the rich Richard Kingsley and his family on board. And speaking of family, Richard and his young wife have been joined by both sons; their wives; and, we hear, his estranged daughter, Sibley, and her date. Even on a yacht the size of his, there's nowhere to hide when the family is all together. One big happy family reunion—or is it something more? Our tipster seems to think there is trouble brewing in addition to the high surf and the stormy weather. I'm certain the Kingsley crew will be on the island at some point. If you spot them, let us know. Send photos, fans.

21

PAIGE

In my dreams, I'm lying in a hammock, swinging back and forth between two palm trees on a deserted island. Dappled sunshine warms my legs. I wrap my arms around Ted's neck as he gently kisses my lips.

I open my eyes. I'm lying in bed in a dark cabin. The entire room is bouncing back and forth. Beside me, Ted sleeps like a baby. I may as well face it: I'm awake. I climb out of bed. The boat pitches to the side, and I grab the door of the cabin. I need to get out of here.

Up on deck, I feel better. The storm clouds have passed, and the sky is a bright, friendly blue. But the ocean still looks furious. I find a cushioned bench seat and a fluffy navy cashmere throw. I pull the blanket around my shoulders.

"Well, you're up early," Richard says, appearing in front of me.

Startled, I scramble to stand.

"Relax, please. Stay warm," he says. He's wearing what appear to be his pajamas—silk, navy, with the *Splendid Seas* logo embroidered on the breast pocket.

I'm wearing sweatpants and a sweatshirt and his cashmere blanket. "Hi, yes. Couldn't sleep," I say, pulling the throw up to my neck. "Is it always this rough?"

"Never had this before. Ever," Richard says. "But it does sort of fit the weekend, doesn't it? Turbulent, lots of undercurrents. Ha."

Despite his jovial demeanor, I look at him more closely and realize he doesn't look healthy. His eyes are ringed with black circles, his face is a strange, sickly hue. The whites of his eyes are pale yellow.

"Are you doing OK this morning?" I ask, likely overstepping. But we *are* family . . . sort of.

Richard turns to look at me, tilts his head. "Sure. I'm good, Paige. How are you doing?"

I think he's lying—that in fact, he may be more gravely ill than he is telling us, but I shouldn't press him. I need to play good cop, compliant daughter-in-law. I'll tell Ted and he can figure it out. As for me, I just want to know Richard's plans.

"Would you like to join me?" I ask, patting the cushion next to me as if it's a casual offer. It's not. I need this talk, just Richard and me. It may be our last chance.

"Sure, thank you, dear," Richard says. "It's nice to spend some time with you, with all of you. I need to size everyone up. Take the pulse of the family. Make some decisions. Like I said, when a doctor informs you of your imminent demise, it makes you think, dear. Consider who is important, who has been true," he says. He pats the top of my hand. "So far, you're doing just fine, Paige. I have always liked you and your two girls. And that capital campaign you led for the food bank—well, it was the talk of the town. You somehow got funding from even the cheapest CEOs, and that new building is phenomenal."

I had no idea he knew about my work for the food bank. "We are going to eliminate hunger in Orange County, thanks to the generosity of all those business leaders," I say.

"You're impressive, Paige. Teddy is, too, of course. All good. I like the package. And just so you know, dear, you will be taken care of generously in my will," Richard says, standing up.

I realize he is walking away. "Wait, please. Can I ask you something?"

"Of course, dear," he says and rejoins me on the bench seat as a big wave rolls under us. "That was a doozy. What's up?"

Despite my best attempt at stoicism, tears spring to my eyes. "I'm so sorry about the diagnosis," I say. I feel his hand on my shoulder, and he gives me another light pat.

"All right, dear, I need you to pull yourself together. You're as surprised as I am; I understand that."

I force myself to make eye contact. "I also want you to know if you pick Ted, I'll be with him, by his side, every step of the way. I was vice president of marketing when I got pregnant with the girls. I know it has been a while, but I love the company. I know Ted and I will make a great team and make you proud."

"We'd be lucky to have you. You're quite convincing when you are closing the deal, I've heard," Richard says. His voice is kind and causes another river of tears. I can't believe he is dying. "No matter who I choose to run the company, you're welcome to step back in."

He's very serious. I nod. "OK, thank you. I can start as soon as the girls graduate—or sooner, if you prefer. Really, whenever you'd like," I say. Ted is going to be thrilled, I think. We'll be running Kingsley as a team. His dad just confirmed it, at least *my* role in it.

"Sooner, I'd advise, just to get going in your career again, dear," Richard says.

"Yes, thank you. This is so exciting," I say, wiping the tears again with the blanket.

"I've lived a good—well, a *full* life. I want to enjoy however long I have left, with those I care about. Like you, dear," he says. We both sit in silence as his words resonate. "It seems the old saying is true: 'Life is short.' Too short, it turns out."

I touch his hand. It's cold. He should go back inside. I don't want to make this about me, but I need to ask him something.

"Is there anything I should know about Ted? Please, you can tell me. I can handle it," I say, even as I'm dreading the answer to my question.

Richard takes my hand in his. "No, dear, I have no doubt you can handle anything, but I'm afraid I have nothing to tell you right now."

"OK, thank you. And could you please not tell Ted about our chat?" I ask.

"Yes, let's not mention your executive-level job at Kingsley to anyone just yet. I must sort through my children first. But you're special, Paige. You are," Richard says.

"Thank you. I won't say a word to anyone. Not until you tell me it's OK. And thank you for the girls' future, for including us in the will. It means so much to all of us. You'll have two granddaughters who will carry on your legacy with pride," I say.

"Pride and a sizable trust fund. Be sure you protect it for them, as money has a way of evaporating—right under your nose, sometimes," he says with a wink. "See you at breakfast." And then he walks back inside, disappearing into the ship.

I inhale deeply and smile. I cannot believe I had the courage to ask Richard for a job, and I'm more than relieved he will make sure our family is well taken care of in his will. The girls are set for a happy life. Briefly, I worry Ted will be angry because I talked to his dad without him and because I only talked about a position for myself. But Ted must stand on his own two feet. And he will.

Was I disloyal to Ted? I don't think so. He never told me about depleting the fund; he certainly doesn't seem to have a plan to refill it himself. He's only focused on being the successor. I suppose he assumes that money won't be a problem any longer, should we win the role.

But what if he doesn't? Richard doesn't know about the college fund being emptied. If he did, what would he think? Does he trust Ted enough to turn over the company to him? Who knows what is in Richard's heart. He seems to like me, and he believes I'm qualified to be an executive at Kingsley with the high-profile charity work I've been doing in the community. He's noticed, and he's heard great things. I can't help but be pleased and a bit proud of myself.

Nobody, including Ted, knows I've taken online MBA courses for a few years now, at night, when everybody's asleep, and I'm about six months away from earning my degree. It was something I did for me because I knew I would reenter the workforce once the girls were raised. The master's degree should help offset some of the work gap—at least, that's what my professors have told me. I can't wait to surprise Ted and the girls with the graduation announcement. I hope Richard lives long enough to be there, too.

Another huge wave rolls under the boat. I look to my right and spot the famous Catalina Casino, lit up and glowing on the brightening but still murky horizon. I hear something banging against the side of the ship and the churning, rolling sound of the water. I think of Natalie Wood, her fingernails digging into the side of the dinghy as she tried desperately to save herself from drowning.

Despite the joy I feel after my chat with Richard, I decide it's too creepy to be out here alone.

22

JOHN

"I need to get out of this cabin. Let's go up to breakfast," Rachel says when I open my eyes. "You'll go meet with your dad, and I'll save you a seat. You're ready, right?"

"More than," I say. We dress quickly and head out the door. We walk past Sibley's cabin, and I think about her rather abrupt appearance here, one that underscored Dad's complete lack of civility and decorum. Screwing a pole dancer is one thing; getting her pregnant is a joke. Sibley is a joke. A bad one.

"John, Rachel, so happy you could join us," Richard says as we make it to the table. Ted tosses a smirk our way. How did he beat us up here again?

"It's not easy walking with this swell," Rachel says by way of explanation as I pull her chair out for her.

It's clear from the status of their plates that none of them waited for us. "Is it too late to get breakfast served?" I ask. I sound whiny, even to myself.

"'Course not. Here comes Talley now." Richard points to the sliding door, and out walks the crewmember and Serena. "My bride needs to brunch as well. And then we'll go into Avalon for a day of fun."

"What about Sibley and Colson? They're coming to shore, too, right?" Ted says, hands on hips. "I wouldn't leave them on the yacht alone."

Apparently, he shares my dark feelings about our wayward half-sibling and her date.

"None of us think it was a good idea for her to come on board, Richard," Serena says and takes her seat. She's wearing something that is expensive, tight, and white. A jumpsuit that pushes her boobs out to the table. It's ridiculous. I'm sure Dad loves it. She turns to Talley. "One poached egg on spinach, please. No toast."

Whatever. I've never enjoyed being around people who eat so pretentiously. "I'll have three eggs over hard, bacon, toast, coffee, and orange juice," I say.

"Make that two of the same," Rachel says. I don't know where the food goes, since Rachel has managed to stay fit even in middle age. It's good to see that she's feeling better.

Dad pats Serena's hand. "My only daughter—so far—is always welcome, boys, whenever she deems it important to check in."

Serena pulls her hand away from his with a jerk. I wonder what's going on.

"What are you afraid of, Ted? John? Competition? Sibley could be the wild card; she could come here and outshine you both," Richard says, pushing away from the table. "Seriously, though, I made a promise to each of my wives to take care of our children. I've kept that promise. And look, here I am, hosting the likes of you. But you're only two of three. Having her here will give me closure of sorts. Not just the *I'm dying* closure."

Serena tilts her head. "Richard. Sit. What do you mean?"

"Oh, not closure—more like happiness. That's what I mean," Richard says, but I can tell he's not being totally truthful. "John, I believe you and I have a meeting now?"

A huge wave tosses the ship to the right, and Richard loses his hold on the chair, slams into the side of the ship with a thud, and tumbles to the ground.

"Dad!" Ted says, sprinting to his side.

Dad remains collapsed on the deck.

"Shit," I say, hurrying over to him. "Dad, are you OK?"

Richard looks stunned, and his hand trembles in mine.

"I'm fine, boys. I am. Just got the wind knocked out of my sails. Need to remember to hold on tight in these types of conditions. Good warning to me, and for all of us. Never know when a rogue wave will hit you."

Ted and I help Dad to his feet. All I can think is Sibley is a rogue wave, and she'll hit soon, very soon. But she'll be easily dealt with. I stare at my brother, over on the other side of my father, and know he's the biggest threat.

23

RICHARD

I make my way slowly to the stern of the yacht, wincing in pain. I may have cracked a rib with that fall. I hang on for dear life now, making sure I'm gripping the railing with each step. John follows behind me, trying to get my attention.

Damn waves better stop, or we're going back to the marina in Newport.

But we can't. I need to finish things, here and now. I need to review things and decide. I finally make it to the outdoor seating area one deck above where breakfast is served and sit down.

John takes a seat across from me.

"I'm so glad we finally have a chance to talk," John says. He wipes his brow with the back of his hand. *Why so nervous?* I want to ask him. It's just little old me. Emphasis on the *old*, unfortunately. I let out a puff of air. Might as well talk to John now.

"Yes, son, of course," I say. "What's on your mind? Money, of course. And power. And one-upping your siblings?"

John's face drains of color.

"It's fine, son. I'd want the same thing." Poor man. He looks physically ill—but of course, that could be the wretched waves tossing us about.

"Dad, look. I have done everything you asked from the time I began at Kingsley," John says. "Even the things no one else can know about except the two of us. I think that deserves to be rewarded."

"It certainly does," I agree. "And you have been. Your salary is quite substantial."

"I'm not unappreciative. But I want to run the company. I want to be named CEO in your succession plan," John says. "I deserve it. I've grown with the business and helped guide the financial decisions for the past few years. I'm a member of the executive team—a *valued* member. Despite my last name, the employees respect me because I've earned my promotions. I've worked my way up. And by keeping me around, you can rest assured none of your secrets will ever be revealed."

"Are you saying you'd start talking if I don't make you my pick?" The sun is warm and hot on my face. I close my eyes. I do not intend to be blackmailed by my own family.

"No, but I am saying I am the keeper of your secrets, so to speak. Take, for instance, Uncle Walter's departure," John says.

He's pushing my buttons. He should watch himself. While I appreciate the bold maneuver, he needs to understand he doesn't have any power in this situation.

"Uh-huh. I know what you've done," I say, standing up. "No need to rehash things."

John grabs my arm. "Dad, I'm just saying there would be trouble if people knew how we pushed him and the others out. You know I kept a dossier on each exit, a secret file on my computer."

"What? Why in the hell would you do that? What if someone finds it? You need to delete that file as soon as we're back to shore. No, as soon as we get internet again. Oh my God." I shake free of his grip and make my way downstairs, wondering why he would put in writing the very things we want no one to discover.

Idiot. What if he were hacked? What if he already has been?

I turn at the top of the steps and stare at my oldest son. "Has anyone else seen those files, those *dossiers*, as you call them?"

He swallows, shielding his eyes from the sun with his hand. "No, of course not."

I don't believe him. I wonder if he knows that in trying to display his power over me, all he's done is prove I could never entrust the company to him. I wonder if he sees how very poorly he's handling things. Likely, he doesn't. The prey never senses its imminent demise until the hunter has him in the crosshairs.

Bang. You're dead, John.

I leave John and make my way slowly back to the library—my happy place. I open the door and discover my daughter snooping around. I catch myself checking her pockets for bulges; she has been known to have sticky fingers. That creep Colson lounges on my couch, making himself right at home. "Can I help you find something?"

"I just need to know you'll help me with Mom," she says, turning around. "It's a lot for just me to handle. She's your responsibility, too."

I think she's trying to cry. But it's not working. Her eyes are tearless.

"Yeah, man, you've got everything. Her mom has jack," Colson says, picking at a black fingernail.

He's on my last nerve. I try to ignore him.

"You should stay away from your mom, for good. She is nothing but trouble. She abandoned you, honey," I say. I try not to let my frustration seep into our conversation. "Look, we are heading over to Catalina Island today. Would you and what's his name want to come, too?" I nod in the creep's direction.

"It's Colson. You know his name is Colson."

I've poked the bear. "Yes, of course. Come. It will be fun." I reach out to hug her, but she moves away, toward the door.

"We'll come. Sure. But you will help me with Mom. You have everything. She has nothing," she says, eyes flashing. Defiant.

"She has nothing because she abandoned you and spent all her money buying drugs. It is all her fault," I say.

"I don't care what you say," Sibley says. "It's your job."

I stare at my daughter with the same fire. She has my eyes, my temper. "I will never help Cassie. Never."

Colson rolls off the couch and stands next to Sibley. His eyes are beady, like a snake's. "You have so much, man."

Captain Bill walks into the library. "Sorry to bother you, sir. I needed to tell you about a small problem with the vessel. I can come back unless I'm needed here?"

"Sibley, go get ready to go ashore," I say. "We're finished discussing your mother."

"You're making a big mistake, Daddy," Sibley says, her voice quivering. She turns and leaves the library. Colson slips out behind her, slamming the door on his way out.

I don't like to be threatened. Not by anyone—certainly, and most especially, not my daughter. I drop into one of the library chairs and realize I must modify some of my plans.

"What is it you wanted to tell me, Captain?" I ask, bracing for bad news.

"Sir, our entire communication system has been taken out by the storm. I'm not certain how long it will take to fix. There isn't anyone in Catalina capable of working on this sort of advanced system, and even if there were, they're all working to fix the cell tower that was destroyed last night."

"Great. So are we trapped here, or what? No phones, no TVs, no internet?" I ask.

"Correct. The CCTVs are operable, but anything requiring a signal off the ship isn't," he says. "I can make it back to Newport, sir. I've navigated these waters without equipment before. We'll be fine, just out of touch with the rest of the world, so to speak."

My whole family is out of touch with reality anyway. I hope this is the last thing that goes wrong on my little getaway trip. But I'm certain it won't be.

"Let's just keep our lack of sophisticated sailing equipment a secret, shall we?" I say. "I don't want to freak out the family. We have some nervous guests on board."

"Yes, sir," the captain says. "For all they know, it's just the cell tower on Catalina. Nothing is wrong on the yacht."

That's the understatement of the trip.

24

JOHN

I join Rachel in our cabin and fill her in on my less-than-rewarding talk with Richard. She tells me to stay confident, that she might have an idea. Before she can share anything, one of the crewmembers knocks on our door and tells us it is time to go ashore.

As we make our way up on deck, Sibley is nowhere to be found. I hope she's not been able to corner Dad. After our talk, I'm unsure what he's thinking—but one thing I am sure of: my sister should not be included in any part of the business-succession planning. Richard would never allow a convicted drug felon to have control of anything. But still, while she is on board, I do need to make sure she will side with me over Ted.

And then, as if my thoughts summoned her, she appears. I watch her saunter onto the deck like she owns the place, her fingers tracing an imaginary line along the railing of the ship. Colson the creep follows closely behind her. I watch Rachel's reaction, distaste clear on her face. Rachel and Sibley are fire and ice. They ignore each other today, as always. Rachel busies herself with something on her phone, even though none of us can get any service, as Sibley stops in front of us. Her shorts are too short, her top is too tight. She thinks she's still a teenager when she should act and dress like an adult. She leans against the railing next to me.

"My cabin is übernice. Across from Ted's. I hear you're down the hall?" Sibley says to me with her signature snark.

Nice of Dad to put her there. "Believe me, I know where your cabin is, Sibley. It would've been a little hard to miss the god-awful death metal you thought was appropriate to blast at top volume at two a.m. Besides, most of the time, we just hang out in all these fabulous open spaces." I gesture to indicate the luxury of the ship, the teak table just inside the main galley adorned with a heavy-looking sculpture of dolphins leaping out of the water in its center, fresh flowers encircling the piece. I stare at it instead of my wayward sister.

"You're not really here to talk about our cabins, are you? What do you want?" I whisper. "Tell me. I'll see if I can get it for you. Are you in trouble? Do you need cash? What is it? I can help you with anything, Sib."

Sibley stretches her arms in front of her. "I don't need anything but love. That's why I'm here. To reconnect."

"Bullshit," Rachel says.

"You've aged a lot since I last saw you," Sibley says to my wife.

Shit. I need to jump in here.

"Sibley, listen, I know you want something," I say, looking around. "Any minute, Ted and Paige will arrive for our shore excursion. I need to be the one in control of this situation. I can get it for you. Whatever you want. But you have to promise to leave."

Sibley laughs. "And miss this family gathering? No way." Her laughter turns to a knowing smile. "Have you spoken to Uncle Walter lately, John? I have."

Uncle Walter hates me, for good reason. After all, I drove him out of the family business at Dad's request. She's trying to stir me up, stir up the past. My heart pounds in my chest, and I try to keep my expression neutral. She's bluffing. "No. Why?"

Sibley laughs. "Hey, Teddy!"

Ted and Paige walk out onto the deck with grim expressions matching ours. For once, my brother and I are on the same page.

"Hey, Sib, John, Rachel," Ted says. "Good morning."

"How's the golden son this fine morning?" Sibley says. "Paige, how are the precious girls? I know—too precious to be exposed to the likes of me ever again, right? The perfect little family, aren't you?"

Paige answers stiffly. "The girls are great, Sibley. Thanks for asking."

Sibley shakes her head as Dad and Serena finally arrive.

"Sibley, are you causing trouble again?" Richard asks, no doubt picking up on the thick air of tension between us. "You can only come to shore if you promise to behave, understood? We cannot afford to have a scene in public. That tabloid paper has eyes and ears on us."

"Promise, Daddy," Sibley says, and none of us believe it. "Colson and I won't be any trouble at all."

Dad stares at Sibley's boyfriend and shakes his head.

"I can behave when I want to," Sibley says. "You *do* know there's not much to do in town? I mean, other than drive a golf cart around and drink beer."

"Exactly," Richard says as a big swell rocks the boat. "Captain Bill and the crew will ferry us over."

With that, Sibley leans back on the railing and smiles. "We'll come with you guys to shore. It will be fun."

"Right, uh-huh," Richard says.

Ted says, "How'd the first of the business meetings go, John? Dad?"

Dad pats me on the shoulder. "Were your ears burning, Ted? Your brother's attempt to do an end run on all of you amused me."

I blink and try to let Dad's patronizing reply roll off my shoulders. I feel my rage simmering even as I try to keep my expression neutral.

"So cheer up," Richard says. "I'm not making any rash decisions, and I'll talk to each of my kids before I reach any conclusions. We have all day, Ted. Sibley."

Ted and I lock eyes. Did our father just say Sibley was in contention? Sure, we knew he was meeting with her, but that was just for appeasement's sake, I thought.

"I'd love to have a father-daughter chat, Daddy. Whenever you'd like," Sibley says. "What's the plan onshore?"

"We'll walk around, grab lunch, play a little golf, and come back to the ship in time for dinner and the crossing back home," Richard says. "Plenty of time to talk to each of you."

Serena says, "Dinner is formal tonight, by the way."

"Oh, whatever. Don't be so pretentious, Serena. Remember where you came from," Sibley snarks.

"Sibley, honestly." Richard shakes his head and says to Serena, "Ignore her, honey."

I'm finished with this discussion. I start toward the back of the yacht. Rachel follows me.

"Oh, Johnny?" Sibley's tone sends a chill down my spine. "Does Daddy know what you did to Uncle Walter?"

"Shut up," I say as I hurry away from her. Of course Dad knows I dealt with his brother. Dad told me to handle him, to get him resettled in Florida, far away from the family and the family business. And I did it. Did he tell me to introduce him to the people who would ruin his life? No. It just happened. I knew some guys, some players. It was Uncle Walter's choice to befriend them. Everything that happened after was Walter's fault, not mine.

At least, most of it was. Sibley can't know anything. She's just trying to scare me. Threatening to tell Dad lies about me. My stomach twists with anger. I will not allow her to undermine my place in this family. I won't.

"Sibley, do try to remember who signs your checks. It's me. You need me on your side. We should be a team," I say.

"You're funny, John," Sibley says. "I don't need a teammate. I'm all set. It's you who should be worried."

I am, Sibley, I want to say but don't. Anger boils up inside me, and I walk away from her before I say anything more.

25

PAIGE

It's so nice to be standing on dry land, I think, climbing out of the water taxi with the rest of the family. Sibley grabs my hand.

"Do you know about your husband's other life?" she whispers in my ear as my blood runs cold. I swallow and pull my hand away.

"Leave me alone. Leave all of us alone," I say.

Next to me, Ted's hands are in fists, as if he could punch his little sister. "Knock it off, Sibley," he says, his voice dark, firm. "Stop trying to stir things up. You have a great deal going. Don't ruin it."

Sibley smiles and pushes past us. "You're the one with the great deal, Teddy," she says.

Ted stands frozen next to me. "What did she say to you?"

"She said something about you having another life," I tell him. My mind races, and my stomach twists into another knot.

"You can't believe a word she says, sweetie," Ted says. "You know that. Remember what she did with Emily? Teaching her how to smoke weed when she was supposed to be babysitting? She got our daughter high. She's completely untrustworthy and a liar."

"OK, I know. You're right," I say. At least, I hope he is. "Don't let her get under your skin."

"Of course not," Ted says. "Let's ignore her, shall we?"

I look at my husband and decide to believe him, not the menace. The pier is packed with tourists. It's a warm day, the storm has moved out to sea, and people are ready to party—or, more to the point, already are.

"Should we be worried that Colson seems to be staying on board the *Splendid Seas*?" I whisper to Ted.

"What? No, don't worry about it." He's distracted again. "I can tell Richard is sick, more than he's letting on. I do need to make a move."

"So do it," I say. Ted nods and hurries to catch Richard.

I try to push Sibley's words out of my head, but as I watch Ted talk to Richard, her accusations ring through my daydreams of a happy empty nest, a happy future: Ted has a secret life? Sure, maybe he has kept some unpleasant secrets about his finances, but that's old news to everyone but me. But everyone also knows he's the nice one, the loving father, the handsome one. I picked the only good apple in a bunch of rotten ones. I must believe that. I hope it's true.

I look at the group of Kingsleys in front of me and realize Sibley has disappeared. I didn't even notice. I need to watch everyone more closely. To my right, a fisherman hoists a huge fish into the air, weighing it and taking photos of the poor doomed creature. I turn away. I guess bad things do happen to some things on this pier. I remind myself this is a fishing village and carry on.

As the pier ends, it's obvious we've reached the main street of Avalon, and we are not alone in our desire to visit this quaint island town. I haven't been here before, but I'm familiar with the picturesque charm of the historic waterfront because the girls both came to science camp on the island. Colorful storefronts spread in both directions around the harbor, and the restaurants and bars are full.

"Right over there," Richard calls out, pointing to a small wooden structure that looks like a home with a sandwich board sign that reads SERGIO'S ITALIAN RESTAURANT, written in clumsy chalk lettering. "Our lunch spot."

I can't believe we're eating again but do as I'm told and follow the family into a small doorway, and I blink in the darkness of what appears to be an ancient bar. Dark wood beams hang low overhead; movie posters from the 1940s adorn the walls.

A short man with a sweaty brow and dirty white apron appears. "Mr. Kingsley, sir, good to see you again. Follow me."

"Sergio, call me Richard, old friend." Richard pats the guy on the back like they're old drinking pals, and they likely are. "Meet my newest bride!"

Sergio looks Serena up and down. "Gorgeous. *Ciao, bella!*"

In front of me, Serena seems perplexed by the welcome. "Hello!" she says to the friendly restaurant owner. To Richard, she says, "You've been here before?"

"Many times. Darling, I did have another life before you," Richard says.

"Oh, yes, he did, ma'am," Sergio says, and he and Richard burst out laughing.

It's creepy. All of it. Beside me, Ted is silent. "Have you been here before?" I ask, wondering if he shares his dad's secret life here on Catalina Island.

"No, of course not. I had no idea Dad was a regular over here," Ted says. "Good news, though. Dad and I will meet after lunch."

"Great," I say as we follow the restaurant owner to a table on the second-floor balcony. I still feel on edge, as if everything has shifted. It's likely because I still feel as if I'm at sea, rolling over the huge waves, even though I'm on solid ground. The small scale of the restaurant isn't helping.

"Paige, sit here next to me. Serena on my other side. The rest of you, fill in wherever," Richard says, pointing to a place next to his. Ted pulls out my chair.

"Fine," Rachel says, clearly offended to not be offered a spot next to Richard. She takes the head of the table opposite him.

Sergio appears on the porch, and Richard nods in his direction. "The lunch will be family-style, just like in the old country. I'll be back with vino and bread."

"Isn't this fun? A family lunch on a channel island in the middle of the Pacific Ocean . . . What could be better?" Richard says. He glances around the table. "Well, I do have one thing that could make the day even more special. Serena, dear, tell them our big news!"

Serena shakes her head and pushes her sunglasses up to reveal her eyes. She's across the table from me, and yet I feel like she isn't here, that her mind is elsewhere. Despite the distance, she seems to snap to attention at Richard's command.

"I'd rather not, Richard. It is our secret," she says.

"We're all family here. No secrets," Richard says.

"Fine. We are having a baby," she says, dropping her sunglasses over her eyes again. She folds her arms across her chest as Sergio reappears and places two small baskets of bread on the table.

"What? Are you serious?" Ted asks.

"Need more bread?" Sergio asks, thinking he's questioning the bread basket.

"No, the bread is fine. Thank you," Ted says.

"Yes, very. I'm about three months along," Serena says, reaching for the bread.

"Serena, Richard, congratulations," I say. "How exciting for the two of you!" Even as I say that, I realize how bittersweet it is that this latest Kingsley offspring won't get to know their father. I guess that's not much different from how any of Richard's other kids grew up.

"Wow, Dad. That's a surprise," John says.

"Congratulations," Rachel manages to say.

Sibley appears and drops into the empty seat across from Ted and me. "Hey, everybody. Did I miss anything juicy?"

"You missed the big announcement, Sib," Richard says. "You're not going to be the youngest Kingsley kid anymore."

"No shit?" Sibley says. "You're pregnant, hooker? It can't be Dad's."

"Sibley, honestly, your mouth," Richard says. "And it's very much mine."

"Ooh, this is a good one," Sibley says.

Serena frowns as she dabs at the corner of her eye. She says, "I told Richard he would be the only one who thought this was a happy surprise, when we're all so distraught over his health. It's just all too much. I wish you hadn't asked me to tell them. It was supposed to be our secret. It's hard to believe I'm bringing another Kingsley heir into the world when Richard's time here is so short. It's such a sad time to be having a baby."

"Don't ruin my happiness, Serena. I, for one, am over the moon. What an unexpected twist in our lives," Richard says in a sharp tone. "We will celebrate things when I say we celebrate things. Understood?"

"You know that's not the way the world works. I'm the one who is pregnant, and you're the one who forced me to tell them when you knew none of them would be happy about another Kingsley offspring, another competitor, so to speak. So I'm the one who is right here—do *you* understand?" Serena says with a huff. "I wish you hadn't forced this. I really do."

"Don't question my decisions, Serena. Unless you would like me to question yours," Richard says. His tone is more sad than angry.

He sounds exhausted, poor man. My heart goes out to him. I look at Serena. It's as if her tragic almost-widow role is a disguise. She meets my stare, and I look away. I need to focus on the business impact of this revelation. What does another heir do to the succession plan?

"There's plenty more wine, so drink up, everyone. Except you, Serena," Richard says. "This wine is exquisite, Sergio. Cheers, everyone!"

Sergio, standing in the corner of the room, looks elated. Serena, the opposite.

We all clink glasses and silently acknowledge a power shift. Richard kisses Serena on the cheek. As he does, she looks at me over Richard's shoulder. Her eyes do look sad. Likely, it's the pregnancy stress, the rocking boat, and having a husband who's not going to be around much for the new baby. Or maybe I'm imagining sadness when there are other things going on.

"I want a glass of wine, too," Serena says. She's whining. It's annoying and selfish.

"You sound like a spoiled child," Richard says.

"I'm in good company with all of yours," Serena says.

"Fine, suit yourself," Richard says. He is even more frustrated with his wife.

Sibley says, "Did you guys know I can captain a yacht? You know, in case something happens to Captain Bill."

"You can captain a yacht?" John says. "I don't believe it."

"Figures you wouldn't. Uncle Walter taught me," Sibley says.

Sergio appears with heaping bowls of salad. There isn't a sound in the room. No one speaks until he departs again.

"Uncle Walter is a great captain himself. He has a yacht almost the size of the *Splendid Seas*," she continues.

"It's smaller. I happen to know," Richard says.

"Why would you be in contact with Uncle Walter?" Ted asks. "You know he was forced out of the family business. Whatever he did was egregious."

"There are two sides to every story, Teddy. You've only heard Dad and John's," Sibley says, refilling her wineglass. "And didn't you get forced out, too, Teddy? For doing something naughty?"

Ted's face darkens, and I touch his thigh. "Breathe," I whisper.

"You're wrong here, Sib," John says. "Uncle Walter got what he deserved."

Sibley laughs. "Not yet—but he will, Johnny."

"Thank you for meeting with Ted after lunch," I whisper to Richard, who nods imperceptibly.

Across the table, Serena leans toward me. "That wasn't fair. You're whispering secrets down here."

"No, I'm not," I say, but I feel my cheeks flush.

"You're a bad liar, Paige," Serena says. "But I really don't care. Do you?" I watch as she grabs the bottle of wine from the table and pours herself a glass.

"Not at all," I say with a grin, trying to show confidence I don't feel. "All's fair in love and war, especially in this family. Congratulations on the baby, though. Should you be drinking so much wine and champagne?"

"She's right, you know. You shouldn't be drinking," Richard says.

"It's a Kingsley family get-together. Alcohol is the only way to survive it," she answers, glaring at both of us. She raises her wineglass to her bloodred lips. "Mind your own business, Paige."

Oh, I plan to, Serena. I plan to manage everyone's business as president of Kingsley Global Enterprises. The thought makes me smile as I raise my glass of wine and take a big sip—because Serena shouldn't, but I can.

26

RICHARD

"Anyone still hungry?" I ask with a laugh. I note the clean plates all around, except for my wife's, who remains distracted, silent, and . . . well, pouting, her ruby-red lips full and shiny. I guess she's angry with me over forcing the baby announcement.

Paige, sensing our awkwardness, has jumped into the conversation with panache, although most of the time, she's speaking only to me. We do enjoy each other's company, and as far as the sons' wives are concerned, she's a clear winner. I'll look forward to welcoming her into the Kingsley management team. And I'm aware she needs the money. Although she didn't mention it, I know Ted has drained the girls' college fund. My second son is terrible with money, rotten. I'll make sure Paige has a great position at Kingsley. That way, she'll be able to stand on her own two feet despite Ted's issues. I can tell she still loves him and has overlooked a lot to keep their marriage alive. And now, with her girls going to college, she'll need Ted by her side more than ever.

"That was a fabulous meal. I felt like I was in Italy, the Amalfi Coast. Remember, Ted?" Paige says, smiling and holding Ted's hand.

"I do," Ted says with something like a smile on his face.

What a happy couple. A golden couple, really. Who could be better to lead Kingsley Global Enterprises? My company needs polish, so to speak. I have a reputation as a bit of a monster, corporately speaking. Paige would certainly soften that by adding a sort of moral compass to our operation. She's earned the respect of the business community with her work for the food bank. And shareholders certainly expect women in leadership roles in companies these days. As for Ted, he'd need to be watched on the money side, but I have people who can do that. People I trust. Ted doesn't want to be sneaky; he has an addiction. I suppose it's filling a space his mother left when she died after he was born—or some such psychoanalysis babble.

Meanwhile, John is a killer. Determined. Focused. Do I need a killer at the top, someone more like me? I like to keep all my options open. Always have, always will. I know it leads to a bit of . . . confusion, let's say, between my offspring. But too bad. Keeping people off-balance is what I do to win.

I look down the table at Sibley and bristle. Whatever she's up to, she should be careful not to push me too far. Sure, she's my only daughter, but a man can only take so much. When I was planning this trip, I did briefly imagine naming my daughter president of the company, a breaking-of-the-glass-ceiling type move. And in addition, she's shrewdly intelligent beneath that wild exterior. But then she shows up with the likes of Colson, pressuring me about supporting her good-for-nothing mother, and makes me doubt her all over again.

By contrast, Paige is a perfect choice. She's had ten years inside the company in the past; she is well liked, smart, and listens before she speaks. Yes, if she were my daughter, she would be a strong contender. It's too bad she isn't my child.

"Anyone need anything else? No?" I ask, pushing away from the table. "Sergio, put a twenty-five percent tip on the bill. Everything was fabulous." I love being the generous restaurant patron. I will miss this when I am too sick to go to restaurants anymore. "So who's up for a round of golf at the local course?"

All my children raise their hands. Good. None of the spouses do. Thankfully, that creature Sibley is with has disappeared. Hopefully, for good.

"Wonderful. We have a foursome. Me and my kids," I say. "First, though, Ted and I are going to have a little meeting. We'll catch up to you all at the course. Serena, darling, feel free to shop or go back to the yacht. Same for you, Paige, Rachel. We'll only play nine holes."

"I'm not going back to that boat until I have to," Rachel says, dour faced as always. "But I'm a scratch golfer. Can I join?"

"No, but thanks for offering," I say. "Captain Bill tells me the seas will begin to calm down this afternoon." I'm relieved, as I know everyone is. I have some work to do, things to review on board, and the violent waves made that impossible yesterday.

"Ready, Dad?" Ted says. I watch as he kisses Paige on the cheek and tells her he'll see her later. She frowns and looks confused.

"There's a lovely walk along the shore," I say to Paige. "And the art museum is surprisingly good."

"Thank you, yes. I'll be fine. It's important for you two to talk, although I'd love to join you. Ted and I are a package deal," Paige says.

I don't want to hurt her, because I don't think she knows Ted the way she thinks she does, and I need to be frank.

"Much as I'd love your company, I've been looking forward to a little one-on-one time with my youngest son. I'm sure you understand, dear," I say.

The rest of the family has left the restaurant, it appears, and Paige is the last to depart. So much for the women sticking together and shopping. Oh well.

"Of course. I'll see you later. And thank you, for everything," Paige says and kisses me on the cheek before Ted and I walk out of the room together.

"Talk to me, son," I say as he and I make our way down the stairs and out onto the crowded sidewalk. "Let's sit over there, on the bench."

"So here is what I know: I'm the only one who can lead Kingsley Global Enterprises into the future. I have the brains, the personality, and the love of the business. And Paige, you love her, I can tell. She'll be part of the package. We're a team. She'll help polish the Kingsley image just by being around at company functions again. Everybody loves her," Ted says. "In comparison, John doesn't have any of that."

I watch a seagull grab a piece of pizza from a child's hand as his mother screams at the bird. The seagull wins. Bold.

"John is nothing like you, that's true. But he is loyal. Trustworthy. Good with my money," I say. "He does whatever I tell him to do without question. And he's never betrayed my trust."

"Dad, if this is about what happened when you fired me—"

"I was thinking about that woman. Marcy."

I feel Ted's body tense next to me. A confirmation. "Look, Dad, I broke that off years ago," he says. He's not making eye contact. "It was a mistake. A onetime thing. It will never happen again. You've got to believe me."

"That betrayal was to your wife, not me. You know I'm the last to throw stones at adulterers, with my record. But the fact is, you're also a thief, son," I say.

"One bloated expense report doesn't make me a thief." Ted puffs out his chest defensively.

"It was more than one, son. And the gambling debt?" I ask. I hate to be hard on him, but he can't run my company with a gambling problem. I have decided to forgive him for his past transgressions—I have. But it must all be in the past.

"All cleared. I am paid up and straightened up. I know what I have with Paige and my girls. I'm a model family guy these days," he says. "I promise. I've quit gambling for good. I'm in a program."

"I hope so. You know the truth always comes out eventually, right?" I say. "I might not be around long enough to find out whatever truths you may be withholding, but I'll haunt you from the grave if you're lying. And your brother is a watchdog. Don't lie to me, son. Not now.

This is an important decision for me. The most important of my life. Can I trust you? Are you telling the truth?"

"I am," Ted says, leaning forward. "I swear. I'm the guy you need. I'll make you proud as you look down from heaven."

"Ha. Heaven, sure," I say.

"I'll take care of Serena and her baby, too. Don't worry about them," Ted says. "Even John. I'll find a place at Kingsley for John."

I lean back on the bench. "What about Sibley?"

I stare into the harbor, and out in the distance, I see the gleaming *Splendid Seas*.

"It's sad, you know it is. You invite her on board, and she's trouble from the moment she arrives. I'm afraid if we allow her to be a part of the company, she'll find a way to ruin it," Ted says. "I hate to say it, but that's what I believe."

I take a deep breath, ready to move, to go play some golf. "I'll need to figure out a Sibley solution before I die. I need to take care of her—I want to, and she is smart. She could be an asset to the company if she wanted to be."

"If you tell me she needs to have a position, I will do as you wish, Dad," Ted says as we stand up. "If you put me in charge, you won't have to worry about anything. You can enjoy the rest of your life and know that you're leaving things in good hands with an honorable son." He pulls me into a hug. "I love you, Dad, despite all we've been through, despite the mistakes we've both made. Going forward, it's smooth sailing."

I look at my middle child, my golden boy. I am starting to believe he is right. "OK, stop with the sales pitch. Let's go play some golf." I take a moment to look out to the sparkling harbor, the boats riding the swell. I know we'll find the rest of the kids at the golf cart rental.

As we start the short walk to the green, I say, "I like Paige, son. She's normal. We don't have a lot of normal in this group."

"I know. She's great. I've been a jerk," Ted says.

Is he the most like me? Is he the one? I think so, despite his problems with gambling. Maybe he really has quit. I look into his bright-
blue eyes and decide to believe he is what he says he is. I do need to talk
to Sibley, but I can't imagine her changing my mind.

"Ted, I know you drained your daughters' college fund," I say.
"That was wrong on so many levels." I watch as his face flushes red. At
least he has shame—something I can't seem to muster anymore.

"I always meant to repay it. It just, I don't know what to say. I used it to
pay off my gambling debts. I meant to replenish it, but I haven't been able
to save enough money yet to make up the difference," Ted says. He looks
deflated, defeated. "I'm sorry. I am. I'll fix it. I've planned on fixing it all."

"I'm going to put the money back in, but only Paige will have access
to it. Your girls will need the money starting in the fall. You don't have
time to find that kind of cash," I say.

"I've changed, Dad. I really have. I'm the man you want me to be
now," Ted says.

"We'll put this behind us, too, if you can accept that Paige will have
control of their trust," I say. "That is my condition."

"Yes, of course. Thank you. But how did you find out? Did Paige
tell you?" Ted asks. I hear the edge in his voice.

"I told you, I find out everything, eventually," I say. "She didn't tell
me, but she must know the account is empty and she's protecting you.
As always."

"Yes, of course. Paige is so devoted to me. She'll be by my side at
Kingsley. Remember how everyone loved her in marketing?" he says.

"Yes, I do. And, son, it's never a good idea to try to hide things from
me. Never a good idea to sneak around."

"I have nothing else to hide, Dad," Ted says.

"If that's true, then you're in great shape, as far as the company is
concerned," I say. *As long as you are telling the truth.* I stare at my second
son one last time.

I'll believe him for now, until I have the proof he's lying to me
again.

27

JOHN

I'm flooring it, but the golf cart won't go any faster. In front of us, Sibley's driving the golf cart, with Dad riding in it, like a race car driver.

"Hurry!" Ted says. "We don't know where we're going."

"I have it floored. Slow down!" I yell. Sibley looks back and flips her middle finger at me.

Ted seems to be in a great mood—much happier than I was after my talk with Richard. I need to find out what happened, although I can tell the tides have shifted in his favor by the stupid grin on his face.

Rachel will kill me if I lose to Ted. She just will. And now Sibley is alone with Dad, probably pleading her case. I push down on the pedal as hard as I can, but we're still puttering along.

"You know, there can't be more than one public course on this island. It's fine. We'll find it. Don't worry," Ted says, his sunny golden-boy demeanor grating on my last nerve.

I wish Sibley wasn't so erratic, and I wish we had a better connection. I should have faked kindness with her when she was young. But I didn't. So I guess I'm the hypocrite here, and it's my fault. I still kind of think she may be on my side in all this, but I can't tell for sure. And that is not helpful.

What's also not helpful is being hacked. Much like my dad suspected when he berated me this morning, the dossiers on my computer have been compromised. I don't know how, or by who, or why, but for the past two years, I've been paying hush money, and a lot of it, to keep my dirty deeds secret. The hackers found the list of the people I pushed out of the company—including Ted and Uncle Walter—and how I framed them, pumping up the actual truth. A little exaggeration here, a couple of extra digits there. The hackers found the deals I'd ruined, on Richard's request, and my hit list of potential people to get out of the way—in the business sense, of course.

So far, the hackers have kept their end of the bargain. No one is the wiser. Of course, Ted assumes I pushed him out, but he doesn't know the depth of the lies I told about him to Richard. Ted was hardly innocent, after all, and deserved what he got. I just made Dad's choice to exit him from the company clearer by exaggerating his crimes a bit. I knew from the moment I joined the company that I'd need to find a way to get Ted out. He helped me out so much, little Ted.

As for Uncle Walter, that was all Richard's doing. I just facilitated the setup, the ousting, and the cover-up. It's not our fault Uncle Walter moved to Florida and fell in with some bad guys. Rachel says they're white-collar criminals, but no one has been busted yet. All I know is, he had money—a lot of it—and he didn't get it from Dad or Kingsley Global Enterprises. Dad cut him off. I wonder why Sibley is close to Uncle Walter. She must have a reason.

"I hope Uncle Walter isn't going to be a problem." I realize too late I said that aloud.

"I can't see that. Dad hates him. Certainly, he's taken measures to be sure Uncle Walter can't come back into play at the company. Besides, Richard and the future of Kingsley Global Enterprises need someone with strength and character," Ted says. "Someone like me, actually."

I shake my head. "Whatever. He needs someone who knows the company, who has been a loyal soldier and trusted employee. Someone who has never let him down, never stolen from him. Someone like me."

"Oh, that's ancient history. Dad's forgiven me; he told me that. What he needs is new energy, someone with charisma," Ted says. "A family man who can be the face of the future."

"A *family* man. That's rich. You're just a pretty face, Ted. That's all. No one has time for that anymore. We're a global company with an intricate web of complicated financial holdings. There's a reason you're not a part of it," I say and turn into the golf course parking lot.

"Yeah, I know why I'm not a part of it: you pushed me out. You framed me, made my little expense-account padding into something much bigger. I know it. Dad knows it, too. Someday, I'll be able to prove it," Ted says. His voice is shaking, and his confidence seems to be zapped.

"It was far more than expense-account padding, Teddy. We both know that. Even if I did set you up, you deserved it. You're a thief," I say. Lucky for me, Ted doesn't know about the hacker. He'd have all the proof he needed that he is correct. I did all that to him and more. But he doesn't have anything. "Poor Ted. His big brother outsmarted him again." I slam on the brakes, and we both jump out. We could fight each other right here, right now. We both feel it.

"Boys!" Richard calls. "Over here."

Sibley grins, sensing the tension between us and loving it, no doubt. She hits her vape pen, smoke swirling from her nostrils like a warning. She and Dad stand beside two new golf carts labeled AVALON GOLF CLUB, each with two golf bags strapped to the back. "Hi, guys. What's wrong? Did you two have a little fight on the ride over?"

Dad looks at both of us. Ted shrugs and I shake my head.

"Good," Richard says. "Sibley and I will be riding together. You two will share a cart and try to get along."

"Daddy and I are going to have a nice, long talk about the company and my future. Right, Daddy?" Sibley asks.

Richard laughs. "Yes, let's go, dear. May the best person win. Right, boys?"

"You can't," Ted says.

"You wouldn't," I say.

"He could," Sibley says, punching the gas pedal on the cart, splattering us with mud as she floors it through a puddle created from last night's rain. We both hear her laughter; it's directed at us. If I had cell service, I'd call Rachel, tell her we're in trouble. I saw Ted's face after his meeting with Richard. And now Richard is listening to Sibley.

We need to do something, something surprising, and Rachel is the one who comes up with strong and surprising. I need to talk to my wife.

"Do we actually have to play? The course is soaking wet," Ted whines.

"We aren't leaving them alone for nine holes. Get in," I tell him. "And, Ted, leaders don't whine. They take charge. So shut up."

He's no leader. I am.

28

RICHARD

I walk behind my daughter up to the first tee, marveling at her non–golf appropriate attire—ripped black shorts, black tank top—and stop to enjoy the scenery. This golf course is the oldest one west of the Rockies, built in the 1800s.

"Sibley, isn't this canyon beautiful?" I ask.

"Sure, it's great, Dad," she says, placing her ball on the tee and whacking her drive. I'm impressed.

"Have you been playing golf?" I ask, stunned.

"I have," she says. "Uncle Walter taught me."

"He taught you how to captain a boat and how to play golf," I say, trying to keep my voice neutral. "You must be spending a lot of time together. Anything else he's been teaching you?"

"So much," Sibley says.

I place my ball on the tee and line up. It feels good to hold the driver in my hands. I take a breath and swing, enjoying the cracking sound as I make contact and the ball takes flight. Not bad for an old guy. An old, *dying* guy.

We walk back to the golf cart as Ted and John approach the tee box.

"Nice shot, Sib," Ted says. "Who would have guessed you're a golfer? You're full of surprises."

"Thanks, Teddy. I am that," Sibley says. "Daddy appreciates my talents. Don't you?"

"You do have some hidden talents, dear. Like the stock you've been acquiring with my no-good brother. Planning a little corporate take-over, are you?" I might as well drop the bomb in front of the boys. I need to remind them not to underestimate their sister.

Sibley's face falls to a frown, but she recovers quickly.

John says, "Are you serious about this, Dad?"

"You're kidding," Ted says.

"It's not for a takeover, Daddy. We just believe in the future of Kingsley Global Enterprises, that's all," Sibley says. No doubt she and Walter practiced those words just in case the truth came out.

"Creative name for the shell company buying the stock, I must tell you," I say.

"All in the Family Incorporated, you mean? Oh, it's nothing. Just a little joke, you know. I'm impressed you figured out the truth," Sibley says. She points to her brothers. "Shouldn't you guys hit your shots? There's another foursome waiting."

To their credit, my sons look sufficiently stunned, which lets me know they have nothing to do with their sister's scheme.

"When did you figure it out, Daddy?" Sibley asks. "Before or after you invited me on the yacht? I'm surprised you were one step ahead of me. I thought I got you!"

This is all Walter's doing, but my daughter seems quite proud of herself. I must admit, it was a smart move. I just wonder where she got the extra loot to make this grand play. I'm sure Walter put a lot of his own money in, but this took more than just his cash. I wonder who else is on her team.

"Oh, my dear, I'm always one step ahead—but it was an impressive scheme. It seems I have another contender for taking over the business. She's shown a knack for thinking outside the box, and she has a lot of stock. So many choices. Anyway, you guys go take your shots. We'll see you on the fairway," I say to Ted and John, then follow Sibley to the cart.

"Wow, you really will consider me to succeed you. Even though you know about the stock," Sibley says, her oversize sunglasses masking her eyes, her thoughts. "I'm really touched that you think I'm smart. I wanted to prove to you I could do impressive things. I'm glad you aren't mad."

"No, Sibley, not mad. Disappointed," I say. "And certainly, impressed with your resourcefulness."

"I'd make a great president or CEO. The first woman to run Kingsley. I'm smart and driven and creative. Imagine all the adoring press," Sibley says, stopping the cart on the path near where my ball has landed. Hers is farther up the fairway. It's impressive that she outdrove me. And she thinks she's outsmarted me, too. But it's time to put an end to this farce.

I climb out of the cart and pull my seven iron from the rental bag. I walk over to the driver's side. "Perhaps you would have been a good CEO. You're a talented young woman, and it's clear you inherited enough of my ruthlessness to keep those around you on their toes. But you sided with my brother, and he has corrupted you, and I cannot abide by that. You will have no part in my company."

Sibley shakes her head in surprise but quickly covers her emotions. She smiles and pulls off the ridiculous sunglasses. "That's not entirely your choice. We have a lot of stock. And, Daddy, I did it because I believe in Kingsley's future. And I want to be a part of it."

I smirk. Lean closer. "You already were a part of it, Sib. I value loyalty, and you have betrayed me. You went behind my back, partnering with my enemy, my brother. I'm impressed you had the nerve to show your face on board my yacht." I realize I'm feeling a bit faint, but I need to finish this.

As I stare at my only daughter, her mask finally drops as she realizes she's lost. I watch as she nibbles her thumbnail. "I wanted to see if your yacht was as big as Uncle Walter's," she says, taunting me to cover for the panic she must be feeling. "You'll be pleased to know it's bigger."

"Of course it is. I always win. That's why I'll be doing a reverse stock split, and I will dilute your ill-gotten shares. And in time, you will come to appreciate all you've lost." I smile but it's an effort. I need to hit my ball and get off this course. I feel awful, sweaty and shaky. The anger I feel, the disappointment in her, and the fact that I'm dying are a toxic combination.

"You can't do that. You wouldn't. Daddy?" Sibley jumps out of the cart, hands on her hips. "Come back here. We're not finished. I didn't mean to hurt you, just—you know . . . show you how smart I am. You like that. You've got so much, anyway. Uncle Walter and I didn't do anything wrong. John did."

"Leave John out of this," I tell her. I'm tired of her games.

"John kept a dossier of everyone you exited on his computer, the idiot, including your brother," Sibley says. "Hackers love that stuff."

My side throbs as I consider her latest bombshell. John knows he's made a mistake, and he's paid dearly for it, although he doesn't think I know that. He is paying the bribes to protect me and to shelter all the deeds I've instructed him to do. Now I know who he has been paying. And now I know how she got the money to buy the stock: extorting her own brother. This will end now.

"I don't know how hackers would be alerted to such a thing's existence, but it's unethical to steal files, Sibley. I wouldn't want to be associated with anyone who would do such a thing. The extortion will stop immediately," I say. "If not, you are cut off for life. No more money, no more credit card. Nothing."

"Daddy! Honestly?" she huffs. "I haven't done anything wrong!"

"Stop lying! You're blackmailing your own brother!" I yell, unable to control my rage. I shake my head, turn away from her, and walk to my ball.

Ted stands nearby, about to hit his ball.

"Son," I call to him, unable to bear the pain any longer. "Could you take me back to the yacht? I'm getting overheated in this canyon." I pick up my ball.

"Yes, of course," he says. "You don't look well."

"Tell John to carry on—play with his sister, if he'd like," I add.

"No, we'll all go back. The two of them will kill each other if we leave them alone," Ted says.

"Yes, in all likelihood, there would be some intense words," I say. Especially once John discovers his sister is the one behind the blackmailing scheme. I'm not going to be the one to tell him. Not now. I double over with the pain.

"Dad, my God, hang in there," Ted says, patting my back. "John! Hurry!" Ted waves his hand in the air and motions for John to bring the cart. As bad as I feel, I'm still shocked Ted is allowing John to drive me back instead of playing the hero himself. I wonder what's happening here.

"What's wrong?" John says, driving on the fairway despite rules against it. He'll do anything for me, I realize.

"Take Dad back to the dock and the water taxi, as quickly as you can. He isn't feeling well and needs a doctor. I'll call the captain and tell him to arrange for medical assistance on board," Ted says as I climb into the golf cart next to John. "I'll be right behind you with Sibley."

"Better you than me," John says. "Here, Dad, drink some water."

"Thanks, boys," I say as we pull away.

I feel a bit guilty leaving Ted with Sibley. Of course, she'll let him believe she's still in contention. That's what I would do if I were her. Poor Ted will likely believe her.

I chuckle despite the pain in my chest. It's good to keep the kids on their toes.

29

JOHN

Sitting beside me in the golf cart, Richard looks horrible—ghostly white, sweaty. I lean forward, willing the cart to go faster. I can't believe my dad is sick. I can't believe he's dying. My whole life is built around him.

"Hang in there, Dad. You're going to be OK," I say, speeding down the canyon road. "I'm going to just borrow this cart and drive it all the way to the pier. We'll get someone to return it to the golf course later."

"OK, son," Richard says. "Whatever you say. Just hurry."

"Good, that's great." I drive fast but cautiously. I don't want an accident with Dad on board. To take my mind off his frailty, I remind myself of my sister's one-on-one with him. He can't possibly choose her, could he? "So are you serious about Sibley? Considering her for the CEO?"

"Can we not talk business right now?" Richard says. "I mean, you have an impressive one-track mind, son, but I'm not feeling so great."

"Oh, sure, sorry. Thought it would take your mind off your pain," I say. We reach the last street where any type of golf cart is allowed. I park and help him out. We need to cross Main Street, and then we'll be at the pier.

Up ahead, in the crowd, I spot Rachel, walking alone, about to start down the pier.

"Rachel!" I call out. She sees me and Richard. She starts walking back toward us. Beside me, Richard is limping and is slumped on his right side, likely from the fall he took on the boat. He's a bastard and a terrible father, but he's mine.

Rachel reaches us. "Richard, what's wrong? Let me help. Where's Serena?"

"Oh, I've been a fool. Thought I could handle a round of golf, but I'm just too tired and banged up," he says. "As for Serena, who knows? Probably off sulking somewhere because I jumped the gun on the baby announcement."

I don't like the way he looks and wish I could find a bench so he could sit. "Ted has found a landline at the club and called the Coast Guard to tell Captain Bill to come get you, or would you like the water taxi?"

"Either one." Richard's voice is quiet, weak.

For once, he's leaning against me, allowing me to help him.

Below us, at the pier, I scan the dinghies tossing and bumping into each other and spot the captain. I don't think Dad should ride in that dinghy in his condition.

"Let's take the water taxi. It's safer and easier," I say. "Captain Bill, we'll take the water taxi. Please make sure the doctor is coming now."

"OK. And yes, the doctor is on his way," Captain Bill yells as we walk past him down to the end of the pier. The taxi is idling and ready for us as we climb aboard.

"Back to the *Splendid Seas*?" the water taxi captain who brought us ashore asks.

"Yes, please, and please hurry," I say.

"We can head over in about twenty minutes. Need to wait for some more customers who are on their way," the water taxi captain says.

"Fine, thank you," I say. I help Dad onto the bench seat and sit beside him, my arm around his waist. He leans against me. Rachel takes a seat on the other side of him. She looks tense, worried.

"You're going to be OK, Dad," I say to Richard. But he's not OK. Nothing is.

30

SERENA

As the water taxi exits the Avalon marina heading toward our mooring in front of Descanso Beach, I spot scuba divers' markers bobbing in the water in front of the casino. A chill runs down my spine just imagining being under this cold, dark water. I pull my sunglasses off and dry my eyes.

I'll put on a happy face for Richard and calm the storm between us. Then I'll decide my next steps. Unless Richard decides them for me.

"Here we are, ma'am—the *Splendid Seas*," the water taxi's captain says with a wink. "Must be nice to cruise around in that thing. Do enjoy yourself and watch your step."

I feel his eyes on me as I leap onto the deck. I'm proud of my sea legs—I'm proud of my legs *always*, and they're looking good on these rough seas. I remind myself to focus. I need to make up with Richard.

I head up to our stateroom. It's strange with nobody else aboard the yacht. For a moment, an irrational thought races through my mind: What if they left me, hopped on helicopters, and flew back to Newport Beach without me? I mean, when I look at the situation rationally, I realize Richard is the only one truly on my side, and now I've angered him.

I race through the door to our cabin, hoping against hope to find him there. It's empty. The room has been perfectly made up, as if no one had slept here last night. Flowers fresh, linens pressed. Beautiful perfection, like me. I decide on a change of clothes and fresh makeup to welcome Richard back to the yacht after golf. The moment I step inside my walk-in closet, I know something is wrong. Someone has been in here; someone has touched my things. Goose bumps dot my arms. I punch in the numbers for the safe and pull on the door.

It's empty. My jewelry, my prized possessions, are gone. The thief left only one thing inside. I grab it. It's a tiny camera, the size of a button. Someone has smashed it. I drop to the floor, unable to move or breathe.

I open my hand and stare at the camera. If there is one of these hidden on the yacht, are there more? Why was it smashed and left for me to find in the safe? Could someone be trying to send me a message? I pull myself up to standing and slip the camera into my pocket. I reach into the safe and find it still empty. This isn't a bad nightmare; this is happening to me. I wrap my arms around myself to keep from falling apart again.

I turn to look at the rest of the closet, the rest of my beautiful things.

"Oh my God!" I rush to the first beautiful gown, a silk ocean-blue dress—one of my favorites. It has been slashed with a knife. The next gown, a light-peach dress by my favorite designer. Slashed, too. Not only was my safe robbed, but all my beautiful gowns and dresses have been ruined, shredded with a knife. I begin sobbing, rushing from dress to dress, examining the damage. They're all destroyed. My frustration and fury get the best of me. I realize I'm screaming with rage.

There is a knock on the door. I clamp my hand over my mouth.

"Dr. Barton here to examine Richard Kingsley," a man says.

Richard isn't here. What has happened to Richard? I must pull myself together. I wipe the mascara away from under my eyes, take a deep breath, and step out of my closet.

"Are you all right, ma'am? I'm Dr. Barton. I heard you screaming," he says, forehead wrinkled with concern. "Mrs. Kingsley, are you hurt?"

I meet his eyes and take a deep breath. "No. I'm sorry. I am just worried about my husband. It's making me a little bit crazy. Do you know what happened? What's wrong with him?"

"I don't. Something happened on the golf course. I received an emergency message and headed right out," Dr. Barton says. I watch as he takes in the scene beyond my open closet door: ripped clothing tossed on the floor; my designer shoes thrown into a hapless pile; my safe, open and empty.

"Your husband will be fine, Mrs. Kingsley. Perhaps you should come sit down," he says before backing out of my closet, pretending he didn't see the carnage inside.

"Yes, thank you. Good idea," I say, pulling the closet door closed and following him into the stateroom. I take a seat as instructed.

Of course, this was Sibley's doing, her and her boyfriend. The doctor hands me a glass of water, and I take a big sip.

"Thank you. I'm fine," I say, although he knows better. Our wealth buys his discretion, I hope. I take a deep breath. Richard will handle Sibley once he feels better. My clothes are all replaceable. My jewelry is still on the boat, likely in their stateroom. I will not be a victim for long. I take another drink of water. I hear Richard's voice in the hallway. I will turn my focus to my husband, where it belongs.

"Thank you both. I can take it from here," Richard says as he limps into our stateroom.

"My darling, you're hurt," I say and rush to his side. The doctor helps me get Richard to the bed. John and Rachel stand in the doorway, gawking. I take Richard's hand in mine as he gets comfortable.

"It's just my rib, Sisi, that's all," Richard says.

"I'm going to give you something for the pain, sir. And then I'll examine you to make sure nothing is broken," Dr. Barton says. "You fell, is that right?"

"Damn waves," Richard says.

"Tell him you're dying," I say. Dr. Barton looks up at me.

"We all are, Sisi. Please, no more of that kind of talk," Richard says. It is then that I realize no one else will know about Richard's diagnosis. Just the family. Always only the family, despite how they treat each other. At the end, they do seem to come together somehow.

"Is there a diagnosis here I should be aware of?" Dr. Barton asks.

"No. He's good as gold," I say and pat Richard's hand.

I watch, my heart racing, as the doctor examines Richard. I hope he's going to heal. This was the last thing he needed with his failing health. The doctor wraps a bandage around Richard's chest, listens to his traitorous heart before closing his medical bag.

"He needs a couple of hours of rest with no disruptions," the doctor says, making his point clear. "His rib is banged up, and his heart rate is elevated. I've treated both, but please be sure he isn't upset by anything or anyone for the rest of the evening. He should heal up just fine. I'll let myself out."

"Thank you, Doctor, for everything," I say, curling up next to Richard on the bed.

How exactly will I keep him from being upset by anyone? This is a family cruise full of scheming people. For starters, I won't tell him about what has happened in the closet.

How could I? If I told him about it now, the stress of the robbery could kill him.

31

PAIGE

Even though I wasn't invited to play golf, I'm having fun, drinking buffalo milk at a beach bar by myself. I can't remember the last time I did something like this. And that's where Ted and Sibley find me, relaxing with my toes in the sand.

They are anything but relaxed.

"What's wrong?" I ask as soon as they make it to my table.

"We need to go back to the yacht. Dad's sick. Sibley caused it," Ted says, tossing some cash on the table as I gather my things.

"Is it his heart? Oh my gosh," I say. "Did you upset him, Sibley? Poor Richard."

"I didn't do anything to him," Sibley says, hands on hips, pouting like a child.

"Did you call an ambulance?" I say to Ted.

"No, he was able to make it back to the yacht. A doctor is meeting him there. He was holding his side, so I don't think it's his heart. It could be from the fall. I'm not sure what happened, except he found out Sibley and Uncle Walter were trying to be corporate raiders," Ted says.

"So Dad told you about my little plan. You guys always do underestimate me, and that gives me room to swoop in," Sibley says with a laugh.

"Surprising, I'll give you that," Ted says as we make our way to the dock.

Sibley takes off her sunglasses and stares at me. "But you don't underestimate me, Paige. Do you? You're just a little bit afraid of me. And I love that. Boo!"

Yes, I jump. But my mind is soaked with an ice-cream-sundae-like drink that is loaded with alcohol. She can't bother me right now. I'm looking forward to getting back to the yacht and checking on Richard.

As the water taxi brings us closer to the *Splendid Seas*, I think about Sibley, who is sitting next to me, and Colson, waiting for her on board. I dread another tense and combative dinner with the two of them. Maybe with Richard's injury, we should just go back to Newport Beach.

"Here you go, y'all," the water taxi captain calls out. "Enjoy your time. Looks like an amazing yacht."

I look up as the captain pulls alongside the yacht. I see motion on the second level, on the balcony. *Our* balcony. Is it a crewmember cleaning the cabin or someone else? Has someone broken into our room?

Sibley jumps from the taxi onto the yacht first and lands gracefully on board. I try to mimic her moves but feel clumsy as soon as my feet land on the deck. Ted pays the taxi captain and then joins me on the yacht. I realize the sea has calmed, and for once, I stand easily, without swaying or hanging on to anything, on the deck. Maybe I am earning my sea legs, I think, until I remember there is someone on our balcony.

"Let's go freshen up," I say to Ted, grabbing his arm and forcing him to walk fast toward the stairs. Sibley is racing up the stairs ahead of us.

We make it up the stairs right behind her. Sibley ducks into her cabin, slamming the door behind her. I slip the key into the cabin door and push the door open with a force I didn't know I had, hurrying inside, ready for a confrontation.

"What's wrong?" Ted asks as I check the bathroom. There's no one here, not on the balcony and nowhere in the room.

"They're gone."

"Who's gone?" Ted asks. "You're worrying me. What did you see?"

"I saw someone on our balcony. I swear I did," I say. We lock eyes at the same time. Ted is first to spot the envelope that must have been slipped under our door or left by the intruder.

"What is this?" he asks, handing the white envelope to me.

"No idea," I say, handing it back to him. Unease rolls down my spine as I watch him rip it open.

He pulls out a piece of paper. Written in Sharpie, in all capital letters, is a threat: A FAMILY IS ONLY AS STRONG AS ITS WEAKEST LINK. I KNOW WHAT YOU'VE DONE.

"Who would do this? It's got to be one of your siblings, resorting to childish pranks. They are beyond annoying," I say.

"I don't know," Ted says.

"Do you think this is a threat to expose your embezzling to the public?" I ask.

"No, of course not. That's private. Family. And it wasn't a big deal," Ted says.

"Can you think of anything else that you've been hiding that your siblings can threaten to expose?"

Ted looks me straight in the eye. "No, nothing."

I bite my lip but decide to say it. "What about that time when you cheated on me with Marcy, in Vegas?" I say the words quietly, my voice shaking. The anger and the hurt bubbling through every word, the alcohol loosening my tongue.

I've never confronted Ted about his indiscretion. I never told him I found the love notes Marcy sent him, the ones I destroyed. I never wanted to talk about it.

"Ted?" I ask. He stares at me with unblinking eyes. Clearly, he's shocked I know this secret. "I know it was more than a one-night stand. I read the letters she wrote you."

"Oh my God, Paige," Ted says. "I'm sorry. It was a mistake. I didn't tell you about that because it's over, and I'm ashamed."

I guess I decided long ago that whatever happened on Ted's business trips was separate from our life together. That those things didn't impact our love, our family, our real life. I was in denial. The woman named Marcy, who wrote him the love notes, made me see that he wasn't just having sex outside our marriage—he was having a relationship. He caused some other woman to fall in love with him. And instead of being angry at him, I turned on myself. I decided I wasn't good enough for him, that I must be letting him down. And I focused on being the best mom I could be, because if I wasn't enough for him, I had to be more than enough for my girls.

But now I realize this wasn't my fault. This wasn't my indiscretion, wasn't my affair. I see the truth now. It wasn't about me. It was all about Ted and his weakness. I refuse to stay angry at myself. And I've grown stronger, started taking classes toward my MBA, started stepping into my power. My role with the food bank helps save people from hunger, and maybe it saved me, too. I take a deep breath. We need to change the subject before I say something I'll regret.

I can't look Ted in the eye right now. We will need to work through all this, as two equals, but not today. We need to focus on Richard and on the mess this family cruise has become. We need to secure our future, and then we'll tackle the past.

"John could have left the note. He feels threatened by you, and he's been back on board for a while with your dad," I say. "And Sibley. She said something about you having secrets, remember? She could have had Colson drop the note off."

"What are you talking about?" Ted asks, his voice tense. I've set him on edge by bringing up his secret lover, and someone else is threatening more. But I don't know what.

"I don't even know what's real or who is telling the truth," I say. My heart sinks with this realization. I shake my head, walk to the balcony door, and open it.

"Paige, wait, please. You can believe in me. It's never happened again. And it never will. Promise. And as for the note, John has been with me all day, until he brought Dad back to the boat. So I guess it could be him," Ted says. "You know, I decided I'm not worried about John. And Dad figured out Sibley's scheme, so I think I'm his only option."

I decide to leave the discussion of his affair for another day, once we're back on solid ground. I take a deep breath and turn around to face him.

"OK, let's go check on Richard, see how he's doing," I say. "But we will need to discuss your affair when we get home. I don't want to sweep things under the rug anymore."

He makes eye contact, clearly relieved I am dropping the subject, for now.

"Sure, yes. Whatever you want. Let's go check on Dad," he says. "You did have two of those drinks, though."

"I'm fine." When I look at my husband just now, I see something I don't like. He's still hiding something. Is it gambling? I don't know. "Where does all our money go?"

My pleasant drunk feeling is beginning to turn into a headache.

"I'm sorry. I really am," Ted says. "Please, we've been through too much this weekend to have any more heavy conversations, but as soon as we get home, we'll talk. I'll tell you everything you want to know. I love you, and I promise you this," Ted says.

I pull the cabin door open. "I hope Richard is OK."

"Me too," he says. "Forgive me, Paige?"

Somehow, I find the strength to walk away without answering. I don't trust anyone or anything right now. It's not the way it should be on a family weekend, but it's the way it is with the Kingsleys. Across the hall, Sibley's cabin door is closed. I put my ear up to it but can't hear anyone inside. I step back and turn to walk down the hall when Sibley's cabin door opens.

"Whatcha doing?" Sibley asks, stepping into the hallway and closing her cabin door behind her. "Were you eavesdropping?"

I feel my face flush. "No, what? Of course not."

"Such a good liar. Maybe that's why you and Ted make such a good team. Your precious husband should come clean, for everyone's sake—even yours. Maybe especially yours," Sibley says, staring at me with her dark-blue vampire eyes. She must have twenty more tattoos since I last saw her. I try to remember when I last saw her and cannot. Not since I kicked her out of our house four years ago, I guess. It was the right call, after walking in on Sibley with a thirteen-year-old Emily smoking weed.

"You're the one who is trouble, and you know it. I'll never forget what you did, under my roof, to Emily. She was a child," I say.

"Emily smokes weed all the time now. I can tell," Sibley says with a laugh. "I was helping her learn how to smoke responsibly."

"I can't go there with you. Not now. It's not worth it," I say, fighting to keep my temper under control. "Did you tell Colson to break into our cabin while we were onshore? Did you tell him to leave us a threatening note?"

"Why would Colson be in your cabin? I mean, you two aren't glamorous, and you don't wear much jewelry—nothing a pro would be interested in. That would be a worthless break-in, wouldn't it?" Sibley rolls her eyes, laughs, and slips back into her cabin. I hear the door lock.

I will deal with her later. I hurry upstairs into the library and on through to Richard's cabin. I'm about to knock when the door opens, and a man wearing a white coat steps out, followed by John.

"Thank you, Dr. Barton," John says as they walk past me.

"What happened to Richard? I know he wasn't feeling well, but will he recover?" I ask, following behind them.

"He's going to be fine for now. Just needs some rest. I taped his cracked rib. Needs to be careful with these swells and relax more, for his heart," Dr. Barton says. "Seas are calming down now, so tonight's crossing should be more peaceful."

The doctor does not know the dynamics of our family will preclude peace, likely forever.

John says, "I'll show you downstairs. The water taxi will be here for you in a moment."

I knock on the open door and walk into Richard's room. I'm startled to find him propped up in bed, Serena beside him.

"How's our patient doing? I hear you've had an eventful afternoon," I say before noticing his eyes are closed.

Richard opens his eyes. "Ah, Paige, I can always count on you to be the princess in the family of hardheaded Kingsleys. But if you're here to continue our delightful tête-à-tête from this morning, I'm afraid now's not a good time. Don't worry your pretty head, though, my dear. Everything will be just fine. You'll see. Due time, my dear." Richard's eyes close again.

Serena puts her finger to her lips and waves me out of the room. I nod and put both hands up. Everything can wait, for now. I think of Richard as indestructible. But just now, he looks fragile and old, and even though he's a pain in the ass, I am not ready to lose him. The girls do love their grandfather.

I walk softly out of their cabin and close the door behind me. Maybe that is the secret to surviving this final evening together. Maybe we should all just stay in our cabins. When we're back in the harbor in Newport Beach tonight, we can make a plan. Pick a time to sit down and talk about the business and succession on solid ground.

That would be a logical plan, but this family is anything but.

Ted waits for me in the hallway. "How is he?"

"Resting. Sounds like he'll be fine," I say.

"Did he say anything else?" Ted asks.

"No," I say, but that's not true. I think, just now, Richard made me a promise. I believe he is a man of his word, at least when it's important.

Somebody needs to be.

32

JOHN

I'm holding on to the railing of the ship to keep from cracking a rib like Dad did.

The doctor departed on the water taxi, and the captain has left the ship with the dinghy again. I swear he's off this boat more than he is on it. I wonder where Dad found him. I wonder if he's even good at what he does. I guess it's a bit late to wonder about that now. He and Sibley's date seem friendly. That's disturbing.

Sibley says she knows how to drive this thing, but I don't believe her. Part of me wishes we could just go back to Newport Beach now. Forget all this nonsense and the final dinner. I'm angry, angrier than I have ever been in my life. I feel as if my chances at leading Kingsley are slipping away by the minute. Ted and Sibley have both undermined me. Dad hates the fact I kept files, despite the reality I was following his orders—*his* files, details I needed to save. Although now it's clear I shouldn't have. I feel sweat running down my back. My hands clench into fists. I want off this stupid boat. Now.

But Dad insists we're staying on this mooring until he says we're leaving, despite his rib. So here I am, on the middle deck, pondering my options. Someone put a threatening letter under our door—likely my sister messing with me, as usual. My dad is hurt. Serena is pregnant.

Sibley is dangerous and volatile and still on board, and Ted is still irritatingly around and in consideration.

The sun is setting, and the water is turning shades of pink and orange. Technicolor and strange. Everything seemed off from the moment I helped Dad back onto the yacht. I can't put my finger on it, but there was something thick in the air on board. Rachel noticed it, too; at least, she said she did. Now she's getting dressed and ready for our formal dinner tonight—something I should do soon.

"John!" When I turn around, I see Ted. "We need to talk!"

I'd rather not, but here I am, trapped. The only way to get off this deck is up the steps, where he is standing.

"Sure, Ted, what's on your mind?" I ask. As if I care.

"How's Dad? Really?" he asks.

"Come on. We both know we don't really care, right? I mean, this isn't about caring for the old man; this is about the company," I say and turn to look at the beach off the back of the ship. Partiers are beginning to arrive, and the music is cranking up louder with the sunset. Tiki torches illuminate the beach.

"Sure, fine, it is about that. But he looked bad on the golf course. I mean, is it more than his rib?" Ted looks like a schoolboy, shocked to learn that people grow old and die.

"He's dying, Teddy. He told us that. We all are. Look, I need to go change for dinner," I say and start walking toward him.

"So dinner is still on?" he asks.

"Of course. You know Serena—she loves to dress up," I say. "And Dad didn't mention any change of plans. Not that that means anything, I suppose. He changes his mind all the time these days. Like with the company. That's what you really want to talk to me about, right? So let me make this conversation short and sweet: I'm the one who should be in charge, and you know it."

"I don't know any such thing," he says and takes a step down, so we are eye to eye.

I'm not afraid of him. Ted's weak and inferior at heart. And although others do, he doesn't have anything to use against me. "I've been groomed by Dad. I know the business inside out. I'm a CPA and a fixer. Dad could never get rid of me because I know too much. I know where all the skeletons are buried," I say. "Including yours."

Ted shakes his head. "You're the most selfish jerk I've ever known. The company is big enough for both of us, and you know it." He wipes his forehead with his hand. He's sweating because he's desperate.

I realize I'm sweating, too.

I tilt my head and smile. "Oh, I know why you're acting so frantic. I know about the gambling problem. Dad doesn't yet; he thinks you've quit all that. But he will find out the truth if you push me too hard. You don't want that to happen, do you? I know your wife and daughters don't want to lose their home. Heck, if I know Paige, she's dreaming of moving to an oceanfront property as soon as Dad croaks. Am I right?"

"Leave Paige out of this," Ted says, but he looks like a scared little boy. "Look, let's join forces. We're stronger together. Sibley needs to go. We both know that. We can go to Dad and tell him we're a package deal. Please?"

It's a little sad, this Ted. I'm rather used to his pompous playboy demeanor, his *I'm so much better than you* swagger. This Ted, well, he's pathetic. A ghost of himself.

"After all these years and all the stuff you've put me through. Remember when you told Dad I embarrassed you around your friends? Remember when you called me a mama's boy and told Dad not to come to our wedding? Do you think Rachel would ever forgive you for calling her a ball buster? Rachel and I are the package deal. You are just some sorry excuse for a half brother. A broke, cheating, sorry excuse for a half brother."

As Ted blinks and takes a step back, I pass in front of him and start up the steps. "Surprised? Yes, I know about your affair. Sounds like you broke that woman Marcy's heart, you bastard."

I keep walking up the steps to the level where our lousy cabin is located. I don't look back at Ted. I don't need to.

The door to our cabin is ajar, so I push it open, feeling proud of myself. I'm still not certain how to use everything Rachel uncovered on Ted, but I've put him on notice.

"Rachel, baby, your guy hit the nail on the head with Teddy," I say as she jumps up from the bed.

"Did you tell him what my investigator found?" Rachel asks with a gleam in her eye. She has one of the best PIs in Southern California on retainer. He had fun tailing ol' Teddy. Has for years.

"I may have mentioned some of it," I say, pulling her in for a hug.

"Did he freak out?"

"In a Ted way, yes. He looked shocked and colorless, quite like a piece of white bread. He knows he's toast," I say, laughing.

Rachel smirks. "Good. They should back off now, and Richard will see you are the only choice. You told Ted that in no uncertain terms, right?"

"He got the message," I say.

"Just so you know, someone tried to break into the safe," Rachel says nonchalantly. "I used my extra lock and security protocol, so they couldn't get in, thank God."

"What? Are you sure?" I ask, but I know she is. In her line of work, secrecy and security are paramount.

"I have a lot of my trial prep in there, among other things. I don't know if that's what they wanted or something else. But they didn't get in," she says.

"You didn't bring any extra jewelry or valuables?" I ask.

"Nope. Just important documents. But they're safe," she says. There's a loud thump on the wall. "That keeps happening. Like someone is jumping off a bed or something? There's music, too. Just wait, you'll hear it. Do you think Ted and Paige are having some kind of party?" Rachel points to the door.

People certainly have a lot of questions for me all of a sudden. It makes me feel as if I'm in command. And maybe I am. I'm the oldest child, the natural heir. Maybe I will take charge and make it so.

"I do hear the music, but Ted's cabin is on the other side," I say, wondering if Sibley is throwing another dance party. "Probably Sibley and Colson. I guess since Dad is under the weather, I am in charge."

"Could you go find out what time dinner is? And, John, I'd like to meet with Richard. Just you and me. Can you finagle a meeting like that before dinner?" Rachel says.

"Why?" I ask.

"I discovered something important to share with both of you," Rachel says, looking strong and talented and powerful. "It can change everything. It *will* change everything for you. What I have will convince Richard to name you his successor once and for all."

"Hmm, you've got my attention. I'll go check on Dad and ask him to carve out a few minutes before dinner for your surprise. You're something, Rachel." I puff out my chest and feel proud of myself and my wife. We've got this.

Rachel kisses my cheek. "Go get 'em, tiger. With any luck, Ted has decided to agree you're the only choice for president in return for your discretion, and we will arrive back in Newport Beach richer than our wildest dreams. In fact, I'm certain of it. Go get that little meeting."

"On it. And you know, it's too bad. I was just getting used to you being my sugar mama," I say as I walk out into the hall. "Lock this, OK? I don't like the undercurrents on this yacht right now."

"I never have. Your family? They're horrible," Rachel says.

I don't say anything, but I must agree. In fact, I may be the most horrible one of all.

33

PAIGE

I stand on the balcony of our cabin and notice a growing chill in the air. The waves seem to have diminished, but with the motion of the boat, it could be a mirage. I do know the wind has picked up, and I'm cold. A thick fog has descended over us, making everything beyond my balcony railing disappear. I'm alone in a cloud.

I hurry inside the cabin and slide the glass door to the balcony closed. I don't know where Ted is, but I do know we are leaving Catalina Island and we'll be back home soon. I cannot wait.

I've pulled on my new cocktail dress for tonight's dinner, a shiny blue silk dress from Mark's store, and hope I look OK compared to Sibley and Serena. They do tend to suck all the life and attention out of a room.

I turn away from the sliding glass door and try to ignore the dark water surrounding us, the lack of any landmass in view. I spot Ted's phone on his nightstand. I'm surprised he's forgotten it, but I suppose without service, it's of little use.

There's a knock on the cabin door. Who could it possibly be? I open it and hear a party. Loud music like the type my daughters play fills the corridor. It's Sibley, wearing a tiny skintight black dress, jumping up and down and flinging her arms in the air.

"Hey! Want to party with us?" she yells in my face.

"What? No? Who all are you with in there?" I ask. She tries to look inside my cabin. I step into the hallway and pull the door closed behind me.

"Just Colson and I," Sibley says, still spinning and jumping in front of me. Colson—the tall, gangly guy with white hair, dark-brown eyes—wraps his arms around Sibley as she continues to dance/grind against him.

"Hey, babe, come back to our room now. I think you're disturbing people," he says, loud enough to be heard over the music. "Sorry." He pulls Sibley, still dancing, backward toward their cabin. "Is that the one you're blackmailing?"

Sibley grins at me. "No, it's the other one." And then they're back in their cabin and the door slams shut. This doesn't make sense. How can Sibley blackmail John?

I need to find Ted.

I hurry down the hallway and can't decide where to go. I take the stairs down to the marina level and find Ted, alone, leaning on the railing, staring down at the dark, tumultuous water swirling below us. His body is shaking.

"Ted, my God, what is happening? What's wrong?" I rush to his side and my heart cracks. He's crying.

"Ted, what is it?" I ask again, and my stomach clenches as I reach out and touch his shoulder.

"John and Rachel are telling lies about me. So is Sibley," Ted says flatly. "And I let them. Because I'm weak." He kicks at the railing with his shoe, misses, and his foot flies out over the water. "God, I can't do anything right."

I try to remember the times I've seen Ted cry. I can only think of when Emily and Amy were born. He cried tears of joy. I've never seen him like this, though. These tears are different. These are for himself. He feels sorry for himself.

"Take a deep breath and tell me what's happened," I say. I'm speaking calmly, using my mom voice. I don't know what else to do. "Let's go to our cabin, OK? So no one sees us like this?"

"It doesn't matter. It's over. It's all over," Ted says.

"Hey, you guys should be careful out here after dark. The swells have died down, but there could be a big set at any time. I'd feel better if you were inside," Captain Bill says, appearing behind us.

"We were just heading back to our cabin to get ready for dinner," I say. I wait for the captain to walk away. "Ted, I talked to your dad. He's going to pick you; I'm sure of it."

Ted turns to me. "Really? But there's so much against me."

"Everybody's got something," I say. I hope it calms him down. "Sibley has something on John, I think?"

"What does she have?" Ted asks.

"I have no idea. Just something her boyfriend said to me," I answer with a shrug.

"I need to talk to Sibley," he says.

"Tonight at dinner, you can. Things will get settled." Although I'm not positive, but I believe I'm right. We will find out soon enough. But for now, Ted needs to pull himself together, and if a little white lie helps, so be it.

34

RICHARD

Where am I?

"Richard! Oh my gosh, you're awake. Thank goodness," Serena says, touching my forehead and kissing me like a baby.

"Stop it already," I say, although I enjoy the attention immensely. I need to figure out why I'm lying in bed, with my day clothes on while it's dark outside. I roll onto my side and wince at the jabbing rib. I reach down and feel the tape. The doctor was here; now I remember. He must have administered something to make me sleep. I'm fine. I'm alive. I make it to standing and manage to smile at my beautiful bride.

"I was so worried about you," she says. "I hate that we fought and that you were hurt. I'm so sorry. Will you forgive me? Please, darling?"

"Stop, Serena, please. Our little spat earlier isn't important," I say. I realize I haven't watched the videos Captain Bill prepared for me from yesterday, and I need to do that before dinner tonight. "How long until dinner?"

"You have about an hour to get ready, but we can push it later if you need more time," Serena says. I can tell she's been crying. It's nice to know she does love and care about me, at least a little bit. My experience with love over seven decades has taught me it is a scarce, fleeting commodity.

"Darling, I need to tend to some things in my study. Why don't you get ready, and I'll be back in twenty minutes," I say, heading out the door. I enter my office and find that indeed Captain Bill has queued up all the closed-circuit television feeds since my family arrived on the yacht. I hired a professional team to install cameras everywhere on the yacht before this family cruise. I click on the first camera's feed and start the show. Twenty minutes later, I'm furious, for several reasons. And something more. After rewinding and watching one of the feeds repeatedly, I sigh.

Sometimes I hate being right.

"Who would possibly do that?" I mutter, gathering my thoughts. For a moment, I feel like a schoolboy caught by my boarding school headmaster. For another moment, I flash back to my parents' faces. My loving mom. My demanding dad. The way they were when I lost them. The cause of the crash remains undetermined. The pilot, my mom, my dad, and the real estate investor my dad was showing a ranch to. The pilot had been drinking, the coroner decided. Either that or the engine failed. Or he had been showing off his part-time crop-dusting job and dropped too low, unable to recover. Having three different scenarios of your parents' last moments is a living hell I wouldn't wish on my worst enemy. I shake away the rest of the nightmares associated with their terrifying demise.

I focus on shutting down the monitor and making my way back to the stateroom. It's time to get dressed for tonight's dinner. This will, I imagine, be the last time I see some of these people ever.

I step into the cabin, and Serena greets me with a kiss on the cheek. She's wearing an uncharacteristically conservative outfit: a silk blouse and black pants.

"You look, well . . . casual," I say.

I watch as tears fall from her eyes. "I've been robbed. All my jewelry is gone, my dresses and gowns slashed. This is all that's left. I didn't want to tell you, to stress you out."

I wonder briefly if she did it herself and decide she would never destroy her beloved wardrobe. No, on this point, she's telling the truth.

"Interesting," I say. "Well, it's just things. Replaceable."

"What? No, some of my jewels are one of a kind—my dresses, too," she says, dabbing at her eyes. "I found this, smashed, inside the safe."

The crooks found one of my hidden cameras. "What is that?" I ask.

"It looks like a camera. Are there more of these?" Serena asks.

"I have no idea," I answer, lying. It's my turn.

"You will report this to the police. It had to be an inside job. It had to be Colson and Sibley." Serena turns from sad to angry in a flash. "I want them arrested."

Yes, I'm sure it was them, too. But *c'est la vie*. "Likely, she did it. She wants her mom to have some nice jewelry," I say. I'm as nonchalant about this as I seem. I don't care.

"But those are my pieces," Serena says. Hands on hips. "I want them back. I demand to get them back. I'll press charges."

"No, you won't. You'll let it go. Go check on the meal plans with the chef. Be sure everything is as planned," I say. I have dismissed her.

Serena looks at me, aghast and mostly jewelry free. She still wears her large wedding ring and sparkly diamond-stud earrings, together worth more than most women will have in a lifetime.

"Yes, fine. I'll go check in on the meal with the chef," she says and walks out the door.

It's dark, the blackest of black, outside our windows, and we're moving, under full engine power, but I did not instruct anyone to pull the anchor. Should I be concerned that someone else is calling the shots this evening? A chill begins to form at the bottom of my neck as I inhale the familiar perfume Serena has left in her wake.

There's a knock on my cabin door.

"Go away!" I yell.

"Dad, it's John. Can Rachel and I meet with you before dinner, privately?" he yells through the door. "It's important."

"No!" I yell. "Go away!"

I walk into my huge master suite bathroom, but I don't see the grandeur, don't admire the luxuries. When I look in the mirror, I see the face of an old, angry man. A man who is dying. In front of me, on the bathroom counter, a single red rose floats in a crystal vase. Beautiful, perfect, like Serena.

I pick up the vase and hurl it at the mirror, watching as the mirror cracks and the vase fractures into tiny shards. When the rose falls to the bathroom floor, I crush it under my slipper.

35

JOHN

As I walk back to our cabin, I practice deep breathing, trying to calm down. Dad rudely refused a before-dinner meeting with me and Rachel. I take another deep breath and feel myself relax a bit. Everything is fine. Rachel is on my side. And she's the only one.

For a moment I wonder if Ted is where I left him, dejected, busted, and looking like he was about to throw himself overboard. I don't really care if he does. Would make Dad's decision that much easier.

I pass by Sibley's cabin and hear music thumping. She's such an annoyance. When I get to our room, I find Rachel excited, pacing inside our cabin, anxious to close the deal.

"He says he's too busy to meet with us before dinner," I say. I hate disappointing her, but I have again.

"That's unacceptable. I'll go find him. I'll handle it myself," she says.

"No. Don't. He's in a bad mood. It's likely better to wait until after dinner, at least after cocktails. Let me change into my tux, and we'll go together and find him, hopefully drinking a large vodka on the rocks. Whatever you have, it better be good," I say. Dad will not listen to Rachel without me; I know that much. "I wish you'd tell me what it is."

"Trust me," she says.

"I don't have a choice, do I?" I shrug, but I'm smiling.

"Nope. It's big, John. I'm so excited," Rachel says.

I need to change into my tux. "You look lovely, Rachel." And she does. She's wearing a tight-fitting sequined silver dress, a copy of her red dress from last night. She has a set style, and it works for her. The last time I saw her in this dress was the emerald-green version for the company holiday party. Hopefully, Dad won't notice the social faux pas of a repeat dress. He likely will.

In the bathroom I look out the window. It's eerie to be out at sea in the darkness this thick fog provides. I can't see land; I can't see anything. I check out my reflection. My hair sticks up straight, so I pat it back down.

"Rachel, why don't you open some champagne, a little liquid courage for tonight?" I call to her in the other room. I'm not worried. Not really. There is only one choice. I helped Dad back to the yacht this afternoon. He was thankful—grateful, even.

After all I've done, he won't disappoint me. And now Rachel has a discovery to solidify my position. I glance at my reflection, register my own doubt.

"Here you are," Rachel says, carrying a flute of champagne through the door. "Hurry and dress. We should try to be the first to arrive."

"Thank you. Yes, the early bird and the worm," I agree. "Cheers!"

It's time for me to be in charge. It must happen tonight. I don't know what will happen if he picks one of the others. But I'm not worried. Of course everything will go my way.

I imagine sitting behind Dad's large mahogany desk, inside the biggest office at Kingsley, and I'm the happiest man on Earth.

36

SERENA

A quick check on the chef calmed my mind. Richard is right, as always: everything is replaceable. He'll buy me even brighter, better baubles if I ask for them. Or, after he dies, I will buy them for myself. It will all be fine. Except for the fact that, as always, Sibley is getting away with stealing and property damage, and she won't be held accountable.

But she will be gone soon, returning with that awful boyfriend to their life in the Florida swamps, and I will be here, with Richard. I have won already. I review the menu one more time. The four-course dinner is coming together exactly as planned. The aroma of fresh garlic and lemon makes my stomach growl. Everything will work out just fine—I know it.

I will make Richard's last few months on Earth happy and comfortable. And then my baby will be born into the lap of luxury, wanting for nothing, surrounded by love. I walk into the formal dining room, admiring the crystal and china place settings, the fresh flowers—red roses, my favorite—adorning the table. We even have name cards at each seat.

I'm worried about Richard. As the doctor this afternoon warned, this stress cannot be good for him, having his sons and daughter lobbying him constantly. Instead, they should take his decision in stride. Nothing much has been asked of them all their spoiled lives.

They should feel grateful. I know it's hard. I forgot this lesson during lunch. I decide to go check on Richard, make sure he doesn't need my help getting dressed. I touch the elegant white silk tablecloth as I pass through the room. It's all perfect—from the outside, at least.

I reach the door and Richard appears. I kiss him on the cheek. "Don't you look handsome," I say.

He nods. "Is everything in order? Ready for a final dinner?"

"More than ready," I answer. "Next time we take this thing out to sea, it's just you and me. Promise me?"

Richard winks at me and says, "Would you like a drink? Maybe orange juice or sparkling water?"

"I have champagne," I answer.

Richard walks to the bar and pours himself a tall glass of vodka. He adds two ice cubes.

"That's a big pour. Are you sure you should have that much before dinner?" I ask.

"I could ask you the same thing—and already did at lunch, as I recall. You shouldn't be drinking at all. Not with a baby on board," he says.

"I know. It's just for this weekend, and then no more until it's born," I answer.

"How noble," Richard says, taking a seat in one of the club chairs in the lounge area. I study him, notice something is amiss. But before I can ask him anything, Rachel and John appear.

She looks ridiculous in a too-tight dress just like the one she wore last night and to the company Christmas party, where it also was inappropriate. Same dress, just different colors. Tonight's is silver and gaudy. John looks . . . well, like John in a tux.

"Hello," I say, resuming my greeting duties. "Hope you both had fun on the island. And you both look so nice for our final dinner. Come in and help yourself to a cocktail."

John and Rachel pass by me as if I'm not even here. I guess I don't blame them, since I'm wearing a boring blouse and pants, the only things not shredded in my closet.

"Dad, will you join us please, for a little talk?" John asks. Rachel kisses Richard on the cheek when he stands to greet them.

"You know what, son? Not now. After dinner," Richard says. "Oh no, look what the cat dragged in."

We all see them at the same time. Colson and Sibley stroll into the formal living room, wearing jeans, T-shirts, and drunk grins.

"Sibley, Colson. You need to dress for dinner. Have you forgotten all your manners, young lady?" Richard bellows across the room. I worry about his heart. This is the stress he is to avoid.

Sibley slinks across the room like a stray cat; Colson follows behind her. They also ignore me and approach Richard. I catch a glimpse of a diamond tennis necklace around Colson's neck. Oh my God. It's mine. I'm sure of it.

"Don't worry, Daddy. In a few minutes, neither of us is going to be on your boat," Sibley says. "It's been fun but not real fun. We're leaving. The water taxi will be here soon." Sibley smiles and turns to face her brother. "I hope you keep getting what you deserve, John. I do admire your ruthless dedication. And yours, too, Daddy."

Rachel steps forward. "Sibley, did you and Colson break into our cabin?"

"That's a good one," Sibley says. "What would we want from you?"

Colson's face hardens. They broke into John and Rachel's cabin, too.

"You're wearing my tennis necklace, Colson," I say.

He smirks and pulls his shirt up to cover it. "No, I'm not."

"Seems to be a bit of a crime spree on board." I stare at Sibley, and she laughs.

"Wow, how interesting. Criminals lurking on this mega-yacht? If only the OC Scoop knew about this, they'd love it, I'd imagine, although I'd have no idea," Sibley says.

"Did you find anything, you know, under your door, Rachel?" Colson asks.

I have no idea what he's talking about.

"Oh, your childish note?" she asks, shaking her head. Rachel turns to me. "Nothing was taken from our safe. We have extra security measures in place whenever we travel, and I'm working on a case. Which is always. I have some important documents in that safe. Things I need to share privately with you, Richard."

"Not now, I said," Richard says. His voice is raised; he's clearly very angry at John or Sibley or all of us.

"Oh, aren't you so smart, Rachel? But still, Daddy doesn't want you to even speak to him. I don't think he likes you very much. Right, Daddy? And he doesn't want to see whatever you want to show him. Frustrating," Sibley says. "On the other hand, hooker, Daddy does listen to you, and you have been taking him for a big ride. So many jewels, so little time."

"Don't talk about my wife that way, Sibley," John says. "You're a rotten person, you know that?"

"Don't talk to my girlfriend that way, dude," Colson says, closing the distance between him and John in a second. He pokes John's chest with his finger. "Did you hear what I said? I mean it. Don't talk to Sibs like that."

Colson towers over John, his dark eyes flashing, his right hand reaching into his back pocket. I know he has a knife.

"I can talk however I want to," John says and takes a swing at Colson's cheek.

Before I know it, the two men are exchanging punches. Sibley screams and yells for Colson to stop. Rachel pushes Colson and then John, trying to force them apart.

"Enough!" Richard roars, and the men disengage. "Colson, Sibley. Get the hell off my yacht. Now!"

"We're leaving," Sibley says. "Oh, look, there's Teddy. He looks a little sad, worried, doesn't he? I mean, that doesn't count for much in this group, as you all look a bit—what's the word?—scared."

All I can do is glare at her. If it wouldn't upset Richard, I swear I would punch the spoiled little creature in the face, grab her backpack, and take my jewelry back. But I can't.

Meanwhile, Ted and Paige draw everyone's attention. Ted in a tux is mesmerizing, I must admit. Paige doesn't look too frumpy herself. She really has stepped up her game on this trip. Of course, she doesn't hold a candle to me, even in pants and a simple blouse, but that's to be expected. She's old; I'm young and I'm having a baby. She's waiting on grandbabies. Ha.

Ted hurries across the room to where we all stand, greeting me with barely a nod. Rude.

"Sibley, what are you doing now?" Ted asks. "Please don't cause more trouble. John, are you bleeding?"

"This piece of shit hit me," John says, using his handkerchief to dab at the blood flowing from the cut on his lip.

"He started it," Sibley says, pointing at John. "We're leaving. You all are just as crazy as Uncle Walter says you are. Maybe worse. The last thing we want to do is suffer through another Kingsley family meal. Besides, I need to take some things to my mom."

"My things, you little tramp? Thief!" I yell before I can stop myself and lunge at Sibley, trying to snatch the backpack.

Sibley grabs Colson's hand and hurries out the door. "Nice try, hooker!"

"Serena, don't lower yourself any further," Richard says. "Let them go."

"I'm sorry, I just—it's my things," I say to Richard. "I'll be right back." I hurry out the door, but I'm too late. They're already boarding the water taxi. I hear them but can't see them with this fog.

"Bye, hooker!" Sibley yells.

I turn around and head back inside. At least she's gone. I will forbid Richard from ever seeing her again. This is the last straw. I remind myself I have Richard's love. Sibley only has his pity.

That, and all my jewelry, the thief.

37

SIBLEY

We climb onto the water taxi, and I'm still not speaking to Colson. He's such an idiot. He almost told them I was behind the little notes in their cabins. *We admit to nothing,* I reminded him.

I mean, they must all know we pulled off the attempted robbery in John's room and the successful one in the hooker's closet. It's strange but typical that Dad didn't confront me, that he just allowed Colson and me to sail off into the sunset. Actually, off into the fog bank. It's sort of scary out here.

I guess that's really what dear old Dad wanted all along: to let me know he was onto my corporate-takeover scheme, the blackmail of John, all of it. It's fine, though. He'd never cut me off. He made a promise, and he kept it. For Dad, I will stop blackmailing John. I'll think of some other way to mess with my brothers. I think of the bag of jewelry in my backpack and must congratulate myself on my revenge on the hooker.

"I had fun breaking into all their rooms," Colson says. "I mean, you know your dad's not going to do anything to us."

"I just don't want you to be so obvious. And you didn't need to slash the hooker's outfits," I say. "That's juvenile."

"It was fun. I couldn't help myself," he says.

"I can't believe you didn't take anything from Rachel and John," I say.

"I tried, babe, I did," he says. "I couldn't crack their safe. That Rachel is intense. She got me. And the other two didn't have anything inside their safe."

"Whatever. It's fine. We got what we came for and more," I say. I just wanted to mess with them, keep them on edge. I knew they wouldn't take my threats seriously. They all think they're Teflon. Anything they do wrong won't stick. They are all so lame.

Uncle Walter will love hearing all about this little family trip. My entire reason for coming was to size them all up, find out what Daddy knew. Turns out, he knew too much about our plans. I need to get back to Florida and make a pivot with Uncle Walter before my dad renders our stock worthless.

We're not finished messing with my family yet—not by a long shot. I still have John to take money from, even though dear old Dad told me to leave him and that computer file of his that I stole alone. Fine. It's lucrative to mess with him, and I'm sure there are more secrets out there. If Ted had any money, I'd do it to him, too.

Besides, what I told Teddy during our little cocktail hour should help him blow apart this little reunion even further. I smile at the thought.

"Bye, hooker!" I yell into the fog. She tried to grab my backpack, but I'm too fast for her. And I win again.

"They're probably happy to see us go, babe," Colson says.

He's on my last nerve, and I don't need him or his breaking-and-entering skills anymore. We'll be finished once we reach Catalina. I flirted with him once I'd discovered he knew the captain of the *Splendid Seas*, that they were old roommates. I wanted to be sure all my bases were covered, that I would have at least one person on my side on the yacht. And Bill has been great, even flirted with me a few times when no one was watching.

But just like Colson, I'm finished with him, too. I need to get back to Florida and make my next plan. I'll be sure to drop by and see my mom, give her the necklace I saw Serena wearing yesterday evening. That will keep Cassie comfortable and off my back for a while. I'll let Colson keep the diamond tennis necklace to remember our time together.

Family . . . It's so complicated.

38

RICHARD

"Before we dig into this scrumptious meal, I have a little announcement to make," I say. I'm seated at the head of the table, Serena at the other end. Beside me are Paige and Rachel. The boys are next to their wives. It's much more manageable without Sibley and Colson. Much. I can feel Rachel staring at me, begging me to talk to her in private. She is the least of my worries at the moment.

I look around at their eager faces, my sons and their wives, their stress and concern. One couple will be happy and one, I'm afraid, disappointed for life. It's just the way the world works. I stand up to get their attention.

"I want to thank you all for your patience during this trip while I tried to make the most informed decision I could. I've enjoyed spending time with all of you, and I've been grateful for your support following my unfortunate diagnosis," I say. I take a breath and look around the table. "I've decided that Ted will be my successor at Kingsley Global Enterprises. Congratulations, Ted," I say and hold my drink in the air. "He's a natural salesman who people are attracted to. He's proven himself outside the company, and he has a loyal, trusting wife, and that counts for a lot in my book—loyalty. Cheers!" I sit back down and wait for the fireworks to begin.

It doesn't take long.

John jumps to his feet, throwing his napkin on the table. His face is red with fury. "Dad, really? You can't be serious. You know Ted is compromised. The affair, the gambling debts. How can you possibly trust him?"

I watch Paige's face pale. It appears she didn't know about some of that. My kindhearted princess among the Kingsleys, always wanting to see the best in people. I pat her hand on the table.

"You know, John, Ted can be a monster like me, sometimes, but he has charm to smooth it over, and he has sweet Paige by his side. You on the other hand . . . ," I say. The look in John's eyes turns even darker. He's furious.

I watch Rachel take his hand, squeeze it twice. I do realize she has been a loyal wife to my oldest son. I just don't like her. Sorry, Rachel.

"You're making a huge mistake, Dad. Bigger than you could ever know. I have been by your side for years. I've been your troubleshooter, doing all the dirty work. You and the company have benefited enormously from my loyalty. Meanwhile, Ted has been playing the field, playing cards, and basically being an embarrassment. You're an embarrassment to this family, Ted."

"Don't speak like that in front of Paige," Ted says, glaring at his brother across the table. "That's all in the past. No need to dig any of that up. Besides, Sibley told me you're the one who's compromised, Johnny. Someone hacked your secret dossiers?"

Wow, I can't believe Sibley gave Ted that information. Nice of her—to help Ted, that is, not the part where she's been blackmailing John. That's definitely not nice.

I still cannot believe John created that file. So ill advised. "John, is that true? Have you been compromised? Are you paying blackmail?"

"No," he says, too quickly. I know he's lying. I've seen the money trail. Interesting, all the deceptions. I take a sip of wine from the crystal glass. I'm enjoying the show, sort of. John was such an idiot to make a file of our exits, and Sibley and whoever she found to help her were brilliant for exploiting his mistake. I shake my head and stare at John. I do not want my reputation, my legacy, tarnished by information about my unscrupulous business dealings—dealings that never should have been written down for posterity by my oldest son.

John says, "Look, Dad. First you had me thinking you'd pick Sibley."

"Your sister and my brother are in cahoots. I'd never trust her with anything," I say. "It was just a test. I wanted to have Sibley confess to what she was up to, and I wanted to see how you boys would react if you thought Sibley was a legitimate competitor."

"So this—picking Ted—is a test, too!" John yells. The cut on his lip is bleeding again. "Why are you testing me after everything I've done for you? I can't take more tests! I am the heir to the Kingsley empire. I have been, I am, and I will be. Anything else is simply a ridiculous game, and you know it, Dad." John storms out of the room. Rachel stays seated, staring at me.

"Well, temper is not attractive in a leader," I say.

Serena says, "Darling, while you're in decision-making mode, you are making plans for our unborn child, aren't you? Your final heir deserves something formalized. Don't you agree?"

Ted exhales. "Serena, you don't need to worry about that. I told Dad I would take care of you and the baby when I'm CEO of Kingsley, and I will."

"Yes, Ted has been quite adamant about that," I say.

"OK, that's enough," Rachel says, standing up. "I demand to speak to you in private, Richard. Now."

As if. I will not be bossed around on my own vessel by anyone, let alone John's dour wife.

"Sit down, please. Anything you have to say to me can be said in front of all the family," I say. Next to me, Paige looks angry, hands clenched in fists at her side. She has a good reason to be furious.

I think she just realized what a bastard her husband is.

39

PAIGE

At least I know the whole truth. The truth is here, right in front of me at the table, out in the open. I can't be in denial—not anymore. I feel Ted watching me. I look to my right. I meet his eyes. He leans in close.

"Paige, this is it, our next chapter," he whispers. "I cannot thank you enough for helping me secure the job from Richard. I am going to run Kingsley. I'll be the perfect husband. We are going to be so happy—you'll see. We'll take a trip together, travel to all our Kingsley offices abroad. It will be like a second honeymoon."

"You told me we'd run the company together," I say. "Remember, CEO and president?"

"Well, sweetie, I mean, I think with all the stress and secrets that revolve around the company, it's best to keep you away from all of it. You and the girls stay pure, so to speak, not tarnished by any of this company mess. You can stay focused on your charity work," Ted says. "It's best to just keep you out of it. It's for you."

"I don't believe anything you say, and I never will again," I whisper back, my heart crumbling. He lied to me, again. He never intended for us to be a team and run the company.

Across the table, Rachel stands and begins pacing back and forth the length of the dining table. "You really want me to do this? In front of everyone?" she says, looking at Richard. "Are you sure? Because once everyone knows, they'll know. And as far as I can tell, you can't trust a single one of them."

"So much drama, Rachel. We aren't in a courtroom; we're trying to enjoy our meals," Richard says. He is, I notice, the only person eating. He sticks a huge prawn in his mouth, severing the tail off with his teeth before dropping it onto a silver platter. He hasn't lost his vigor for eating, that much is clear.

Richard leans close to me and says, "Paige, dear, hang in there. Eat a shrimp. It will help; I guarantee it. Besides, you should be happy. Ted seems to have won the job."

I nod and pick up one of the shrimp from the cocktail and try to eat it. Ted shouldn't win. Ted shouldn't get anything. Why did Richard pick him, anyway? What could he be thinking, when apparently everyone knew he is a cheater and a gambler. Now I know where the girls' college fund money really went.

Rachel stops pacing and stands behind her chair, like she's at a lectern in the courtroom. She stares at me a moment and moves on to Ted and Serena, then finally locks eyes with Richard.

"All of the years you have spent pitting your children against each other, making them compete for your love and attention. Guess what? It was all for nothing," Rachel says. John appears behind her, having slipped into the room while we were watching her speech, I guess.

"What are you doing?" John says. He's lost his tux jacket and bow tie. His dress shirt's top few buttons are open, sleeves rolled up to his elbows. He looks like he's itching for another fight.

"Please sit down," Rachel says.

"Everyone in this family is shit," he says and looks like he's going to punch someone, but he drops into his seat. "This better be good."

"John doesn't know the information I'm about to share. No one does. But that will change if our demands aren't met. The information I have would make a front-page story, a breaking-news headline if it were to be made public," Rachel says.

Richard sighs. "Very cloak-and-dagger of you. Can you please get to the point?"

Rachel nods and takes a breath. "Girls, can you excuse us? And please wait to serve the next course until I give the OK."

Talley and Halley stop in their tracks, salads in their hands. Serena waves them away. We are all curious about what Rachel knows. Can it be worse than what I now know about Ted?

"All of this posturing, all of this competition and mutual destruction will be for nothing if what I found becomes public, because there won't be a company anymore," Rachel says.

"What the hell are you talking about?" Ted asks.

"While doing due diligence on a wrongful death case I've been defending, I discovered Kingsley Global Enterprises' terrible past. The company, back then called Kingsley Chemicals, had its employees transport barrels of DDT and acid sludge waste from the company's Torrance facility to barges where they were dumped into the ocean near Catalina Island. As many as half a million barrels could be underwater today, just a few miles away from us. Generations of people have died due to these chemicals being in our water supply. My client's dad for one. Kingsley Chemicals' pollution is bubbling out of those barrels, three thousand feet under the sea right now, poisoning another generation."

We're all silent. I'm still processing what Rachel is saying. The family business has created a toxic dump in this ocean, close to where we are right now, next to this island.

"I don't understand. We're a multinational conglomerate focused on finance and real estate holdings. We have nothing to do with chemicals," Ted says.

"Yes, that's what all the manufacturers did when the chemical DDT, or dichlorodiphenyltrichloroethane, was banned more than fifty years ago. They dumped the chemicals, often in the ocean, changed their names, changed their focus. But eventually, the truth always comes out. The company—*this* company—could be held liable for this cleanup if an investigation is launched. And if that's the case, it will reach levels of personal liability. You could all lose everything," she says.

Richard picks up another prawn and dips it into the bloodred cocktail sauce.

"That company was dissolved. There is no liability for my company here. That was under my grandfather's watch, back in the late 1940s and 1950s," Richard says. "Besides, all this talk of some sort of chemical dump is just a nasty rumor. You have no proof. And you're terrible for bringing it up. I want my salad."

I'm sitting here, listening to Rachel, and realize that, just like normal people, the Kingsleys could lose everything. I never imagined them being vulnerable, wealth wise, to anything or anyone. I must admit I'm in shock. I stare at Rachel with a newfound sense of awe and fear.

"You're wrong, Richard. There is proof. I found it. I found the only copy of the company's shipping logs, handwritten by your grandfather's CFO. The Kingsley Chemicals logo on top of every page. I have the proof to trace the dumping back to this company—direct proof. You're screwed if this comes out," Rachel says. She's smiling.

She's scary. I would not want to go against her in court. Beside me, Richard grumbles. And then roars.

"Let me see them!" Richard says, smacking his hand on the table. I jump like someone shot a gun.

"They are tucked away in a safe place. I'll hand them over to you when you give the company to John," she answers. "Do we have a deal? I'm sure we do."

I glance at John, who looks both stunned and proud. He starts clapping his hands, slowly at first but then with gusto. "Bravo, dear! What a performance. What a find. You amaze me, you really do. I had no idea you were this ruthless."

Richard stands and walks to Rachel's chair. "How dare you? No one forces my hand. Ever."

If Richard spoke that way to me, I'd crumble, but Rachel stands her ground.

"I'm sorry, but it had to be done. Ted is inept, Sibley is a joke. John is the rightful heir, if there is to be a company, that is," Rachel says.

Ted says, "Do you actually believe this, Dad? Can this possibly be true?"

Richard looks at me and then Ted. I can't believe all the secrets in this family. My head is spinning.

Richard smiles in grim recognition and says, "Yes, Rachel is right. I did know about this—mostly my dad and his dad whispering, leaving the room quickly. They told me it was nothing, that there was no proof this dumping of chemicals ever happened. I worked hard to make sure my version of the company was clean, distancing it from that tragic history, distancing it from what it was. That's the thing with dirty little secrets, though: they always come to light."

40

SERENA

Rachel is threatening to bankrupt the company and all of us. I can't let that happen.

"What will be left for me and the baby, darling?" I say to Richard, who ignores me. He and Rachel are locked in a standoff; both have their arms folded across their chests. The only movement in the room is the sparkle of light the silver sequins of Rachel's ridiculous dress send darting each time a wave rolls under us.

"Why don't you all sit? Let's work this out. Rachel isn't going to tell anyone what she has. This is her piggy bank, too," Ted says.

Rachel laughs. "Ted, I'm likely the only one at this table who doesn't need this company or this family for anything. I'm a partner in a successful law firm. I'm doing this for John because he is the right man for the job." She pulls out her chair and sits down. She pats John on the shoulder. "John will be CEO of Kingsley Global Enterprises, formerly known as Kingsley Chemicals. Cheers!"

I feel like I've been plunked down in an episode of a courtroom drama, and Rachel just gave the closing argument and won.

"Richard," Paige says. I note she's calm, collected. Still, if she was in the dark about Ted's waning affections, she has no one to blame but herself, in my opinion. You need to keep a close eye on your man if you want to keep him. She took her eye off the ball, focused on her girls. Big mistake.

"Yes, dear," Richard says distractedly. He doesn't seem to have the patience for sweet Paige.

"What are we going to do? We can't let her ruin everything," Paige says. "You've worked too hard. You shouldn't make a decision based on blackmail, though. Take your time. You deserve it. We all love you."

Beside her, Ted jumps up, clutching his stomach, and hurries from the room.

Richard laughs and says, "Thank you, dear. And my apologies for my second son. Ted has a lot of, well, weaknesses. I know you see that now—at least, I hope you do. But Rachel! Wow! Never saw her coming! Ha!"

Richard's maniacal laugh continues. A feeling of dread rolls through the room and lands in the pit of my stomach.

"Dad, stop making that sound," John says. "Look, let's go to the library, work things out. Rachel is more than happy to work with you on this. She won't tell anyone what she discovered. She will destroy the documents. Everything will be fine. I'm handling it."

"You're handling it," Richard says, still laughing, tears rolling down his cheeks. "Oh, what a relief. My son the self-proclaimed troubleshooter is handling it. Hallelujah, I can rest easy now. Be sure to make a record of it and save it on your computer so you can be blackmailed some more. Ha!"

I stand up and walk to his end of the table, place a calming hand on his shoulder. "Darling, maybe we should go to the stateroom, take a little break. I'm not feeling so well—morning sickness, I believe, even though it's nighttime."

"Oh, grand idea," Richard says. "A break from this folly is just what the doctor ordered. We'll see you all later for final cocktails in the library. In an hour. Enjoy your meals."

I try to slip my hand into Richard's, but all he does is laugh again as he walks away.

Richard finally gets ahold of himself when we reach our stateroom. Rachel must have really rocked his world. As we walk inside, I hear the engines come to life. It's time for the crossing, thank goodness. Another reason to smile, because I've realized now that if Richard is finished with his children as heirs, he will select me.

"Darling, I'm so sorry your children have been such a disappointment," I say, pouring us each a glass of champagne. "I assure you, that will not be the case with this one." I rub my small baby bump and grin.

"Oh, Serena, that's impossible. All children disappoint their parents. That I won't be around long enough to be disappointed doesn't mean that your tiny one won't . . . Well, he or she will disappoint you, too," Richard says. He takes the champagne from my hand and loosens his bow tie.

I take the club seat across from him and lean forward. I want to calm him down, offer him solutions. "I want you to know I am more than ready to step into the role as president or CEO. I will be a place-holder until the baby grows into the job."

I watch Richard's face as it turns from amused to laughter. Not that again.

"Richard, stop it. I'm serious," I say.

"Oh, I'm sure you are. Say, how would you like to watch some reality TV?" Richard says.

He's never watched reality TV in his life. "What are you talking about?"

"I had Captain Bill splice together some of the special footage from the last two days. I thought we could watch the highlights of the voyage together. You know, before I share it with the rest of the family," Richard says.

"Sure," I say, although a knot forms in my stomach. Something is wrong. Something in his tone is off. I wonder what footage he has. How many cameras are hidden on this boat? I think of the smashed camera in my safe. He never answered the question whether he knew if there were more. I swallow as my heart races.

Richard walks to the corner of the room and turns on the flat-screen TV. "Let me see if I can do this right. Bill had to do it for me earlier," Richard says, fumbling with the remote.

"We can watch later, when we're back home. Yes, why don't we do that?" I suggest, crossing the room to stand next to him.

"Here we go!"

The screen bursts to life, and my stomach drops. There's a close-up of me and Ted, just after we all boarded the yacht. We're in the back hallway. We're alone. We're holding hands.

A bead of sweat rolls down the back of my neck.

The video cuts to Ted and me, not long after we began the crossing. I know what happens. I cover my mouth as the camera zooms in for our kiss. A passionate, embarrassing kiss I instigated.

"Richard, I can explain," I say. Panic rises like a fire in my heart. My mouth is dry. "Please stop the video."

"But there's so much more footage of you two. I mean, I give you both credit: Paige and I are sometimes just feet away, and you're pulling this. Did it make you happy to have a tryst right under your spouses' noses? Does he make you happy?"

"Richard, I'm so sorry. It's . . . it doesn't mean anything. I think you're misinterpreting things. Ted was helping me. I thought you were leaving me; I thought you had another woman. He comforted me," I say.

"*Comforted.* Is that what it's called these days?" Richard shakes his head. "He's the father, right? It's his baby. A Kingsley baby but not mine." He clicks off the television. "You see, dear, I was fixed after Sibley. I just didn't want to deal with this anymore. But I'll admit, even I was enthralled by the notion of another Kingsley, imagining my vasectomy failed, imagining my virility intact."

"Ted and I never slept together. It was a flirtation. Nothing more," I say. "The baby is yours. It is."

"I don't believe you, Serena. How could I believe anything you say after watching you two together? Disgusting," Richard says.

I don't answer him. I can't. I turn away, tears springing to my eyes. I think about my future, my baby's future, and I know now it will be much different from what I imagined. I hear the door of the stateroom open, and he's gone.

41

JOHN

I'm on my way to find my father in his stateroom, hoping to pry him away from Serena, and here he is, alone, in the hallway. "Dad, let's work this out."

Dad tilts his head. "Can you and Rachel please join me on the middle deck? We'll have a meeting of sorts. Just the three of us. Poor Serena won't be attending. She's feeling terrible. And Paige and Ted, well . . . they have their own issues."

"Actually, Dad, Rachel and I would like to speak with you inside, perhaps the library. It's chilly outside," I say.

"No, we'll meet outside, away from the prying eyes and ears of the crew," Richard says. "Be there in ten minutes. And, son?"

"Yes, sir?" I swallow, knowing his anger is just below the surface, like mine.

"You need to control your wife. She is a clear and present threat. She must be stopped. How can I ever trust her to keep that big of a secret? I refuse to let her burn my legacy to the ground. Even if she gives me what she says is the only copy of the shipping log? All of this, all we have built, can be ruined by your wife—like that." Richard snaps his fingers and I jump.

"I understand, sir. I didn't know what she found. I had nothing to do with it," I say, my voice shaking. Rachel can't ruin our company. She won't. My anger and resolve ignite. "I will fix this."

"See that you do," Richard says.

I turn and hurry away, down the hall and down the steps to our stateroom level. I burst through our cabin door. "Rachel, we need to go to the middle deck. Dad's called a meeting."

"Why outside? It's freezing," she says.

"So the crew can't listen in," I say. "Change into warm clothes. Hurry."

Rachel hurries into the dressing area and reemerges without the sequined dress. She's pulled on a navy sweater and jeans.

"You're proud of me, right?" she asks. "I mean, I got the company for you."

I swallow. Yes, of course it's great, because once I run the company, I'll be able to pay off the hackers. But then, what she's found could also ruin us all. And Dad? He's furious. That's not good. "I am so proud. But Dad is beside himself."

"Too bad," she says. "It's hard when someone shakes your family tree and toxic chemicals spill out. But like I said, his family secrets—*our* family secrets—are safe with me."

I take a deep breath. This is one of those times when it doesn't pay to have a wife smarter than you, a wife your father despises, more so now. My heart races. I need to fix this. I promised Dad I'd fix it. God, how did everything get so complicated? I realize my hands are in fists and release them at my sides.

"Come on, it's time to go," I tell her and lead the way out the door, dread and panic washing over me every step.

42

RICHARD

The wind whips around the deck like it's propelled by a large invisible fan. The fog sends its chilly tendrils to your spine. I pull my *Splendid Seas*–branded windbreaker tighter, glad I added a layer to my tux.

Rachel appears at the top of the stairs, dressed in jeans and a sweater, as if her job impressing me—us—is over. It is. John is behind her. The gang is all here. Rachel shivers, and I point to a nearby closet.

"Grab one of these windbreakers. It will do the job," I tell her. She wordlessly does as I say. Out of the corner of my eye, I see Serena has joined us on deck. Splendid.

"Now that we've all had a little time to calm down from the evening's adventures, I thought it was important to clear the air," I begin, addressing John and Rachel. "You should know I'd never pick Ted to be the CEO of Kingsley Global Enterprises, even though I announced it at dinner to get a reaction. And reactions I got, that's for sure. As you know, Ted is a liar and a cheat and has no credibility with me. Sibley, well, my mention of her was just to stir the pot. As for you, John . . . I was leaning your way until now."

"Oh my God, you were picking me! I knew it," John says. His eyes are beady, manic. "Don't worry, Rachel won't say anything. Dad, really. I can handle this."

"Rachel, I'm sure you thought you could get away with this type of extortion, but you can't. Shame on you. I am so disappointed that my own daughter-in-law would betray me in this, the worst of ways. I mean, how will I ever be able to trust you with this hanging over my head? You will ruin this family," I say. I am using my fiercest boss voice to make myself heard above the wind. I want her to be afraid of me like my children are—like she *should* be.

She backs away and stands at the railing. "Are you serious? You're threatening me when I'm the one who has the proof to ruin you? I have the only document. Me. I've been nothing but discreet. I've told no one, not even John, until I could tell you face-to-face."

"I'm afraid I don't believe you," I say. "And that isn't good. John, what are you going to do about this? Your wife is out of control."

Beside me, John puffs out his chest like he's a superhero or something. He turns to me and says, "I hear you loud and clear, Dad. This is my final test, and this time I'm going to pass." He turns to gaze apologetically at his wife. "I'm sorry, Rachel. I don't believe you, either. How can we ever know who else you've told about this?" In a moment, he's crossed the deck and lunged at his wife.

In one quick move, he flips her over the railing and into the cold, dark sea below. All that remains of Rachel is a terrifying, guttural scream.

43

RICHARD

What just happened? My brain cannot compute what my eyes saw. It seems like time has slowed to a crawl, that the world has stopped. My God. We're in the middle of one of the biggest shipping channels in the world, at night, in the fog. John just pushed Rachel overboard, to most certain death. I turn around and realize we are not alone on the deck. In addition to Serena, Ted has also followed us here. They saw what happened.

Serena screams as she rushes to the railing. "Rachel, my God. It's so far down there. She can't swim."

I join the others at the railing, looking down. She can't swim, but it wouldn't matter. She likely died from the fall. In the thick fog, you can't see the ocean. It looks as if Rachel disappeared into a dark cloud. The woman was on my last nerve, but she didn't deserve this. And John didn't mean to do this. It was impulsive, a mistake. He loved her; I know he did. My God.

"Come away from the railing, son," I say to John. He's frozen, likely in shock.

I look over and see Ted comforting Serena, and I feel nothing but disgust.

"It was an accident, right?" I ask John quietly. "What were you thinking?"

"You told me to handle it. I heard you, loud and clear," John says, eyes large and glassy, as they would be when you murder your wife in cold blood. "I passed the test, right? Can I be CEO now?"

What? Did he just ask me that? I'm shaking with rage. I explode.

"Holy shit, son, I didn't mean kill your wife. I never said that. Christ almighty. A temper like that will get you put in jail, not at the head of a company. Why did you go rogue instead of waiting for my orders? I just wanted you to control her—the situation she put us in was unacceptable." I let out a breath and look around.

John puts his face in his hands and says, "Rachel, what have I done? Oh my God. I love you, Rachel. I need you. You're my partner. My best friend. Oh my God. I'm going to jail for murder."

He would—and did—do anything for me, poor misguided man. It's a pity, really. I pat John on the shoulder. "Look. Jail, that's not going to happen, son. Calm down. Rachel fell overboard. It was a tragic accident," I say. He needs counseling—help, not prison. What an idiot. I look around to be sure Serena and Ted heard our story: Rachel fell overboard.

Serena and Ted have separated, made space between them, I notice.

Serena says, "I'm going to go inform Captain Bill that one of our guests has fallen overboard."

Ted says, "Babe, let Richard handle it. It's his mess to clean up. His and John's."

Paige arrives in time to hear what her husband just said to Serena. I watch her face as the realization hits. Her husband just called my wife—his stepmother—*babe*. I put my arm around her shaking shoulders.

"Yes, my dear, it's true. Ted is worse than me, I'm afraid," I say, a feeble attempt to soften the blow of what she has overheard. Well, I suppose that settles it. I have only one choice. I've decided who will be my heir, my successor. The only one of this family I still trust. I extend my hand to Paige. She looks confused but takes my hand in hers. "Congratulations, Paige."

"For what? I don't understand," Paige says, eyes wide.

"You will be president of Kingsley Global Enterprises," I say. "I'll be around as CEO long enough to make sure you get the support and respect you deserve from the board, so don't worry. As for my marriage . . . time for a change, wouldn't you say?"

Serena stares at me, her mouth open. Beside me, Paige is silent and shaking. It's freezing out here, and terrifying for many reasons. Paige does not need to know about what happened to Rachel. Not now, at least.

"Paige, listen, it's not what it seems," Ted says, rushing over to us. "I was just comforting Serena. It's nothing. You and me, we're a team, Paige. Sweetie. We'll run Kingsley together, remember?"

"Son, Paige has impressed the entire community's business leaders with her handling of the food bank's capital campaign, and she did that without your help. She is loyal, smart, and trustworthy. Much more than I can say about you. Let's get inside," I say to Paige, ignoring Ted. "I'll inform the captain there has been a terrible accident. Somebody make sure John doesn't fling himself over, too. Get the man inside, Ted, Serena. Do that for me. Now."

The traitors do as I instruct and hurry to John's side.

"Paige, come with me," I say, taking her by the arm.

Paige nods. Poor girl is in shock. In addition to Rachel's rather violent demise—the cause of which, she fortunately didn't witness—the revelation of Ted's latest betrayal isn't easy to deal with, let me tell you, and I've had a few hours to process things. I suspected Serena wasn't being true, but I had no proof. Not until Captain Bill arranged for the closed-circuit TV. I'll admit, that was the real impetus for the trip. Sure, I wanted one last family trip, but I also wanted to spy on my family.

Unfortunately, it's dangerous and disappointing to look too closely at the things and people you love—or, I should say, *loved*.

44

JOHN

I hold on to the railing and stare down at the cold, dark nothing where Rachel fell.

"Rachel! I'm coming!" What have I done? Oh my God. Rachel, my partner, my all. I climb the railing, and I'm about to step over, to follow Rachel, to find Rachel.

"John, no!" Ted yells and grabs me around the waist, pulling me back onto the yacht as we fall together onto the deck.

"Let go of me!" I scream, fighting him with whatever strength I have left. Ted keeps me wrapped in a tight hold. I cannot overpower him. I give up. My everything is gone. A sob racks my body, and I shake all over.

"Let's get you inside, John," Serena says. She extends her hand, and I take it. Ted pulls me to my feet, his firm grip under my arm. "We aren't going to let go of you. Come on. This was an accident, do you hear me?"

"It wasn't your fault, John," Ted says as we make it inside the yacht.

I can't stop crying. I can't speak. Ted and Serena take me to the yacht's grand living room and settle me on the couch. Serena brings me a drink.

"Chug this," she says.

I do as she says; the bitter, potent taste of tequila explodes in my mouth. I lean back on the couch, shaking uncontrollably.

"You should stay with him, Ted," Serena says. "I'll let the captain know where you both are. I have to go."

"There's nowhere to go. We're on a yacht in the middle of the channel," Ted says. I feel his hand on my shoulder. "Brother, you need to pull yourself together. Want another shot?"

I nod and close my eyes, but when I do, all I see is Rachel falling into the dark, foggy night. I open my eyes.

Oh my God. I've killed the love of my life.

Ted hands me a glass and I chug it. "Thanks," I manage.

He sits down beside me. "Tell yourself you did what you had to do. That's the only way through this."

"For Dad," I say. "I did this for Dad." I hear Richard's voice in my head: *Holy shit, son, I didn't mean kill your wife.* "I was just so angry, and Dad told me to handle things, to get back in control, and I panicked, and I just couldn't see another solution. I didn't think. I just acted. I'm a murderer."

"You're not. Dad got in your head and lit the fuse of the Kingsley anger we all know so well," Ted says. "We all know what happens when that rage comes. It blocks out everything, all reason goes away. That's why the story is she fell overboard. We all will stick to the story. OK? You did what you had to do, and now we'll all do what we have to do."

"Lie for me," I say.

"Protect you, for the good of the family," Ted says. "You'd do the same."

No, I don't think I would.

"Thanks, Teddy. For saving me earlier." I look at Ted, and for once, I see a brother instead of a rival. I wonder how long that will last.

Dad appears. "Ted, give us the room. In fact, as soon as we dock, you get off. Stay at a hotel tonight. Do you understand?"

"Yes, OK, sure," Ted says and hurries out of the room.

Dad stares at me. A look of dark concern, perhaps?

"I'm fine," I say. "I mean, I'll be fine. Don't worry."

"Good. Here is what is going to happen. Our communication system is down, knocked out by the storm, so we cannot summon the Coast Guard until we get to the marina. But once we reach the dock, you and the captain will alert the Coast Guard and do whatever they instruct. You will tell them how she fell, that it was an accident," Richard says.

"Yes. OK. Got it," I say.

"I need you to go to your room and get the document Rachel was referring to. I'm assuming it is in your safe. Get it. Destroy it. Do you understand?" Richard says.

And just like that, I'm back under his command. As always. Forever. "I understand."

"Get going, son. Now. And pack up your things and Rachel's," Richard says. "She won't be needing them, but, um, just take her possessions home with you."

I stand while fighting the urge to vomit as Dad turns and leaves. I make my way slowly through the yacht, heading to my cabin to do exactly what my dad instructed. But this time is different.

I almost can't bear to step inside our cabin, knowing she should be next to me, knowing she never will be again, and I have no one to blame but myself.

45

PAIGE

I sit in Richard's library, wrapped in a light-blue cashmere blanket. Richard and I are the only ones in the room. The search for Rachel's body will be handled by the Coast Guard, Richard and Captain Bill inform me, and as soon as we reach the dock, we will alert them. It seems our yacht's entire communication system was destroyed by the storm, a fact Richard kept from all of us.

I am so cold; chills run up and down my body. I know I'm in shock. Rachel somehow fell overboard and likely died. And, at about the same moment, I discovered that my husband and his stepmother have been having some sort of relationship, right under our noses. Ted called Serena *babe*. I'm devastated.

"How did Rachel fall overboard?" I ask. "The railings are high enough, right?"

"I'm not sure anyone saw it, quite frankly. She was there one moment, and the next, she was gone. We heard her screaming. She must have slipped or leaned over the railing too far," Richard says. "It's a tragedy, for sure. But accidents do happen."

"I can't imagine it," I say, another chill rolling down my spine. "And we just left her out there."

"I'm sure she will be found," Richard says. "Best to put the horror of it all out of your mind."

"I'm so glad I didn't see it," I say. I take a deep breath, turning to the other shocking revelation I'm having trouble processing. "I cannot believe Ted and Serena?"

"Dear, I know this has been a terrible evening, to put it mildly," Richard says. "But let's focus on the future. You will make a fine president, and if things go the way I hope, the eventual CEO. I just wish you were flesh-and-blood family, but we have Ted around for that."

"What? No, Richard, Ted has been with Serena. I can't stay with him," I say.

"I'm afraid that's going to have to be a condition of your appointment. You need to keep him around. He's lost, Paige. He needs you," Richard says. "I blame myself. I've been a terrible role model, an absentee father. Ted loves you, and he loves those girls of yours. He's not a perfect man—but really, none of us are. You two have a special connection. He just needs to appreciate it, nourish it. I know he can be better, do better. He's my son, after all."

I'm speechless. I have seen through all the illusions I'd cloaked our lives in. The girls and I will be fine. I know that. I will lead Kingsley. I knew about Ted's other affair and carried on. I won't do it again.

"How long did you know about Ted and Serena?" I ask when I can finally bear it.

"Not long. I was suspicious, but I had no proof until I reviewed the footage tonight. For the record, I don't think they slept together," he says. "I think Serena was bored with me flying around the world, trying to find a cure for my heart. She thought I was leaving her, so she turned her attention to Ted, and others. I can show you the video, but it's not important now. Ted will apologize to you, and you will accept that. It's the only way to keep the Kingsley blood involved in the company. Make him sleep in the pool house—for years or forever, if you'd like—but it is my one stipulation. He will be at the company, reporting to you."

"I don't know if I can do that," I say.

"You've been in denial about his actions for years, dear. Now you see him clearly, but I know you still love him. And he needs you. I need you to forgive him, eventually, for the bigger plan," Richard says.

He's right, of course. I do still love Ted, but do I love him enough to ever forgive him? Forgiving Ted seems impossible right now, but for the chance to run the company, have an exciting future of my own making, I'll need to make it work. We will be together for appearance's sake only. I do like Richard's idea of making Ted sleep in the pool house. I take a deep breath.

"OK, I'll do it. I'll stay married to Ted but only for show. He will move into the pool house," I say. "And he'll agree to counseling. That's my condition."

"Agreed! That's the spirit! Tonight, he will stay at a hotel, per my instructions. Tomorrow he can move into the pool house while you and I meet and go over the details for your appointment and the press announcement. We're almost back to the dock, dear. I'll have one of my drivers take you home to the girls. Say, would you like me to talk with them?" he asks.

"No, it's OK. I can handle it. I can't wait to tell them I'm going to be president of Kingsley. They won't believe it. They would love to see you, whenever you'd like. Thank you again, really, for everything," I say.

"Of course, dear," he says. "I'm lucky to have you and those girls. You did a good job raising them, and I'm certain it was mostly alone. As for my parenting track record, John's a ball of anger; Ted's a lying, gambling cheater; Sibley's a burglar. I don't think I'm going to win any Father of the Year awards. Maybe in whatever time I have left, I'll work on being a better grandpa. I don't think I can do too much damage to your girls."

Despite myself, and everything that's happened, I start to laugh. And as I do, I realize I'm going to be OK. That I'm actually better off than I was before this trip. I'd turned a blind eye to reality. Ted and I looked so perfect from the outside, but our relationship was not what it seemed. Now it's all out in the open. Richard has empowered me in ways I could never have imagined. For once, I am in the power position. And it feels good.

"What are your plans?" I ask him.

"Well, I'll give Serena a day to move out of my house, what I'd recommend you do for Ted. You and I will focus on making the succession announcement as big as it can be. I think the team will really enjoy having you as their boss. It will be quite a change from yours truly."

"I promise to make you proud, Richard. You know, I've almost earned my MBA," I say. "I graduate next month." It feels good to finally share my secret with someone.

"That's fantastic. More proof you're the right pick. Ted will be vice president of sales. Sound OK? If he does one thing out of line, he's gone. Agreed?"

"Agreed," I say. "And John?"

"You should keep him around as CFO. He knows where all the bodies are buried, so to speak," Richard says. "And not just his wife's."

A chill sweeps over me again. "What really happened to Rachel?"

Richard tilts his head. "I'm not sure you need the details, dear."

"You just made me president of your company. I need to know," I say, sounding braver than I feel.

"She fell overboard. That's all there is to it," Richard says. "Let's just say we all need to rally around supporting John."

I look at his face. "John loved Rachel. I know he did."

"Yes, he did. And he loves this company and will do anything to protect it," Richard says. "He needs to keep his place at the company. That will keep him sane. As the president, you can tell him what to do. And he'll do it. He's loyal like that."

"He's going to need help," I say. I simply cannot imagine watching your spouse fall to her death, no matter how it happened. All my doomsday worries about this trip came true. I wasn't crazy to worry about the crossing, to read about all the deaths that have happened here. Another chill ripples down my spine at the thought of Rachel in that cold, dark, deep ocean channel.

There's a knock on the door, and I jump. I hope it's not Ted. I cannot see his face right now. Richard told me Ted and Serena will leave the ship as soon as we dock, but I wouldn't put anything past Ted. Not ever again.

"Come in!" Richard yells.

It's Talley. I chastise myself for worrying that she was flirting with Ted. So ridiculous. Ted was already taken. By his own stepmother. It's all so sordid it makes my stomach turn. And makes my resolve firm. We're over. We'll stay married per Richard's request, but he's fooled me one too many times.

"We're docking, sir," Talley says. I notice she's dressed in a light-green sundress, not the usual blue-and-white *Splendid Seas* uniform.

"Fabulous. Let's allow all the others to go ashore, and we can finally have that dinner together?"

"I'd like that," she says. "I'll be back."

I shake my head and grin. "That was fast."

"I don't have much time, dear. And I don't want to be alone in my final days," Richard says. "Although, I guarantee there will not be a next wife. My marrying days are over."

I nod my head as I stand up to leave. "Thank you, I think, for an eye-opening trip. And for trusting me to lead the company with you. I'll see you tomorrow, for lunch at the office." I kiss him on the cheek. "Poor Rachel. Such a tragedy."

"I know. A tragic accident," Richard says.

I don't say anything more. Of all the lies and secrets this family keeps, I suppose how exactly Rachel fell to her death is just another mark on the ledger. Maybe it's all the secrets and lies that hold them together. In my mind, family members should be bonded by love and shared memories. Not this one, that's for sure.

"Richard, whatever document Rachel had, do you have it now?" I ask. "The proof. The trackable history?"

"By now, it has been destroyed. It's over. It died with her. You, dear, you'll start with a fresh slate. No skeletons in the company closet anymore," he says. "And don't worry. I predict I'll be around to watch over you for quite some time."

"I hope so." We both know most of what he just said can't be true. I take a deep breath and open the door. The marina is glowing with lights from other boats, the fog has dissipated, and stars twinkle in the sky.

There are no other guests left on board. John departed with the captain to meet with the Coast Guard. Serena and Ted slipped away as soon as we docked, the cowards. I listened in as Richard called Sibley, making sure she made it back to the mainland safely and telling her about the tragic accident aboard. And I heard him tell her to stop blackmailing John, or she'd have to deal with him directly.

"John's too fragile to be messed with anymore, do you understand? He just lost his wife," Richard said in that tone that scares people. I can only assume she understood. Whatever she has planned next for revenge—notes or blackmail or hostile takeovers—I'll be the one who will have to stop her. I'm in charge now. "And Sibley," Richard added. "I assume some of that jewelry was for your no-good mother?"

He winks at me. I wish I could hear what Sibley was saying, how she was justifying herself.

"Yes, that's what I figured, and that's why I let you have it. I didn't appreciate the clothes slashing, though. Quite childish," Richard said. "I know you'll blame it on that boyfriend."

This family. What a mess.

"Good. I'm glad you dumped him. Behave, Sibs, and I'll keep you in the will. Oh, and I'm naming Paige as the new president of Kingsley. Good night," Richard said, hanging up—but not before I heard Sibley scream, "What? No!"

Richard laughed. "She told me to tell you congratulations," he said with a wink.

It's hard to wrap your mind around this weird family with too much money and too many secrets, but I know I'm lucky to still be in Richard's favor. I take a moment to breathe in the sea air and remind myself to be thankful. I'm stepping off the finest yacht in the harbor. A uniformed driver holds a sign with my name on it and waits for me in the parking lot, luggage already loaded in the limo's trunk. It's another perfect Southern California night. Soon, I will be announced as the leader of a huge multinational company. I have it all.

At least, you could believe that if you didn't look beneath the surface.

SIX MONTHS LATER

OC SCOOP

Tipsters tell us *Splendid Seas* has been SOLD! The mega-yacht, owned by Newport Beach's own Richard Kingsley, also was the scene of a tragedy, you'll recall, when Rachel Dilmer Kingsley, 45, fell overboard and drowned. We hear the Kingsley family just couldn't bear to climb aboard after such a horrible death took place. The buyer, a wealthy German financier, doesn't seem to mind that the yacht has a dark past, and will relocate the vessel to Montenegro, sources say. The private transaction for the mega-yacht was rumored to be $20 million.

Speaking of Kingsleys, you'll note that for the first time, the company named a woman president. Daughter-in-law Paige Kingsley of Laguna Beach got the nod, much to the shock, we hear, of the two sons, John and Ted. Richard Kingsley remains, at 79, the CEO. We've had a tip that King Richard's health is on the fritz, but other sources say he's happy and squiring a new young thing around town. Sounds like Richard is doing just fine after his recent divorce. Keeping up with the Kingsleys is what we do. Send us your tips.

46

JOHN

I sit in my chair, in my office, and stare out the window. Today is the six-month anniversary of my wife's accident. I must think of it in those terms to make it through each day. My faith in God and talks with my mom have helped. If I stay focused on work, I'm fine. It's the evenings and the nights that haunt me.

It's still hard for me to walk down the hall and see Paige sitting in Uncle Walter's huge office—the biggest office, except for Dad's. It should be mine. She looks small in there; the furniture scale is all off. I heard rumors she was going to do some redecorating. I guess she can do whatever she'd like. Seems she's the boss, for now. Dad has backed her, and the board seems to like her. But the shine will wear off. It always does.

I pick up the photo of me and Rachel from earlier days, happier days. Oh, Rachel. I miss you. I blink and force the tears away. Some days, it still seems as if the yacht weekend was a bad dream. Most days, though, I know it was a living nightmare.

I put the photo away in a drawer and remind myself to focus on work. Paige said she wants to work with me and will keep me in my position as CFO because Dad told her I know "where all the bodies are buried." She said it with a wink. She thinks it's a euphemism, God save my soul. And I've made it clear to Sibley and Uncle Walter that I won't be paying another dime, not anymore. If they try to go public, they know what I'll do to them. Sibley is synonymous with that horrible trip. For some reason, she's backed off. I don't know if it's forever, but for now it's good.

I'm profoundly changed. Not simply because I murdered my wife because I was convinced that's what my dad wanted and I'd do anything for him. But also because I lost everything. I lost the last shreds of my father's trust, and I lost Rachel, the only real family I had. The Coast Guard eventually found her body, or what was left of it. A shudder rolls down my spine at the memory. I take a moment to pray for forgiveness once again.

I've found Jesus—or I guess He found me. When you're at your lowest, that's when He appears, like a miracle. I've been saved by the Church of the Sea, and I have found my home.

Ted knocks and walks through the door. "Hey, can I have a minute?"

"Sure," I say as he takes the seat across the desk. He's vice president of sales again, reporting up to his wife. The situation has to be awkward for a guy like him, but it's what Dad wants, and Dad always gets what he wants. Every day, Ted brings Paige a different flower arrangement or gift. He tells me he's going to make Paige love him again, no matter how long it takes. For now, though, he's still sleeping in the pool house, and his only company is his dog, Peanut.

Ted's office is next door—a little smaller than mine, which befits the younger son. But I'm trying to let go of those rivalries. We are, for once in our sibling lives, a team, the plan Ted had suggested all along. Despite the fact he was sleeping with our father's wife. Best not to think about that.

"So I've got some great news," Ted says with a smile. "The land deal is a go."

"I can't believe it. It's the biggest deal in the company's history. Congratulations," I say. "Did you tell Dad? Paige?"

"Dad's thrilled, and Paige said she was. It's hard to tell, really, what she's thinking. She's really working the whole corporate-executive thing, complete with poker faces, fancy suits, the works," Ted says. "It's like she's a whole new person."

A person moving on from Ted, I presume. I stand up from my desk and walk to my brother's side and we shake hands. "Congratulations on the deal. That's the best news I've had in months. Maybe this will be enough to get you back in his good graces."

We lock eyes. "Nah, probably not," we say in unison.

Ted's face has turned pale. I can tell he's reliving that weekend. "I was such a jerk to Paige. For too long. And Serena. That was meaningless. Just stupid. I don't know how I'll ever get Paige to forgive me, but I'm going to keep trying. I've changed since that trip. I have."

"I know. Have a seat. Talk to me. Nothing you've done compares to what I did." We have each other's backs now. No one else will ever know the true story. As far as the world is concerned, Rachel slipped and fell overboard in the foggy night crossing. A tragedy.

Another Kingsley cover-up.

"I know. We are both horrible," Ted says.

"We learned from the best," I say, pointing at Dad's portrait on the wall across from my desk.

"I guess we did," Ted says.

"Speak of the devil," I say as Dad strolls into my office without a knock. His typical entrance. He's followed by a new assistant, Gina. Young and gorgeous, of course.

"Boys, Paige is calling a meeting in twenty minutes to review the deal Ted landed," Dad says. "She has a few concerns she's expressed to me. We'll see if she'll ultimately get behind it."

"Wait. She has to. This deal is huge," Ted says, snapping out of his sorrow.

Dad grins. "Son, she's the president. She'll make the call. See you in the conference room. Gina, let's go." And just like that, we're both deflated. But not defeated. No, never that. Not at the office.

"Take a deep breath, Ted," I say. "I'll help her see what a great deal it is."

"Thanks, John. I need this to go through," he says. "I need to have a win."

"I know," I say. "I'll help."

We've been doing a lot of that lately—helping each other. We took care of Ted's gambling debt quietly, without involving Paige or Dad, just shifting some accounts. Ted has promised he's quit; he's in some program for gambling addicts, and it's working. As for me, I called Uncle Walter and asked for a truce. I told him I'd like to see him sometime if he's ever in Southern California. And I apologized for running him out of town all those years ago. I'm not sure I made things up to him, but it ended the blackmail. Hopefully, for good.

Dad decided, with Paige's urging, that half of Sibley's monthly payments will be used to take care of Serena's family for life. It is more than enough to put Serena's sister's kids through college, take care of her parents, and more. The money Dad wasted on Sibley will finally be put to good use. Serena's parents have a nice new home on the coast, courtesy of the Kingsleys. Sibley still receives more than enough, especially after the jewelry heist she pulled off. She's doing just fine. Serena, too, although of course Dad divorced her and invoked his ironclad prenup. He even blocked her baby-to-be, who will arrive any day, from inheriting any of his estate. Guess that shouldn't be a surprise, given the circumstances. It worries me to think that baby could be Ted's, despite his denial of anything more than flirtation and a couple of kisses. Paige is suspicious, too, and told Ted she will demand a paternity test as part of her healing process. Time will tell, I suppose. Serena's set for life no matter what.

"Want to come over for dinner tonight in the pool house?" Ted says, heading for the door. "It'll be me and Peanut. She's my only date these days."

"Thanks, but I have a thing at church tonight," I say. "We should head down to the conference room. Talk to Paige and try to get this deal back on track."

"OK, let's go," Ted says and leads the way.

I'd like to think Dad is happy with how the two of us settled things, if they are in fact settled, which always remains to be seen, of course. We are Kingsleys, after all. Until the reign of Queen Paige comes to an end, I'll be the loyal foot soldier Dad pays me to be. I always do what he says, except in rare instances.

Dad seems to be enjoying himself these days. His sons back at the company, his daughter-in-law running the show under his guidance, him stepping aside when the time is right. Just the perfect happy family, running the perfect conglomerate—at least, that's the story. I glance at the copy of the newspaper carrying the profile piece on Paige's appointment as president. Dad and Paige sitting side by side on a couch in his office, Ted and me flanking them like noble servants.

Dad loves the photo. He felt good that day. In fact, if I didn't know he was dying, I would think he's just the same old grumpy, domineering guy he's always been. In the photo, he's smiling, happy, in control. And, as always, one step ahead.

I shake my head as I walk into the conference room and force a neutral expression. The truth is, despite my newfound religion, I can't help but imagine Paige messing something up, by accident or with some help. Dad needing me to step up. So I'm biding my time.

Amen to that.

47

SERENA

I did love Richard—I did. Until he stopped paying as much attention to me. I'll admit, I am a fan of the spotlight. I didn't know Richard was traveling the globe to find a doctor to save his life. I thought he'd found his next wife and was just waiting for the right moment to cast me aside. So I turned my attention to Ted. It was wrong, and he tried to tell me no. But I'm very persuasive when I want to be. Ted and I were nothing. Sure, I flirted with him on the ship, but he was focused on winning the company. I was just playing around.

Ted lost a lot when he let me kiss him on the yacht. Of course, I lost a lot, too, including Richard. I was a bit concerned about keeping what I'd worked for in the Kingsley family. But it all turned out so well. Despite the prenup, I still walked away from the marriage with more money than I know how to spend. The Kingsleys were also surprisingly generous with my family, and my parents have moved into their own house. And now, good riddance. It's time to be finished with the Kingsleys.

They want me to keep quiet, and for the money, I did. I also agreed to have a paternity test done on the baby when she is born. I already know who the father is.

Thankfully, this child will not be a Kingsley. She will be a Marino.

I've found a real man, Roman Marino, and I will be leaving on the last flight from LAX to Milan tonight. Tomorrow, I will meet his family. And this weekend, I will become his bride.

Do I feel guilty about Ted? Did Ted feel bad for Paige and his children?

No, not at all.

I hope Paige doesn't take him back. I hope she has found her spine by now, poor dear. I hope she's a badass woman boss. I try to imagine it, and I suppose I can. I wonder if she'll end up getting so powerful she could fire Ted and John. The thought makes me happy.

"Hey, beautiful, *mi amore*," Roman says, joining me in the kitchen. "I cannot wait to leave this place and start our life in Italy."

I feel his strong arms around me and relax. My Kingsley-free life is just about to begin.

48

PAIGE

Ted's betrayal is not so painful. Not anymore. Even now, just before I go to sleep, when I glance over at what was his side of the bed, I realize I'm doing fine. Therapy helps. And my friends. Turns out I have more than most people, and it's likely because I lost the connection with my husband along the way. That much was obvious to everybody, and now it is to me, too. Ted wants to work on getting back to us. He has apologized repeatedly, explained that Serena came on to him and that he was weak, that they never slept together, that the baby couldn't be his, that his gambling days are over, he's in treatment, that he is who I deserve now. Time and the paternity test will tell.

Frankly, I've been focusing on myself. I love my job. Richard and the Kingsley executive team have been so welcoming, helping me learn the ropes. Even Ted and John are seemingly respectful of my position and defer to me on all decisions. I've revitalized our charitable giving, and we're already making positive things happen in the community. I pinch myself every day. It wasn't hard to get back into the nine-to-five routine, and the twins seem quite proud of their professional mom.

Next up is to decide who to invite to the corporate party this year. Typically, the entire family is invited. I'm not so sure that's a good idea, given all that's happened, even though Richard usually keeps everyone in line. We'll see. John is pushing for the status quo. Ted says he'll support whatever decision I make if Sibley isn't included. But when I challenged his statement, he backed down.

"Your call," he said.

And he's right.

Richard made having dinners with me and the girls a priority, and they've bonded with their grandfather. He's a big teddy bear as far as his granddaughters are concerned, something I wouldn't have said or believed before the weekend on the yacht.

The girls are thriving and loving college life. Over their holiday break, they took on temporary internships at the company, which was so wonderful for me. They both expressed interest in coming back for summer internships at Kingsley. Like mother, like daughters, I suppose.

They're accustomed to Ted's pool-house residence, although they do feel a bit sorry for him out there. I tell them not to worry. He's fine. Besides, Peanut has chosen to live with Ted, the little traitor, so he's not alone.

I don't know what the future holds for us, but he has been more attentive than ever in our relationship. I suppose that's something. I'm going to take things slowly and make him go to marriage counseling with me when I decide the time is right. It's not time yet. Maybe it never will be. Maybe we just keep things as they are, at least until a new generation of Kingsleys are ready to step up and run the company. I think about the twins as co-CEOs and my heart is happy.

My phone lights up. It's a message from Ted.

I sit in our bed—my bed—and can't help but smile thinking of him out back in the doghouse. I have moved past the shock of his betrayal to more of a calm anger. My therapist says that's healthy, as long as I move out of the anger phase at some point soon.

He texts: Can I call you or come over? We could have wine . . .

I text: Not tonight.

He texts: Hope you have a good night's sleep, beautiful

I text: Thanks you too

I take a deep breath and put my phone on Do Not Disturb. It's strange, I don't feel guilty about saying no to Ted, not at all. When it comes to confidence, I know I'm building mine back up in so many areas. We looked perfect on the outside, but our relationship was built on a lot of lies. And I was too weak to push for the truth. To be fair, he is a product of his family. His upbringing didn't provide the stability or character-building he needed, nor did it provide love. He didn't learn to be honorable, and so he didn't behave honorably. I was too weak to push him to change. All I could offer him was unconditional love. But that was not enough. I should have expected more in return, should have seen him for who he really was and helped him to become a better version of himself. Perhaps there still is time for him to change, to become the man I know he can be. That will be up to Ted.

As for me, my eyes are wide open now, and I see things clearly.

I guess that really is the secret to a happy life.

ACKNOWLEDGMENTS

I am thrilled *Beneath the Surface* is my tenth novel. I am living the career of my dreams, and all I can say is it keeps getting better. And while writing a novel is a solitary experience, the writing community—authors, reviewers, bloggers, bookstores, and social media friends—feels ever-present, always supportive, whether online or in person. It's a blessing. I wouldn't be able to do what I do without you, the reader. Some of you have been with me from the beginning of my career, more than ten years ago. Thank you for reading, for buying, for checking out my books from the library, for reviewing, and sharing with your friends. I hope to keep entertaining you with my stories for years to come.

To my team at Thomas & Mercer—you are the best. Thanks especially to Gracie Doyle, Megha Parekh, Charlotte Herscher, and Ellie Schaffer. Gratitude also to my agents, Meg Ruley and Annelise Robey, for your thoughtful collaboration and expert advice. I am lucky to have you both on my side. And to Margo Lipschultz, editor and friend, for helping wrangle this story early on. Author friends Kimberly Belle and Heather Gudenkauf and I teamed up to create the Killer Author Club during the pandemic to support each other and other authors. We've had a blast creating a vibrant community of readers and authors, and we would love for you to tune in for an episode. Visit our website, www.killerauthorclub.com, for more.

My husband, Harley, and our kids are my life. I wouldn't be the writer I am without their support and love. And to Tucker, my beloved

Shihpoo, happy twelfth birthday and thank you for being my faithful writing buddy. Being able to pat your little head while you sleep next to me helps keep the muse flowing.

Thank you for reading *Beneath the Surface*. I hope you enjoyed it!

ABOUT THE AUTHOR

Photo © 2018 Kristin Karkoska

Kaira Rouda is a multiple award–winning, *USA Today* bestselling author of contemporary fiction that explores what goes on beneath the surface of seemingly perfect lives. Her novels of domestic suspense include *Somebody's Home*, *The Widow*, *The Next Wife*, *The Favorite Daughter*, *Best Day Ever*, and *All the Difference*. To date, Kaira's work has been translated into more than twelve languages. She lives in Southern California with her family and is working on her next novel. For more information, visit www.kairarouda.com.